Skinny-
dipping

Skinny-dipping

Claire Matturro

wm

WILLIAM MORROW
An Imprint of HarperCollins*Publishers*

SKINNY-DIPPING. Copyright © 2004 by Claire Hamner Matturro. All rights reserved. Printed in the United States of America. No part of this book may be used or reproduced in any manner whatsoever without written permission except in the case of brief quotations embodied in critical articles and reviews. For information address HarperCollins Publishers Inc., 10 East 53rd Street, New York, NY 10022.

HarperCollins books may be purchased for educational, business, or sales promotional use. For information please write: Special Markets Department, HarperCollins Publishers Inc., 10 East 53rd Street, New York, NY 10022.

FIRST EDITION

Designed by Renato Stanisic

Printed on acid-free paper

Library of Congress Cataloging-in-Publication Data

Matturro, Claire Hamner, 1954–
    Skinny-dipping / Claire Hamner Matturro.— 1st ed.
      p. cm.
    ISBN 0-06-056705-8 (acid-free paper)
    1. Women lawyers—Fiction. 2. Canoes and canoeing—Fiction.

  I. Title
  PS3613.A87S56 2004
  813'6—dc22   2003055849

---

04 05 06 07 08 WBC/QWF 10 9 8 7 6 5 4 3 2 1

To Mary Catherine Carter Hamner and William Peter Matturro

Chapter 1

I, Lilly Rose Cleary, have a nearly endless capacity for driving myself crazy.

That's why I ended up in law school, that and a serious lack of any readily discernible talents, despite my being smart and tall for a girl.

That's why I was sitting behind a long wooden table in a courtroom, defending this guy, this person, my client, in a civil lawsuit accusing him of causing this woman, this plaintiff now testifying, to suffer the terrible pain and disability of whiplash.

Kayak whiplash.

From being rear-ended in a kayak. In a mangrove channel off the Intracoastal. On a church outing.

Kayak whiplash invited ridicule. Naturally, I obliged. But after an early deposition round of humiliating the plaintiff, economics brayed and I had offered her twenty thousand dollars, the nuisance value of such a case, to stop being stupid and shut up and settle. But no, she had insisted on her constitutional right to a jury trial, meaning I, the defense attorney, would get the twenty thousand and more for convincing the jury to give her nothing.

In my efforts to persuade the jury to give her precisely that nothing, I was trapped behind this courtroom table while this woman's attorney, Newton "Newly" Moneta, questioned her on direct, trying to nail down her husband's loss of consortium claim. This plaintiff, this woman who couldn't even kayak right, was expounding on why she couldn't have sex with her husband because her neck and shoulders and back and entire torso were a constant spasm of pain because my guy, the defendant, had come around a bend in the mangroves and rear-ended her as she sat, stopped dead, in her kayak.

Listening to this plaintiff pontificate on her lack of a sex life, I thought my head would explode. My legs jiggled under the table, I shifted and sighed, slumped and straightened, and my fingers tapped on the desk until my client frowned at me. So, okay, spank me, I'm not good at sitting still.

Newly took a step back and nodded at me, and it was my turn.

But the plaintiff, thinking, I guess, that the jury might have missed her point, hung her head and said in a little-girl voice, "I mean, I can't even, you know, do him with my hands, because my arm and shoulders hurt so."

Newly whipped around toward her and said, "Thank you," and told "your honor" he was done.

I stood up. Didn't even bother to walk around from behind the table.

"You can't"—I stopped and glanced down to show my own reluctance to pursue this inquiry—"manually stimulate him with your hand?"

She looked wary but nodded.

"Anything wrong with your mouth?" I asked.

Newly objected before he even got back to his table.

The plaintiff jerked her head up, glared at me as if this were all my fault, and said, "I don't have to answer that."

In case the judge had missed it the first time, Newly repeated, "I object, your honor."

Not waiting for the judge to respond, which is bad lawyer etiquette, I said, "Your honor, he opened the door on direct." Lawyer talk for "You started it."

Newly said, "Outside the scope of direct." Lawyer talk for "Did not."

The judge said, "Overruled" and turned to the plaintiff and said, "Yes, you do have to answer that." Judge talk for "I'm the boss."

The plaintiff gave it her best shot at being offended and offered such a nonanswer answer that I said, "I withdraw the question, your honor. No further questions." Lawyer talk for "Never mind, the jury gets my point."

Newly closed the plaintiff's case with a medical whore, who swore a person could actually suffer such a thing as whiplash from a rear-ended kayak. After Newly officially rested his case, I made the standard motion and asked the judge to rule immediately in favor of my guy and deprive the jury of both hearing my defense and reaching its own verdict. To my detailed argument, Judge Goddard responded, "Go to lunch but don't take long." Taking that for a denial of my motion, I gathered up my client as the judge added, "I want this case over with today." We'd been at it for two days before this morning's testimony, and Judge Goddard had apparently had a bellyful.

With Judge Goddard's infamous impatience in mind, I scarfed a banana and a bowl of organic mixed greens with a maple syrup vinaigrette dressing from the Granary, the local health food store, while my client, a guy named Elvis who drove a tow truck and who had the rare good luck of having a personal liability insurance policy that was covering my fees and his lunch, picked at a tofu sandwich and asked, "What is this stuff?"

"It's like tuna," I said, figuring soybean curd was beyond the tolerance of his Florida cracker upbringing.

3

After lunch, I put Elvis on the stand to show the jury that he was a nice, basic guy and then put on our main medical guy. This medical witness was costing my client, or, to be technically correct, the client's liability insurance company, a small fortune, but the doc was great. Soft voice, big medical words explained to a grade-school level without condescension, gray hair, and taupe-colored wire-frame glasses that brought out his blue eyes. Came across like Marcus Welby, M.D. Privately, he'd told me the plaintiff was as healthy as an ox, big as one, and about as dumb, and, by the way, he "really knew how to grill a great steak" if I would like to have dinner with him at his beachfront house. Yeah, sure, dead cow burnt over charcoal to maximize the carcinogenic impact. I said I'd keep his offer in mind for the calm after the trial and suggested that he convey to the jury that the plaintiff was a big, stupid girl making this up. Bless his heart, the doc did just that.

Newly wisely elected to limit his cross-examination to eliciting the amount of money we were paying this guy per hour to testify. I rehabilitated Doc Welby on redirect over Newly's objection and Judge Goddard's explicitly expressed impatience—he tapped his watch twice during my two questions—by having him point out that his hourly rate for testifying was less than that of the plaintiff's medical whore.

After that, I put Elvis on again for a five-minute review of "I'm a nice guy" and "Really, it was just a tap. I mean, I didn't see her and didn't know she was just sitting there in the channel," and I rested my case.

Newly, no doubt having sensed his contingency fee slipping away, was pretty quick in his closing statement. If he had a point, I didn't hear it.

When it was my turn to close, I stood up and walked into the center ring of the courtroom, wearing my pearl gray suit with the demure skirt a modest one inch below the knees because a jury consulting firm had statistics showing that to be the length a jury preferred, and I smiled as if I were the best friend of every person on that jury and I was *so* glad to see them.

And kept smiling until I giggled. Just a little.

"Really!" I said, arching my eyebrows into perfect little black exclamation points of ridicule, and I sat down.

But my tone of voice, which I had practiced in front of every experienced trial attorney in my law firm, conveyed the whole scope of my contempt for such a silly case.

Newly rose, as if to object, but then sat down.

I won, of course.

After the foreman read the verdict and the judge thanked the jury, the plaintiff jumped up and waggled her finger at me. "I can appeal. I know my rights. I'm gonna appeal. And then you'll be sorry."

Sorry? An appeal just meant I would double the legal fees I'd draw in.

Behind the plaintiff, Newly, whom I liked despite his occasional tendency to display sociopathic behavior, opened his mouth and made a crude sexual gesture with his lips and tongue, and I burst out laughing.

He smiled and winked. Once, between his wives, we'd had a thing going for a week or two, but I was only a year out of law school and still pretending to be idealistic, and I couldn't get past the fact that he advertised on the local buses. Despite our brief fling, or maybe because of it, we had remained friends. Just last week, he asked me out again after he admitted his current wife (number four) had filed for a divorce. He's a big man, punches the bag and plays raquetball, hides his age, still has all his hair, and he can be both rib-busting funny and toe-curling sexy. We'd had a good time before the bus advertisements shamed me off of him. I told Newly, "You get that divorce, you call me."

I'm big on keeping my options open. And I was years past pretending to be idealistic.

5

. . .

Of course I had to take Elvis out for the obligatory victory drink, and of course he wanted to go to the Cracker Boys Bar, where I nursed a bottled beer, not trusting that anyone had actually washed the glasses, and tried not to touch anything. I was buzzy from my beer when Elvis kissed me good-bye and said thank you about a hundred times as if I'd done all this as a personal favor.

So, it was dark when I walked back to the law offices that I share with my cowboy law partners, and the humid Sarasota, Florida, breeze hit my face and pouffed my hair and warmed me from the artificial cold of the bar. I was thinking about how much I wanted to get out of my damn expensive Italian shoes and wash my face and hands. Cutting through the alley that runs beside my law firm, I crossed over to the back door. I always use the back door unless I have a snooty client with me. The front door, with its gargoyle door handles, creeps me out.

My trial briefcase, which is the size of carry-on luggage, pulled down my right hand, and my purse, which is the size of a normal briefcase, weighted down my shoulder as I punched in the code on the back lock with my left hand. No, as I told the cop later, I wasn't paying attention. This was my territory, and I had just won a case and was thinking that tomorrow morning I would regale the troops with punch line–by–punch line coverage of my courtroom victory. Muggers and descriptions had no place on the mental lists ping-ponging in my brain.

Somebody put a choke hold on me, and my victory-replay fantasy was cut off by the need to breathe. I dropped the briefcase and the purse.

I stomped on my attacker's foot as hard as I could with my own foot and tried to jam my elbows into his rib cage. My reward was only a slight letup in the choking, but that allowed me enough air to scream.

Screaming got me knocked upside the head pretty good by a gloved fist holding something hard and giving off a strange perfumy, chemical smell I couldn't place, but my attacker had to stop choking me to hit me. That was a modest improvement. For a moment I wished I'd spent more time with a boxing bag at the Y instead of the evil Stairmaster as I tried to turn and punch back.

What probably saved me was one of the firm's founding three partners, Ashton Stanley the Second of royal Florida cracker genealogy, driving into the back parking lot. Ashton suspects he might be the Second Coming, but he strikes me as a short maniac with nearly as much hair as I have, only he wears his straight up. Trying to add inches with the pouf in his hair. When Ashton saw what was going on, he honked his horn and activated the burglar alarm in his Lexus.

Of course, he also got out of his gold sedan and gave chase to the bad guy, who naturally got clean away, given the head start Ashton allowed him. I'd have run off too if I could have caught my breath.

Chapter 2

I had learned to wiggle my ears during constitutional law in my second year at a second-tier law school at a football state university, one that *Newsweek* once labeled "*the* biggest party school." While my con law professor was speaking about the penumbras hidden in the Bill of Rights, I kept myself from plopping asleep on my desk by tensing my jaw muscles in a certain way, causing my ears to wiggle.

In the overall scheme of things, this skill proved as useful to me as learning about constitutional penumbras.

So here I was, the morning after my courtroom victory and mugging, wiggling my ears to stay awake as my new client, a desperate orthopedic surgeon who, through a series of events probably not his fault, had nonetheless permanently screwed up his patient's left knee, explained in excruciating detail how he performs a knee replacement operation. Dr. Trusdale was saying, repeatedly, as if I'd never heard this before, that it wasn't his fault the guy on the table got a staph infection, which ate away bone and tissue and required subsequent surgeries until the poor patient had ended up worse off than when he'd begun his odyssey into the world of modern medicine.

Okay, okay, I get it. Not your fault. Not like you went to the bathroom before surgery and didn't wash your hands.

Staph happens.

I'm going to make a line of bumper stickers and T-shirts marketed to medical malpractice attorneys with that in bold orange: STAPH HAPPENS!

"Are you all right?" he asked, interrupting my fantasy of a new business producing witty T-shirts for lawyers, filled with in-house jokes. New client or not, I was already bored with him.

"Sure. Why?"

"You were, ah, twitching your face."

Oh, yeah. Memorandum to file: Stop wiggling your ears when the client is looking at you.

"Fine, sorry. I got mugged last night. Right out back. Believe that? Neck's a bit sore." I rubbed it. It did hurt.

Proving that doctors can be just as self-absorbed as lawyers, Dr. Trusdale said, "Oh, all right, so long as you're listening to me." Then he went back to explaining technical stuff while I bit my tongue to keep from yawning. I willed my ears still, but my legs and fingers started tapping and wiggling. I had a smoldering headache that I could blame on my mugger if anybody cared, but which probably had as much to do with the vodka and Häagen-Dazs Swiss Almond that Ashton and I and his girlfriend, who had beamed in from someplace long after the actual mugging, had consoled ourselves with once the police left. I ate the whole carton. Ashton said the almonds get caught in his teeth, and Jennifer, the girlfriend who's as skinny as a snake but has Barbie-doll breasts, doesn't "do dairy," but they definitely helped with the vodka, so I can't say how much I drank. Jennifer cooed and smothered and tried to act like my best friend, though our previous social exchanges had been to argue over whose turn it was on the Stairmaster at the Y and to trade exercise comments at firm functions ("I can do forty-five minutes on the Stairmaster," she claimed. "How long can you go?")

"Give her a chance," Ashton had begged me. "She's really smart."

Sure thing, and those breasts are real.

But all that was the night before, and now I wanted this doctor to shut up. He was probably a decent enough guy. But his "it's not my fault" mantra was getting old.

Drone. Drone. Drone.

"Un-huh," I threw out now and then, while I was thinking, Yeah, I know, I'd have to learn this stuff if I'm actually going to try this case before a jury, but there'll be months, maybe years, of discovery and dilatory pretrial crap before the judge gets pissed off and makes us actually try the damn thing. If we don't settle. If we don't delay until the plaintiff, the guy with the bum knee, gives up, wears out, runs out of money, or dies (which happens a lot in Sarasota, where the average citizen is a blue-haired Michigander who is 106 years old, drives a big-ass Lincoln Continental, gets her driver's license automatically renewed by mail, and can't see a Honda at five feet). "Justice delayed is justice denied" being a favorite cliché among personal injury and malpractice defense attorneys like us, prospering here in a city grown rich catering to the only technically still alive.

But by catering to professionals and businesses that got sued, often only because they are the deep pocket, not the guilty, my law firm had grown wealthy and taken on an air of uptown. A tony facade. Our sign, a four-foot-high chunk of carved marble that bears an unpleasant resemblance to a gravestone, proclaimed the name of the law firm: Smith, O'Leary, and Stanley, P.A. We obviously never abbreviate the name, though our receptionist is adept at saying the whole firm name as if it is one word. While we are mostly a defense firm, we indulge in a modest real estate practice since all real estate in Sarasota is for sale and has an appreciation rate that blows my mind. We don't handle criminal defense, unless an existing client gets into some kind of discreet trouble, like DWI, but concentrate on medical malpractice and personal injury defense, and we have a host of doctors, hospitals, auto insurance companies, and nursing homes as revolving clients.

These revolving clients crash through our dark oak double doors, angry at us because they've been sued, and we lock them out at night with a ridiculously decorated but quite serious deadbolt lock. The front door is a monster, with door handles designed to look like gargoyles foisted on us by an interior decorator that Ashton Stanley, in the years before he'd taken up with Jennifer the Stairmaster wizard, had been wooing until he found out this interior decorator had begun life as a boy. Ashton's early crush on the decorator also explained why he had a clear plastic table for a desk and a purple rug and black walls. Good thing the decorator stopped playing hard to get before the whole inside of the law firm was mauve and black and plastic.

Thinking I'd rather have a black and plastic office than continue to pretend to listen to my dreary new client pontificate further on the difficulties of his profession and the unfairness of a legal system that actually allowed an injured patient to sue his doctor, I stared at my client and waited for a break. So, when my good orthopod paused to inhale, I gave him an earnest but pain-laden smile (I've learned something from watching Newly's well-rehearsed clients over the years), and I said, "My head and neck really hurt. *Really*. Bad. I'm afraid we'll need to reschedule this so I can give you the attention, the *whole* attention, you deserve." I paused, studied his face, and saw the emerging sympathy.

"Mugged, you said?"

Got him.

I grimaced, rubbed my neck. Exaggerated the mugging experience, with special emphasis on the choke hold and the neck twisting.

"You're a surgeon, so could you, please, maybe, write me a prescription for a pain medicine? That Advil just isn't helping me."

Memo to file: Never ask for a narcotic by name—that tips them off.

By the time he left, I had a prescription for Percocet, a personal narcotic favorite of Elvis Presley's and Dean Martin's.

If I'd known somebody was going to kill Dr. Trusdale later that night by spiking his marijuana with toxic oleander, I'd have listened closer and been nicer.

Chapter 3

Jackson Winchester Smith, the founding and controlling partner at Smith, O'Leary, and Stanley, P.A., charged into my office while I was grinding the beans and heating the Zephyrhills bottled spring water for my second pot of coffee.

"Good win on that kayak whiplash case," he thundered. Jackson never talks, he thunders. He has a portrait of Stonewall Jackson in his office big enough to be a weight-bearing wall, and his favorite quote is "Don't get in a pissing contest with a skunk." It does not worry me in the least that the man who signs my paycheck believes that he is the physical reincarnation of Stonewall Jackson. Despite a certain love-hate cachet to our relationship, he is my hero, my mentor, and the man who single-handedly made me the firm's only woman partner.

Jackson glared at my French press. "What's wrong with the coffee in the lunchroom?"

Oh, please. Shall I start with the dioxin in the bleached paper coffee filters, or the pesticides in the coffee, or the white fake dairy creamer consisting almost entirely of fat, dye, and chemicals? Or limit myself to the apt observation that the stuff tasted like crap?

Smiling, though I felt the muscle spasm kicking in at my jaws, I asked, "Join me?"

I maximized the swing of my hair and my smile while I fixed us both coffee with just a dollop of organic two percent milk. We tipped our coffee cups together like friends toasting with their wine, and I sat down, leaned back in my chair, and waited.

"Ah, sorry about the mugging. You don't need to file a workers' comp claim."

I noted this was a statement, not a question, but nodded and said, "I'm fine" as if he'd asked how I was.

"I've ordered new security lights for the back. Also, I sent out a memo telling people to leave the building in groups of two or more after dark."

Nothing so silly as saying, "Don't work nights anymore."

"A good idea," I answered, sipping my coffee and waiting.

"How's your caseload?"

Aha.

"Heavy." I gave the answer I always give to that question. Not to be overworked is the kiss of demise in a law firm.

"Good," Jackson said, the answer he always gives to assertions of overwork. "I want you to take over my CMV case, the brain-damaged baby case. One with cerebral palsy and mental retardation."

Oh, sure, I thought, now that you've milked thousands of dollars of legal fees out of the discovery stage of the litigation process, dump it on me. So year-end, your computer printout shows you made a ton of money for the firm, and my score sheet shows I lost a multimillion-dollar veggie baby case after a two-week trial.

"I thought you were going to settle that one." The rule of thumb being that a defense attorney always settles a brain-damaged baby case unless the mother is a total pig caught smoking crack on a police video while visibly pregnant and pounding her womb with sharp objects in front of forty bishops, all of whom will testify against her. Not that negligence on the part of the doctor or the hospital has a thing to do with the jury's decision. A sweet young mother, a distraught and earnest father, and a drooling infant dangling his big-eyed, vacant head left and right. No way a jury doesn't give that skewed Norman Rockwell painting some money. Big money.

"Tried to settle it," Jackson said. "Parents' damned attorney has visions of grandeur. Some snotty hotshot out of Miami."

Yeah, I knew the parents' attorney, an arrogant son of a bitch who liked to make sure everybody knew he went to Harvard and who was forever correcting my pronunciation of his name—Steph-fin, not Steve-in. We'd met at some early rounds when Jackson sent me to argue some legal minutia in the case. As I recalled, our theory was that the infant's birth defects were caused by a common virus, CMV, and not mistakes during the delivery. But it was going to be hard to get around the argument that the obstetrician screwed up by not doing an emergency Cesarian when problems developed during labor.

"Up the settlement offer," I said, hoping I didn't sound like I was begging.

"Can't. Already at policy limits."

That was a lot of money thrown at the plaintiffs. Their refusal showed either confidence or stupidity, and where personal injury litigation lottery stakes are at play, the former is often a reflection of the latter. Me, I'm a "bird in the hand beats two in the bush" sort of girl. I would have taken the offer. Never let a jury of strangers decide your fate if you can help it, that would be my advice.

But, of course, the good-parents had not asked me. And now Jackson wanted to hand this mess off to me.

"Sure," I said. It wasn't as if I had a choice, since I was barely even a partner and crap runs downhill, so I might as well pretend to take it with good graces. "Got a trial date yet?"

"End of the month. But I filed a motion for continuance. It's before Judge Goddard. You argue the motion."

"What're the grounds?" I asked, thinking, Other than the usual justice-delayed maxim and the natural human tendency to put off as long as possible anything that was difficult to do.

"The parents' attorney hired off our leading expert witness, and we need to find another one. You'd better hit MEDLINE this afternoon and read up on the literature, find the leading CMV experts. Look for somebody we don't have to fly in from California, all right?"

"You mean our doctor who was so emphatic that this sort of brain damage could only develop in the womb? He bailed on us?" My heart made the kind of conspicuous thump-thump that happens after a loud noise late at night.

"Yeah. For twice our hourly rate. After he changed his mind, I set him up for another deposition. Under oath, son of a bitch says the money Stephen LaBlanc offered him didn't have a thing to do with it. Our doctor's damn insurance company's so cheap we can't even keep a decent expert. Then this overpaid expert says he erred in his initial opinion because we distorted the facts about the microcephaly."

"The what?"

"Microcephaly. You know, kid was born with a small head. You don't remember that?"

Yeah, I remembered the small-head thing, only I called it a small-head thing, not microcephaly.

So we were screwed with that physician whore. Nice trick on Stephen's part, I thought.

"Better get busy." Jackson put down his coffee cup, keeping his eyes even with mine, probably checking for panic. I hoped he couldn't hear the thump-thump-thump of my heart, my now fully activated fight-or-flight response in place. Even my mouth had dried up. I smiled, reassuringly I hoped, to the man who had just ruined my life.

Oh, just frigging great, I thought, as I watched him leave. If I didn't get that continuance, I had less than three weeks to find an expert, hire him, coach him, amend the witness list to include the new expert, set up his deposition so Stephen LeBlanc couldn't bitch "unfair surprise" and keep my expert off the stand, get ready for the trial, and maintain my regular caseload.

My left eye pounded and my shoulders twitched in spasms.

Two minutes after Jackson left my office, I poured another cup of coffee and heaped it with turbinado sugar, the soul food of any personal crisis. I turned on my computer and went online, accepting my karma that I was soon going to know more than anyone could possibly want to about cytomegalovirus, wisely called CMV, and I had better find a good medical expert, quick.

Just what I wanted to be, the law firm's leading expert on an unpronounceable virus. Already my "anything wrong with your mouth" fifteen minutes of pop-star status at my law firm had faded. My law firm, where if you rested on your laurels, somebody would steal your billings and your leather desk chair.

Chapter 4

My full name is Lillian Belle Rosemary Cleary, named after both grand-mothers and a maiden aunt, and I haven't answered to Lilly Belle Rose since I was six and got expelled for hitting a boy who kept calling me that. In even the most modest shoe heel, I'm six feet tall. When I need to project power or instill fear, a black suit and a pair of three-inch heels pretty much do the job. I'm gaining on thirty-five at a rate that has exorbitantly sped up since I turned thirty, and I'm not really that pretty, though often people think I am.

It's my hair, my half a yard of thick, black shiny hair that I can use as a veil in the dance of the seven veils and that stays just the right shade of black, with painfully maintained highlights of burnt sienna to belie the hair dye, courtesy of Brock, my hairdresser and therapist. Except in bouts of high humidity, which in Sarasota is more often than not, my hair keeps just the right pageboy wave. That's why people think I'm pretty. That, and being thin, tall, and having blue eyes. What they call Black Irish, that dark hair, pale skin, and blue eyes. My two brothers are what I guess you'd call Red Irish, big red faces and big heads of red hair, and big, big hearts.

Though my brothers stayed home in south Georgia, I moved to

Sarasota straight out of law school because once when we were children we'd vacationed here with our father. My brothers and I had discovered that if you dug any kind of hole, it would fill up with water from the ground, and there were medieval statues of women and bulls and goddesses in the median of the Tamiami Trail near the John and Mable Ringling Museum of Art, and the beaches went on forever with white sand washed by the turquoise Gulf of Mexico, and elegantly thin royal palms lined the city streets, and, in the bay-front curve of the Tamiami Trail, majestic homes built in the 1920s boom stood in rows of grandeur not contemplated in my native south Georgia town.

All that Sarasota grandeur was gone now. Overdevelopment and progress and retirees seeking high-rise condos and not giving a rat's ass about history or architectural integrity, plus the passage of time itself, had conspired to render it all asunder. Even the high water table was gone, sucked out of the ground by greedy use and years of prolonged drought. But when I was six, I saw the city in the waning days of its glory, and I loved it. I kept that image in my mind, and I wanted out of all that Georgia red dirt anyway, and so I came here to make my way in the world.

And now, eight years later, I stared at my face in the lighted mirror of my own bathroom, and I wondered if the Retin-A was really making any difference. I mean, I still saw those lines around my eyes. And the ones around my mouth.

Sun. The number one cause of wrinkles. Should have stayed out of the sun, the dermatologist had told me. Oh, thanks, that's worth that ninety-five-dollar bill. As if I'd had a choice, growing up in the Deep South. The only people who didn't have sun-damaged skin in my Georgia town were either invalids, rich white ladies, or night-shift workers at the pickle factory who slept days.

Sun. Yeah. To avoid it in Georgia, you have to stay indoors.

And my mother's principal child-raising technique when my brothers and I were children was to open the kitchen door while clutching her first Coca-Cola of the morning and say, "Shoo." In the summer, that meant we played outside in the hot, bright sun until we saw my dad's car come up the driveway at dusk and we went in for supper. My brothers and I stayed sunburned. We'd eat lunch from our weekly allowance, Fudgesicles, Dr Pepper, cheese crackers, and banana Popsicles being the staples of our summer diet. During the school year, we ate the school lunches, the house specialty being lime Jell-O with green peas in it. My mother's idea of cooking dinner was to open cans—canned hash, canned chili, canned pears, canned beans. My father ate his noon meal at the Woolworth lunch counter, and my mother drank Coca-Cola and took pills from a bottle she hid under her mattress. I took one of those pills once when I was nine, and when it hit me I couldn't get up off the floor for over an hour. My brother Delvon took one and smashed his bike into a slash pine. Our middle brother had no imagination and never stole from our mother's stash.

When we got older and the school nurse sent home a note saying our mother should fix us breakfast, she'd put a raw egg in a bottle of Yoo-hoo for us. By the time we were teenagers, she didn't even bother with the cans or the egg in the Yoo-hoo. It's a wonder we didn't all get scurvy.

In that ill-nourished family, I was the baby, and when I graduated from law school, my father, who was himself a lawyer, retired and moved to a fishing camp on a TVA lake, where he sits most of the daylight hours at the end of a dock, wearing a broad-brimmed Tilly hat I gave him and watching the life on the lake play itself out against the sun and the day. He sits so still that once a butterfly landed on his arm. My mother stayed in the house in town, where she never gets out of her pajamas except to go to the occasional funeral.

That's who I am, and that's what I was thinking about when Newly called me up to say that he'd just heard on the police monitor that Dr. Trusdale had some kind of seizure and died, and the police were called to the house to investigate because it could be poison, and wasn't I defending him? And could he come over?

Chapter 5

My first thought, may God forgive me, was to wonder if I could still get Dr. Trusdale's prescription for Percocet filled now that he was dead.

Then, to my modest credit, I felt really bad and asked Newly all the proper questions, interspersed with the proper cries of dismay. Frothing at the mouth, writhing on the floor when his wife came in from her AA meeting. Marijuana smoke in the air, a half-smoked joint on the floor by his hand. Already dying. Paramedics never had a chance.

It never once occurred to me that this had anything at all to do with me. Never once occurred to me to question the source of Newly's details. I mean, he is a prominent plaintiffs' attorney in Sarasota, a big frog in a small pond, with contacts where he needs them to be. I accepted the truth of what he told me, and I let the horror sink in and then dissipate.

The phone call with Newly done, I rushed out to the nearest all-night pharmacy and didn't have a bit of a problem with Dr. Trusdale's prescription, and when I got home, in my driveway Newly was sitting on the hood of his big gold Lexus, a twin of my colleague Ashton's sedan. Must be an amendment I had missed to the *Rules Regulating*

The Florida Bar that now required attorneys to drive imported automobiles costing at a minimum twice the average annual income for the state. I drive a 1987 Honda Accord with 187,000 miles on it. Salesman told me it would go 200,000 miles, and I'm holding the man to his word. Ashton makes fun of my ancient car and my little concrete-block "great starter home," but I have a five-year plan and it doesn't include locking on the golden handcuffs.

Sliding off his imported gold sedan with the "Save the Rain Forest" bumper sticker, Newly held up a single red rose and a bottle of wine.

"I don't need consoling," I told him.

"I do," he said. "After all, you beat me in court. And I'm getting divorced. Again."

"Yeah, I've heard that divorce line before."

Newly pulled out some papers from his jacket pocket. "Here's the notice of my property settlement hearing."

Always the Boy Scout, I thought, looking over the legal papers he had brought to show me.

"That's not all," he said. "Damn Florida Bar's investigating me again on Karen's allegations that I lied about my personal assets to the judge in this divorce."

Karen, his soon-to-be ex-wife, no doubt had an ax to grind, but given Newly's history, I asked, "Any truth to her claims?"

"No. None whatsoever. Totally spurious."

I nodded but didn't wholly believe him.

"If I could just hold you," he said, "I know we'd feel better."

"I feel fine," I said, "and you remember, I've got a strict rule about not messing with married men."

But Newly looked forlorn, and he sweet-talked some more, and I let him inside my pink-tiled, terrazzo-floored house with the big Live Oak in the back and the modest mortgage payment. After all, Newly had brought some good wine and my invitation inside seemed the minimum standard for civilized behavior. We drank the wine while contemplating the specter of Newly's losing his license again. Before I'd come to Sarasota, the Florida Supreme Court had suspended his license to practice law for three years, something to do with suborning perjury. That in and of itself hadn't made much difference in Newly's overall career; he just hired another attorney to sign pleadings and be the face man in court while Newly told everyone but his clients that he was working as a paralegal. Newly's wife was embarrassed by the scandal and left him. And she took his money.

By the time he was back on his feet and married to his second wife, he took on the largest tomato-growing conglomerate in the state on behalf of the migrant workers being systematically poisoned by the illegal use of pesticides. Big class-action suit.

Technically, Newly won both a legal and a moral victory. The EPA shut down the tomato growers, who sold off the fields to a big-ass developer at a profit that shot up the growers' stock. Now modest tract houses lined the streets, acre after acre, where the migrants used to make a meager living picking poisoned tomatoes that were shipped north and sold high in winter to support rich white guys who lived nowhere near the illegal poison dust. Now our tomatoes come from Mexico, where they can legally use the pesticides that are illegal here. The circle of poison Newly didn't dent.

But Newly got some money out of the case and some satisfaction, and maybe some karma credit in heaven. But his second wife felt neglected because that class action took so much of his time, and she left, taking his reaccumulated money with her.

That's when I met him.

Between two and three. Number four was now calculating his net worth and ratting him out to the bar association's ethics division.

For a very smart man, Newly needed to learn a few things. Memo to file, I thought, sipping the good merlot: Tell Newly: 1) you don't have to marry everybody you have sex with (he'd proposed to me after making love the second time); 2) don't ever put anything in joint title unless you're protecting assets from creditors; and 3) get a way better divorce attorney.

While I was thinking who'd be the meanest, nastiest divorce attorney for Newly, I felt the first wave of the wine kick in, that woozy feeling that life is rather splendid after all. Giving in to the buzz, I finished my wine and curled comfortably against Newly on the couch.

"I remember the first thing you ever said to me," he said, putting his hand on my arm and rubbing two fingers up and down on a small warm space of skin.

No way—it'd been eight years since I'd met him. "Yeah? What?"

"That's not your real name. That's the first thing you said to me," Newly insisted.

Well, it *wasn't* his real name. I'd looked up his name-change petition in the courthouse later to be sure. Lester Bagley Ledbetter was the name his parents had stuck him with, and I didn't blame him a bit for upgrading it. But why would he remember my saying that years ago, *if* that's what I had said? Maybe he made it up. Lord knows Newly was the mother of invention. Even allowing for that, something in the tenor of his voice made me look closely at him. Granted, he is the master of artful facial expressions and tones of voice—all good trial attorneys are—but he sounded wistful, like a man carrying a torch.

Rather than pursue that concern, I hinted that Newly should leave now.

"Oh, hon. I hate hotels. Can't I just stay the night?"

"You haven't gotten your own place yet?"

"Aw, my money's all tied up. You know what a divorce is like."

No, I didn't, not personally, though Jackson had made me work on a few rich doctor divorces on the theory that a girl lawyer representing a rich man dumping his wife for a younger model makes the man somehow more sympathetic and strongly suggests by example that a woman can earn her own living and doesn't need alimony. Apparently Newly didn't have a woman lawyer. I frowned by way of an answer.

"Hon, just tonight. For old times'. I'll get a place tomorrow."

Addled by fatigue and wine, I nodded. "One night. On the futon."

He slid his arm around my waist.

"In the guest room," I said.

"Aw, hon."

But I handed him clean sheets and gave cursory instructions on how to unfold the futon from couch to bed, and I headed into my own room and shut my door against him.

The next morning, when the phone rang and I rolled over toward it, I was momentarily stunned to find Newly curled up like a hairy, forty-four-year-old teddy bear on my organic cotton sheets that are dyed with beet juice and cost not much less than what I'd paid for my first car, a 1965 Chrysler Newport that I bought from my brother and never did learn to parallel park.

Sometime during the night, he must have sneaked into bed with me. He's not that light on his feet, and I am not that sound a sleeper. Okay, memo to file: Don't slurp down that much good wine when you want the man to sleep in the guest room. Still, I was certain we hadn't done anything but sleep. The phone rang again.

Some guy from the police department with a name I didn't quite absorb wanted to talk to me about the dead orthopedic doctor and asked if I could come right down to the police department. The half-life of last night's wine made me nasty, and I said something rude that loosely translated to "Hell, no." Newly jerked beside me as I hung up.

I hadn't finished making the coffee before the police officer called back.

"Detective Sam Santuri," he snapped, as if that excused his earlier call.

"So detectives come to work at dawn, like farmers?" I wondered if

I could just chew the coffee grinds instead of waiting for the hot water to soak out the caffeine.

After a long pause, the detective said, "Sorry. Didn't mean to wake you. I thought most professionals were up by seven."

"I usually am," I said, suddenly not wanting this man with the sexy last name and the good bass voice thinking I was a dilettante. "But I had to work late, very late, last night. Trial work, you know."

I cradled the phone between my chin and shoulder and reached to pour my coffee. While Sam breathed into my ear, I sipped the *real* nectar of the gods, and the caffeine seeped into my bloodstream and my brain cells popped into gear. I guessed it was my turn to apologize for yelling.

"Look, perhaps I was . . . snippy when you called earlier. But I'm too busy with my clients to just run over to the police station this morning. Call my office and make an appointment with my secretary. Her name is Bonita." I gave him the number and was satisfied that I'd let him know I was an important person he couldn't be jerking around, calling at all hours of the morning.

While I put down the phone, Newly was sitting at my kitchen table, smiling and looking as if he was expecting breakfast. If the man wanted me to fix him breakfast, he was going to get a raw egg in a Yoo-hoo, but first he would have to go out and buy a Yoo-hoo and a raw egg.

Chapter 6

The law clerks were all in a huddle when I went into the law library first thing, looking for Angela, the associate I was technically supposed to mentor, which in most law firms translates into "work to death."

"We read about, er, your client getting killed," one of the law clerks said.

I rarely bother learning their names. They are only at the law firm for a few months, then gone back to law school or into the great stream of legal commerce elsewhere. They are all either in the top quarter of their class or related to a client or somebody important. They are all eager, healthy, and fundamentally useless in their tender years, with only one or two years of law school under their caps. They are fungible goods. It was Angela, a second-year associate with the perfectionistic work habits of the chronically insecure, that I needed this morning.

But I nodded politely to the law clerk.

Encouraged, the nameless boy said, "They don't even know if it was murder."

"Yes, I read the story," I said, peering over the heads and the law books, looking for orange hair. One thing about Angela, petite though she is, she can't hide from me with that Orphan Annie/Bozo the Clown hair.

"Newspaper quotes an unnamed source, said it looked like poison."

"Yes, I read the story. Anybody seen Angela?"

"Why didn't they mention your name?" the unnamed clerk asked.

"You think that'd be good, free advertising?" I finally focused on him. Blond, square-jawed, tall. Was there a factory somewhere making these boys and importing them without a tariff? The Mattel factory for boy lawyers, located in some Third World country, stocks high on the Dow because cheap, native child labor and creative American accounting maximized profit? Why else would there be so damn many of them?

"Sure. So long as they spell your name right and put in the firm's name and address," the clerk said, too perkily for a boy.

"Sure," I mimicked in his pert tone, waited, then added, with the serious voice of a lecturer, "A dead client is not a good result."

"Oh," he said.

"Angela went over to the courthouse library to look up something in the Federal Register," another nameless boy said.

"Thank you." I left, wondering if the firm would pay for a beeper for Angela.

I stomped toward my own desk through the cubbyhole of my secretary's office and for my greeting said, "Send a runner after Angela, will you? She's at the courthouse."

Bonita, my long-suffering and unnaturally calm secretary, said, "She'll be back by the time you're done with the Evan's file interrogatories on your desk and with Detective Sam Santuri. He's due at eleven. Good morning."

I started to growl, then said, "Good morning." Figuring I might as well get this detective thing over with, I didn't make Bonita change the appointment.

Sam appeared just as I finished churning around on the interrogatories, and Bonita ushered him into my office on her small, light feet.

"Sam Santuri," he repeated as if I might have forgotten his name in the last few hours, and he offered his hand.

Standing in the military "head up, shoulders back" stance, I took Sam's hand with the firm but brief grip Jackson had taught me so I wouldn't "shake hands like a girl," and I looked Sam Santuri straight in the eyes and didn't blink. Now that I'd had my second round of coffee, plus the adrenaline from my irritating but mercifully brief exchange with the nameless law clerk, I was ready for him.

Sam was, I noticed, rather good-looking in that broken nose sort of way that men who have spent too much time outside and led rough lives can be. While unfashionably dressed, he had a Kirk Douglas jaw and a full head of graying black hair and acted all business. I had about five hundred other things I needed to be doing and didn't even think about flirting.

"Dr. Trusdale's appointment with you yesterday, what was that about?" the detective asked after we minimized the polite exchanges to the bare basics.

"What did he die of?" I asked.

"We don't know yet. The autopsy will tell us more. Now, could you answer my question?"

"You're saying it could have been an accident?" I thought it interesting that neither the detective nor the newspaper had mentioned the marijuana roach on the floor by the stricken man's fingers.

While I was thinking about that marijuana, my heart gave a jolt as my mind focused on the impact that half-smoked joint would have on the jury in my bum-knee guy versus the dead orthopod lawsuit. How exactly would I rehabilitate a dead defendant doctor at trial if it became public knowledge he smoked marijuana? A stoned surgeon, now there was a defense attorney's nightmare. I definitely had to settle this case before the investigation went further and produced more publicity.

"Excuse me," I said, punching the phone's intercom. To Bonita,

"Get Henry Platt on the line and set up a face to face with him as soon as possible, but no later than this morning."

Sam looked at his watch, then at me. Behind his head, my imitation heirloom clock, from which I had forcibly removed the chimes one day in a fit of pique, said it was 10:58 A.M. So spank me, I was rude and in a hurry. Detective Santuri didn't need to know that Henry was the claims adjuster in the Trusdale case and the man I needed to authorize a quick settlement.

"What did you ask me?" I looked at him and admired the poker face he maintained.

"Why were you representing him? What was that about?"

"Medical malpractice suit against him. Knee replacement. Plaintiff got a bad infection. Totally messed-up knee now. Would you like a copy of the complaint?"

Sam nodded and made a note.

I punched my phone and asked Bonita to make a copy of the complaint in Dr. Trusdale's case but not until she'd set up the meeting with Henry.

Ten minutes later, after the good detective and I exchanged more questions than answers, Bonita brought in a copy of the complaint and said, "Henry will be here at eleven-thirty. I've ordered two fruit plates from the Granary." Bonita took Sam in with a sideways but practiced study and winked her approval over his head as she passed back out the door. Being a devout widow didn't stop her from admiring a fine-looking man, though the ghost of her late husband seemed to be as real to her as he had been in the flesh. Before he died in an accident at the local orange juice processing plant—an accident so ghastly neither she nor I could drink the stuff to this good day—he and Bonita had had five children, and she never raises her voice to them. There wasn't a man in the law firm who wouldn't jump her if he could, but the five kids and the prominent gold cross around her neck and that "Don't even think it" look she can zap out at the first hint of a flirt kept them off of her. She remained as married to the dead husband as to the live one, as far as I could tell. None of that kept her from admiring Detective Santuri, and she tended to matchmaking for me, thinking I couldn't reach Nirvana until I had a husband and five kids tearing up my house.

As I watched Bonita leave my office, Sam scanned the complaint and asked, "How far along are you?"

I inhaled so I could give him the layman's-introduction-to-litigation speech I use on clients, but before I got past the first ten words, he cut me off.

"When's the trial?"

In about ten years if I get my way, I thought, irritated at being interrupted, but I kept my face neutral and said, "I just filed an answer denying liability. In the normal course of litigation, we dick around a year or two with the plaintiff and his attorney, and then we either settle it or try it in circuit court. Fortunately I'm not hampered by any speedy-trial problems like you are in the criminal courts."

"Dick around, eh? That a new legal term?" He almost grinned.

"Yes, a legal term of art meaning to jerk one's opposing counsel's chain as often as one can while keeping careful billing records of each sparring event. Or, what they call discovery in law school."

"We call it depositions in criminal court, but every now and then in the criminal justice system it actually accomplishes something other than generating fees."

Generating fees, eh? As if my getting paid for hard work is a crime? This guy was definitely irritating. But I nodded and kept my mouth shut.

"Sometimes on our side," Sam said, "it lets our assistant state attorney know if he's got any holes in his case to worry about, and once or twice I've seen it convince a defense attorney to throw in the towel and plea."

Yeah, okay, so Sam knew something about the legal system. Good for him. "Yes. You've no doubt been through depos and trials as a homicide detective."

"Seems like I can remember one or two." He shifted forward in his chair and took a closer look at me.

Caution sensors went off in me.

"You were mugged the other night?"

"Yes. No big deal. How'd you know?"

"We share info at the police station. No profit motive in our business. Think there could be any connection?"

Sharing their info? About me? Why? Not wanting to draw a red circle around it, I didn't ask the detective but made a mental memo to file to ask Newly to find out why somebody was looking into me because the good doc died.

I paused so long wondering why Detective Santuri had asked me that question that he repeated it. "Any possible connection?"

"No."

The good detective Sam Santuri let my "no" sit there in the air long enough that I wondered if I'd been too emphatic, and I watched him watching me. Waiting for what? For me to jump up and confess something? I visualized a crystal blue waterfall and kept my face calm, my shoulders relaxed, and my eyes right on his. They were a kind of deep chocolate color, I noticed.

"Tell me about the mugging?"

I did, including the rescue-by-Ashton story that Ashton was perpetuating to his greater glory.

"Why try to strangle you? Why not just grab your purse or briefcase?"

"Beats me," I said. "I'm a civil defense attorney, not a criminal defense attorney. Don't have a clue how muggers think."

"Any attempt to snatch your purse or briefcase?"

Maybe not. It happened fast. I shrugged, but I was thinking Sam raised a good point. If this was a common mugging gone awry, why had it felt like the mugger wanted to choke me? Why not just grab the purse and run?

"Any attempt to get into the building? Maybe choke you after you'd punched in the lock code, get in, and steal whatever he could grab quickly?"

"Maybe. I don't know. I guess I'm not a good witness."

Sam Santuri sighed. "Most people aren't."

Imagine that, not taking careful notes while being choked and then knocked up the side of the head by a perfect stranger. Shame on me.

Finally Detective Santuri leaned back in his chair and asked, "Who pays your bills, the doctor or the insurance company?"

"Doc's malpractice liability insurance company pays my bills. Plus it pays the settlement or the judgment so long as the amount is within the policy limits."

"Any benefit to the insurance company, Dr. Trusdale getting murdered?"

"You mean, like if he's dead they don't have to pay up?"

"Something like that."

"No. Coverage doesn't go away just because the insured is killed. So long as the premiums are paid." But I made a mental note to check the policy's terms in case there was a new cost-containment rider that precluded coverage in the event the insured died during a lawsuit.

"So the lawsuit continues? Murdering the defendant doesn't end the case?"

"No. I just file a notice of death with the trial court and follow that with a substitution of party, naming the doctor's estate or the executor of the estate as the new defendant."

"How about the plaintiff? Any benefit to him?"

"Just that I can't put Dr. Trusdale on the stand, make him come over to the jury as a nice, competent physician. Nothing direct." Well, that and the fact that it would be virtually impossible to rehabilitate a dead pot-smoking surgeon.

The good detective took another look at the complaint and then pulled out his card. I pulled out my card and we exchanged, and I smiled what I hoped was my nice-girl smile and he nodded and that was that. Or, so I thought.

Sam Santuri hadn't driven off yet before Ashton popped his head into my office.

"Sorry your guy got zapped," he said, fluffing his hair up another inch with his fingers. Somebody should tell him the bouffant on men went out with Elvis Presley's waistline. Ashton's shirttail was half out of his pants and there were little white specks of something in both corners of his mouth, but his maroon silk tie looked tight enough to choke him. "Heard he was smoking a bong of hash when he keeled over."

"I heard it was a marijuana joint," I said. "How'd you hear?"

"Aw, courthouse rumor. You know the girls in Records."

Damn. That meant a very good chance that the bum-knee guy's attorney already knew, or would soon, that the defendant surgeon was a pot smoker. In a conservative community with an average age of 106 and zero tolerance for recreational drugs, the best jury I could draw would still reflect the moral superiority of a generation that survived the Great Depression and World War II and would have great sympathy for a man who had a knee replacement operation and none for a younger, pot-smoking surgeon.

"I have to go," I said to Ashton.

"You'd better settle that sucker, today, right now. Don't even bother looking at the file."

As if Ashton Stanley needed to tell me that.

Henry Platt, the medical malpractice insurance claims adjuster in charge of Dr. Trusdale's case, came pattering into the conference room where I was already inspecting a slice of kiwi from my fruit plate and wondering if the kitchen help had used a clean knife.

He offered his plump little hand, which I shook and held tightly for a moment past the ordinary convention, as if we were old friends.

In a way we were. We'd been through a lot of cases together, the worst being the hysterectomy on the pregnant woman.

"Henry, please have a seat," I said and pointed to his fruit plate and his iced coffee. He'd probably hit the Dairy Queen on the way back to his office, but at least that wouldn't be on my conscience.

"We have a problem," I said, with no smile, "but you know that."

"Yes. I read about Dr. Trusdale in the morning paper. Learn anything more about it?"

Oh, yes, thanks to Newly and the exponentially expanding rumor mill.

"That the good doctor was smoking a marijuana joint at the time he suffered a seizure and collapsed."

"Oh, my Lord," Henry said.

I let that sink in while I wiped off a grape with my napkin and ate it, then sipped my coffee.

Henry is a nice guy, generally neat and careful, and he'd been promoted by the insurance company from his early days largely because he was there and he was nice, but he was way too easy to manipulate for a claims adjuster. Because of that he had now gone as far as he would go with his company, and he knew it but had the serenity to accept the things he couldn't change. Or else he was on Prozac.

"We'll have to settle. Right away. Won't we?" Henry took a bite of his banana muffin, eyeing the fruit as if he wasn't sure what a kiwi was.

"I'll need your authority to go to the policy limits if I have to do so to settle. Now, before the marijuana is common knowledge," I said, hearing the clock ticking. "Before the bum-knee guy's attorney hears about the pot. For all we know, it'll be in the paper tomorrow. Today is my window of opportunity."

"I'll have to ask my boss on the policy limits."

"Henry, I don't have time. We're racing the rumor mill here."

I popped another grape in my mouth and waited for Henry to capitulate.

"All right," he said.

"Here." I shoved a sheet of paper at him. "I need your signature on this authorization to go to policy limits." Bonita had already notarized it. All right, I know you're supposed to wait until the person signs before you notarize things, but time was of the essence.

Whether he noticed this breach or not, Henry signed the authorization and I shoved my Styrofoam container of fruit at him. "Thanks. Take this one too—I've got to get to the bum-knee guy's attorney before he hears about the pot."

"Aw, Lilly, aw, could you, I mean, would you . . . that is, eh, can you . . . will you . . . ? "

Overadrenalinized and cranky with anxiety, I snapped, "Pick a verb, Henry."

"Will you ask Bonita to join me for lunch? Please?"

From inside the doorway, I studied Henry and softened when I saw his naturally pink face had turned a deep red and his Paul Newman blue eyes were downcast with shyness. So, he was smitten. I smiled. "Sure, Henry. I'm sure she'd like that."

I walked back to my office, sent Bonita off to join Henry, and punched in my own telephone numbers to call the bum-knee guy's attorney.

As Bonita nibbled fruit with Henry in the conference room, I hurried my opposing counsel into a hasty settlement conference. Fortunately for me, the bum-knee guy's attorney hadn't heard about the pot yet, and I said a prayer of thanks to God, Buddha, the cosmic forces, the blue god, and the angels of both light and darkness.

Two hours of bickering later, my stomach churning, with nothing in it to digest except two grapes and itself, I had a signed preliminary settlement agreement. It was higher than it would have been if I hadn't known about the marijuana, but lower than the policy limits. Henry should be happy.

Too bad I couldn't be there when the bum-knee guy and his attorney heard about the toxic marijuana and realized they had settled for half of what I would have offered.

When I got back to my office, I found Bonita back at her desk and Olivia, the wife of the second key partner, Fred O'Leary, waiting for me. "Won't take but a second," Olivia said, holding up a form letter and some petitions. "Bastards trying to put up a medical arts building down in Laurel, next to Oscar Scherer Park. Knock out the last great Florida scrub, knock out the last of the scrub jays. You need to write a letter to the planning department and your county commissioner. Then get everybody you see to write one and sign the petition." Fred O'Leary's wife handed me a stack of paper as we stood over Bonita's desk.

"Didn't we do this before?" I remembered Olivia's intense one-woman campaign to save the scrub jays that nested next to Oscar Scherer State Park. Scrub jays are odd bluebirds that for some reason have no fear of man, much, unfortunately, to their detriment, and will land on you in a curiously touching way. They are beautiful, they are friendly, they are industrious, and they are endangered, and, of course, hardly anyone cared. Except Olivia.

"Yeah, we stopped them in 'eighty-six, way before your time, and then again in 'ninety-eight, but now they're at it again. County bought the land in 'eighty-six to protect it but never did anything to tie it up, no conservation restrictions. So every new county commission can sell it or lease it long-term if they want. Value of the property has skyrocketed like you wouldn't believe. These doctors want a thirty-year lease from the county to develop it. Planning board has to okay it first. Lots of pressure on the members of the planning board, you can imagine. In fact, that doctor of yours is one of the main movers and shakers."

Doctor of mine? Did she mean the dermatologist I had dated to much fanfare a few years ago, the one who officially broke my heart when he dumped me for his office nurse, a twenty-one-year-old blonde with nary a blemish or wrinkle, or was she talking about any one of my current or former physician clients?

"Which doc of mine?"

"Dr. Trusdale," Olivia said, as Bonita pointed to the clock on the wall and then to her calendar, her face calm, her eyes almost sleepy.

Oh, the dead doc of mine, I thought, momentarily ignoring Bonita's desultory warning. Did Olivia know Trusdale was dead? She hadn't used the past tense.

"I'll get on it, but first I think Bonita has something for me to do."

"I'm out the door," Olivia said. "You guys come on by, see the dogs anytime." Olivia, aside from trying to save birds, raised and trained Rottweilers.

"I'll put my kids on it. They'll get signatures at the mall and get their teachers to write," Bonita said.

Olivia thanked us and left. Bonita put the "Save the Scrub Jays" materials in a neat pile by her purse so she wouldn't forget to take them home.

"You haven't forgotten Dr. Padar's hearing on the plaintiff's motion for a new trial, have you?" Bonita said. "It's in St. Pete."

"No, I haven't forgotten. Get Angela for me, please. She can drive while I review the file." As if I didn't already know every word in it.

Because the hearing was in St. Petersburg, Angela would have to navigate two interstates plus drive across the Sunshine Skyway, the wicked and beautiful 192-foot-high bridge that spans Tampa Bay and connects St. Pete with Sarasota county and points south. A trip from Sarasota across the Skyway could take anywhere from a half hour to all day depending on wind currents, traffic flow, and whether anyone had rear-ended someone or any suicides had backed up the steady stream of cars. Just last week the bridge was closed all morning while someone in a Spiderman suit scaled down the high bridge only to be arrested by the waiting coast guard and hauled off to jail or the loony bin.

I glanced at the clock and considered that I might be pressing my luck, but I thought a Skyway crossing under a tight time frame would be a good test of Angela's aggressiveness and nerve.

With the wind behind us, and no suicide jumpers or slow tourist gawkers in front of us, Angela whipped us across the Skyway while I flipped through the file. We got to the courthouse in the nick of time, hustled across the genteel old streets of St. Petersburg, smiled through two sets of metal detectors, and ran up the stairs to the courtroom.

At the hearing I said about two hundred dollars' worth of words and won despite my conciseness. So flushed with that easy victory and the Dr. Trusdale settlement, I felt exuberant.

Angela surrendered the keys at my demand, and I blasted back across the Skyway while Angela studied Tampa Bay for dolphins or sharks.

"You reckon it's true, what they say about this bridge?"

"Don't say 'reckon.' It's not sophisticated," I said, echoing the same correction Jackson had drilled into me as a two-month associate after I'd said "reckon" and "fixing to" at a hearing while he bird-dogged me. Jackson had paid for speech and diction lessons for me so I wouldn't sound like a south Georgia hick, but I didn't think I needed to go that far with Angela. "Don't say 'fixing to,' either," I added.

Angela gave me a hurt little look.

"After all, you're not in the South anymore, not in Sarasota." Where the imported carpetbagger culture overruled the geography.

"Do you think it's true, what they say about the Skyway?"

Much better, I thought, and said, "What, you mean about VWs and vans blowing off in the windstorms?"

"No, I meant about the men buried in the concrete supports."

Everything and nothing about the Skyway myths are true, so I just said I didn't know and kept driving as Angela studied the blue waters of Tampa Bay, and then the bridge was behind us and four thousand cars were in front of us.

I hate interstates and swung off at the first chance onto U.S. 301, where there is still some hint of what old Florida must have been. But as I was negotiating the traffic on the way back to Sarasota, Angela piped up and asked, "Can we stop at my apartment a minute? I need to check on Crosby. He's very old."

"Oh, you live with your father?" I realized that though Angela had been working with me for nearly two years I knew very little about her.

"No, Crosby's my dog. He's fifteen."

"That's practically ancient, isn't it? For a dog?"

"Yes."

So, we spun off east to the cheaper apartment complexes and stopped to check on a little rat dog with a fluff of gray hair around his face. Despite his frail look, Crosby engaged us both in a rather lively lick-and-wag session.

Angela's apartment was decorated in Early College Poverty, with a three-legged couch propped up on a brick. But the place was as clean and clear of debris as my own house.

"Don't they pay you?" I asked, looking at the wounded couch, though as a partner I knew perfectly well what she earned. I had argued for her first raise myself.

"I've got a lot of debt. College loans and stuff. And I'm saving up for a down payment on a house."

Good for you, I thought. Get out of debt, don't put on the golden handcuffs, hold out for a real life in a decade or so—exactly my plan, so I approved of the implication that it was also Angela's.

We walked the ancient little rat dog outside in the shade around the Dumpster, where he seemed to be unusually fussy about selecting a place to go, and Angela explained that she hoped Crosby would live until Christmas so she could take him home during the annual law firm holiday shutdown and leave him with her brother so that "when Crosby crosses over, Jimmy can bury him down in the pecan orchard with all the others, exactly like I promised."

Home, from her accent, was obviously somewhere in greater Dixie. I decided not to ask about the rest.

Chapter 7

To counterbalance the otherwise good afternoon, after returning from the Crosby detour I hunched over my desk, reenergized by the panic at the thought of Jackson's veggie baby case, and I began reading MEDLINE literature about CMV. Bonita had gone, but she had left me tomorrow's schedule and an apple with a note that said it was unwaxed, organic, and washed.

Trusting Bonita not to trick me with a waxy pesticide / germ-laden apple, I munched and read. Reading medical literature is a torturous process. Physicians, especially research physicians, tend to use words that normal people naturally will not have a clue about. The article in front of me stated that congenital CMV infections occur in .2 to 2.2 percent of births. Okay, got it. That's English. Approximately 5 to 10 percent of those infants will have classic signs of illness or defects at birth. Okay, got it. Also English. Cerebral palsy and mental retardation are but two of the possible results if a woman develops a primary CMV infection during pregnancy. Okay, got it.

Then the article said, among other incomprehensible phrases, that suggestive findings included hydrops, splenomegaly, chorioretinitis, occlusion of the foramen ovale, cerebral ventriculomegaly, intracranial calcifications, microcephaly, ascites, hyperechoic bowel, brain atrophy, and oligohydramnios. I stifled my urge to scream out loud and reached for my dog-eared medical dictionary, in which the definitions of terms such as *oligohydramnios* usually were made up of still other words I would need to look up. Sometimes the process of understanding one word could suck up half an hour or so of time I didn't have.

After spending an hour on one page, I simply couldn't comprehend any more, and I figured that if I drank another drop of coffee I might as well scrape out the lining of my stomach with a rusty knife. That, and not the darkness outside the window in my corner office, told me it was time to go home.

Having had only two grapes, Bonita's apple, and coffee for nourishment, I was hungry, so I stopped at the Granary and got a wide assortment of fresh, organic vegetables, including some luscious-looking snow peas and a gingerroot so fresh that the scent of it warmed my nose when I sniffed it. I envisioned a big stir-fry over brown rice, spicy with ginger and hot with just a dash of Chinese mustard, and some penoir blanc in a long-stemmed glass.

I forgot about Newly.

He was sitting in my living room, flipping through a file, his briefcase and a stack of transcripts on the floor. Newly, still in his office clothes, kissed me casually on the cheek, like somebody all moved in. He smelled like a courtroom.

"Did I give you a key?"

"Sure, hon."

I knew he was lying, but he smiled sweetly at me. He can look rather winsome for a big alpha-male type. My best guess was that he had taken the spare key out of the kitchen drawer sometime this morning.

"We broke up, you know. About three wives back. Remember?"

"Aw, Lilly. I *never* broke up with you."

I let it pass, for now, as I was too tired and too hungry to get into a discussion of any kind of personal relationship with anyone, especially Newly.

Newly wanted to take me out to dinner, and I debated, but I heard the call of the snow peas and the good wine and the fresh ginger waiting to be sliced. I said I'd cook, knowing even as I said it that this was a mistake.

I can cook, having learned through necessity, not at my mother's knee. But as a general rule I don't let men know I can cook. As soon as you cook a meal for them, before you know it they want you to do laundry, pick up after them, fetch them stuff, and then next thing you know you're cleaning up the bathroom after some large male animal with poor aim.

But I made the offer and edged around Newly's stuff on my floor and headed into the bedroom, where I chewed my lip after seeing suitcases scattered on my clean, bare terrazzo floors. I hung up my jacket and skirt, smashed my other clothes in the hamper, and took a quick shower, heavy with Dr. Bronner's peppermint soap, which, I am convinced, could revive the dead.

Back in the kitchen, Newly hovered, trying to be helpful, so I sent him to move his stuff from my bedroom to the guest room and to shower while I rewashed the vegetables he'd held under the faucet in a clump for a fraction of a second. The rice was on, the garlic browning in a blend of olive oil and tamari, and I had finished slicing the ginger. One of the tiny, expensive jars of hot Chinese mustard, the pale green kind that will sear the roof of your mouth if you aren't careful, was opened on the counter. I like a few drops in the stir-fry to add a kick to the vegetables. Newly came back in the kitchen, wearing a pair of my tap pants in pale pink satin.

"My stuff's all dirty," he explained. "These fit a bit snug," he said, grinning, "but look good."

Well, he did. Look good. He was a fine-looking man, though the pudge around his middle was gaining on his workouts, and the pink complimented his swarthy skin. Tall, dark, and handsome—in my pair of ladies' fancy panties.

Well, okay, I thought, grinning back and giving him a playful tug on the pink satin, then washed my hands and turned back to sauté the shiitake mushrooms.

Newly circled me from behind as I slipped the sliced carrots in the broth in the iron skillet.

"Smells good," he said, his nose deep in my hair.

I took a long slice of fresh ginger in my fingers and turned around. "Here, eat this."

"Hot," he said, sucking air into his mouth.

"Hot," I mimicked, with a seductive tone and come-hither smile to underline the double meaning.

Having obviously gotten Newly excited, though I wasn't at all sure why I had done so, I deliberately turned back to my vegetables, sizzling now in the skillet, and flipped the carrots and mushrooms, the rising steam smelling of spice and earth and food. The snow peas would go in last, just seconds after I turned the heat off, to turn them a bright green from the last of the heat but leave them crisp. Newly hovered, and pressed, and touched. His hands reached under my cotton shirt and touched my bare skin. They were warm. I remembered Newly's hands. Our history and my long dry spell conspired against my better judgment. I let his hands drift upward, his fingers gentle but sure as they tracked my skin and set off little sparks not wholly unlike those from the Chinese mustard.

Long before I got the snow peas in, we hit the cold terrazzo floor in a hot, hard thunk that bruised us both, though we didn't notice until the next morning.

As always with Newly, I was never quite sure how it had happened.

Chapter 8

Practicing law is like juggling a dozen raw eggs, and sooner or later every lawyer drops one.

I heard the sound of splat coming at me.

More precisely, I heard my faithful secretary mutter something like *Madre de Dios,* which I think is Mother of God, or Saints Preserve Us. I get them mixed up, but Bonita doesn't blaspheme lightly and my antennae were up when she came into my office holding a file.

"Jackson's brain-damaged baby case," Bonita said.

Splat, splat, splat, I heard.

"I found the pleadings file on your desk when I came in this morning."

While I'd been playing around with Newly and was late getting in.

"I was going through it, tagging . . ."

"Spit it out."

"Did you know that the plaintiff's motion for a pretrial conference is set for this afternoon?"

"Good God," I blurted, blasphemy coming easier to me, having been raised by heathens.

Bonita handed me the top volume of the veggie baby pleadings file with the notice of hearing faceup, as if perhaps I wouldn't believe her. I read it and handed the file back to her as if it were safer in her hands than mine.

No way on this whole huge green earth could I be ready for a pretrial in that case in a matter of hours.

The phone rang and Bonita eyed it but turned back to me.

All right, think. That's what lawyers do in tough spots. They think.

No, in exigent circumstances, they file paper. "Has Jackson filed the motion for a continuance?"

Flip, flip, flip.

"Yes."

"Is it set for a hearing time yet?"

Flip, flip.

"No."

"Okay, good. File a cross-notice of hearing for this afternoon, same time as the pretrial, telling the plaintiff's attorney, Stephen LaBlanc, and the judge and his judicial assistant that I'm going to argue the motion for continuance at the pretrial. Fax a copy to LaBlanc, the judge, and his J.A."

The phone, which had stopped ringing, started ringing again.

Bonita didn't even blink at the sound, but she nodded at me, a small smile playing about her full lips. "Got it. Take up LaBlanc's time with your motion, argue that if your motion is granted it moots his pretrial. Buys you time to get ready for the pretrial. How about I do the same on the motion to amend the witness list?"

"Excellent. Do it."

Ambush, stall, live to fight another day. Guerrilla litigation tactics were by far the norm and not the exception these days.

Our receptionist's voice cut through the speakerphone. "Bonita, are you there? It's one of your kids. You'd better get this."

Bonita stepped over to my phone, hit a button, and said something sweet-sounding in Spanish, followed by a very American "What's up?"

I chewed my lip and waited.

"All right. Put the tooth in a damp paper towel. No, don't wash it. Wrap it up. Have Benicio drive her to the dentist. I'll call and tell him you're on the way. Pack some cotton on her gums and put a cold compress on her face, you hear?"

I chewed my lip so hard I tasted my own blood and started thinking about which secretary I could commandeer if Bonita insisted on going to the dentist's office herself.

"Yes, I know he's only fourteen, but Benicio knows how to drive. Wear your seat belt and tell him not to speed."

I edged closer to Bonita.

"Yes. I'll call your aunt and she'll meet you at the dentist. I'll be along soon as I can, but I have something here I must finish first."

Oh, bless her, I thought, and stopped chewing my lip.

"No, I'm not mad. I love you all. You tell her that for me." This was followed by something sweet-sounding in Spanish.

"Accident. I'll tell you about it later," Bonita said.

"If it's serious, don't sign anything and call Newly," I said, knowing Bonita knew that.

Bonita only glanced at me as she headed out to her computer, where within seconds after she'd called the dentist's office, I heard the reassuring sound of legal jargon being typed into the computer at an incredibly fast rate of speed.

Stephen LaBlanc, the hotshot Miami attorney representing the veggie baby's good-parents, was already in the hearing room when I tumbled in with my entire entourage of one, Angela, the orange-haired wonder, both of us looking like feverish, crazed women. Naturally, Stephen sat calmly in his chair, posed as if for the cover of *Esquire.* Dapper. The man was dapper. I hate a dapper man. He rose smooth and easy while I struggled with my purse, the five-pound paperback *Florida Rules of Civil Procedure,* the most recent volume of the veggie baby pleadings file, three copies of my amended memorandum of law, and a stack of photocopied cases Angela had jabbed at me as I fled the office for the hot ten-minute walk over here. She had trudged along beside me, twisting her hair with one hand and with the other carrying a briefcase full of the most important summaries of Jackson's discovery in case we actually had to do a real pretrial conference. The humidity had tripled my hair into a kind of wiry, electric-shock punk style, and I was keenly aware that I was visibly sweating. The air-conditioning in the building was set at about zero, which had the immediate effect of stopping up my nose.

When Stephen stuck out his hand, I dropped the *Rules of Civil Procedure* trying to put enough stuff down to shake it.

"Well, I see the bottom of the order is here," he sniped and stepped back. Didn't even pick up the dropped book.

Angela did, and then she took the memoranda and the photocopies out of my other hand and smoothed them out and laid them on the table.

Judge Goddard came into the hearing room. We all rose and I dropped the damn *Rules of Civil Procedure* again. Angela scampered to gather it up.

Judge Goddard nodded at Stephen. To Angela and me, he said, "Good afternoon, ladies. Ms. Harper and Ms. Cleary. Are we ready?"

No, I thought, but that's beside the point.

After introducing himself for the sake of the court reporter and the transcript, Stephen informed the judge the hearing had been set on his motion for a pretrial conference, and that I was improperly trying to piggyback my motions for a continuance and to amend the witness list onto his motion. Stephen maintained that he learned of my plans to argue my motion for a continence only when his secretary had called him on his cell phone just minutes ago.

Oh, yeah, right. As if she'd waited three hours to call him on that.

"But you were served with the original motion for continuance, what, three weeks ago?" Judge Goddard asked.

"Four, your honor," I said.

"And the grounds haven't changed, have they?" The judge peered at Stephen with much the same look I've seen Olivia give one of her Rottweilers after he'd piddled on the Oriental rug.

"Yes, sir, but . . ."

I stopped listening and tried to visualize my safe place, my crystal blue waterfall. I was so wholly unprepared that listening to Stephen prattle wouldn't help me. Nothing would, I thought, as the waterfall crumpled into a vision of canned hash.

Angela nudged me. Judge Goddard looked at me. Stephen had shut up, so it must be my turn to speak.

"Good afternoon, your honor," I said, as Angela shoved a memorandum in front of me. "I have a memorandum of law prepared for you, if I may."

"I trust you have one for me," Stephen said.

"Of course she does," Judge Goddard answered, a hint of a growl deep in his throat.

Okay, this is going all right, I thought, making myself breathe and sliding the copy that had the pages out of order to Stephen and taking the perfect copy to the judge.

"If my motions for a continuance and to amend the expert witness list are granted, your honor, then Mr. LayBlank's pretrial conference would be premature."

"La-Blanc," Stephen corrected. "There is no *y* and no *k* in it."

"What my memorandum establishes is that where a need for a

continuance is occasioned by some fault of the other side, which I can demonstrate here, and there is no undue prejudice to either party, then it is a matter of discretion with a judge to grant a continuance. I refer the court to the case of, er, . . ." Here, I had to stop while Angela turned the page of my copy of the memo and jabbed her finger emphatically at a citation of law on page two.

"That's all right," Judge Goddard said. "I can read. Tell me how this is his fault."

"Well, your honor, Mr. LayBlank here hired away our top medical expert witness by offering him twice the hourly rate the liability insurance company authorized me to pay him, and I am in the process of locating another expert witness. I need—"

"Time," Judge Goddard finished for me and eyed Stephen as if he were guilty of some personal affront against me.

Encouraged by the judge's expression, I wandered through my explanation, pointed out that nobody would be unduly prejudiced by a delay and that justice would be served, et cetera, et cetera, and threw in a couple of the case names that Angela kept waggling her fingers at, and hoped I had made some kind of sense.

The court reporter typed, paused, looked up, and nodded, and Judge Goddard turned to Stephen and said, "Mr. LayBlank."

I noticed Stephen didn't correct that as he launched off without notes or sweat or mispronunciations and slung out rules and citations and hundred-dollar words and then turned and looked at me and said, "Ms. Cleary is clearly engaging in sophistry, your honor, but I must insist. . . ."

Sophistry? I didn't like the sound of that, or the tone of voice Stephen was using, and I checked the stern look on Judge Goddard's face before I jumped up and said, "I object."

Technically you don't object at a hearing, but I'd been reading Judge Goddard's facial expressions for years now and knew I could get away with it.

"You apologize to her, right now, Mr. LayBlank," the good judge said.

"Your honor, all I'm saying is that she is blaming me for the inadequacies of her own case, for her law firm's inexplicable delays, and—"

"That doesn't sound much like 'I'm sorry' to me," Judge Goddard snapped.

Stephen looked at me, then at the court reporter, who had stopped typing and leaned back to watch the show.

"Madam Court Reporter, please make a record of this exchange."

"Yes, Mr. LeeBlink," she said.

"La-Blanc, La-Blanc," Stephen snapped. "Can't anybody in this whole damn county pronounce my name?"

"No reason for profanity, son," Judge Goddard said. Then he slapped down his hand on my memorandum and said, "Motion for continuance granted. Contact my assistant for a new time. Motion to amend the witness list granted. Ms. Cleary, you have thirty days to file an amended list with your new expert witness identified. Pretrial conference will be rescheduled. Now, Mr. LayBlank, you apologize to this woman right now."

"Very well, I see I have no choice but to capitulate to this obvious hometown favoritism. Madam Court Reporter, I will be ordering a transcript."

"Steve," I said, smiling my biggest fake smile, "you have a nice flight home." He never did apologize.

"Steph-fin," he corrected, clueless, still, as to how easy it was for the hometown crowd to play him.

The judge rose to his full five feet five, we stood, and he disappeared through a green curtain into his own chambers. Sort of like the Wizard of Oz, I thought, as I slumped back into a chair while Angela gathered up the strewn papers. Stephen picked up his dapper briefcase and left with a tight-assed smile and the ubiquitous "See you in court" threat.

Madam Court Reporter—Judy, by name—closed her little machine and smiled at me. I take her to lunch regularly at the Ivy Club, charging it, wine and all, to a rotating list of clients, and we gossip like schoolgirls. "I'll let you know if Mr. LaBlanc orders the transcript," she said, winked at me, and left.

Judy gone, I put my head down on the table, and Angela patted my back once and then apparently thought the better of that.

I heard Judge Goddard come back into the hearing room, and I lifted my head.

"Lilly, what happened to you? In all my years of listening to you, I've never known you to be unprepared."

"No sir. It's just . . . you see, it's Jackson's case, and he dumped it on me a couple days ago, but I didn't get the pleadings file until this morning, and I didn't know about the pretrial until mid-morning, and one of my clients got killed, and . . ." Of course, I wasn't going to mention I'd been diddling with Newly instead of working late at night as I usually did.

And I was whining. I stopped.

"I'm sorry, your honor. It won't happen again."

"Lilly, I'm not fussing. Just worried. You're always so overprepared, that's all."

He would have called me "honey" if Angela weren't still in the room.

"Thank you, your honor. I'm fine. And it won't happen again."

"Ms. Harper, we aren't ex parte communicating," he said, nodding at Angela. "We're old friends." The judge glanced at Angela, who nodded, graciously gathering the papers into her arms and taking the trial briefcase, and eased out of the room.

"What the hell is sophistry?" I asked.

"Ten-dollar word for chicanery. Come on, look it up so you'll remember it."

I myself thought *chicanery* was also a ten-dollar word, but I didn't share this with the judge.

Back in Judge Goddard's chambers, I looked up the word Stephen had thrown at me with such contempt. "A plausible but misleading or fallacious argument," the dictionary said.

"That's not so bad," I said.

"Told you it was just a fancy word for chicanery," he said.

He leaned back in his red chair and sighed and closed his eyes. "I hate those know-it-alls from Miami with their big bags of tricks, looking down their big-city noses at us."

"Me, too." But I was studying the judge, thinking how old he looked. Coming up on his mandatory retirement birthday in another few years. The last of the old-fashioned Florida-cracker judges who let common sense and fair play rule and didn't take crap from anybody.

As if reading my mind, Judge Goddard opened his eyes and looked right at me and said, "You know, they'll replace me with somebody like him. Some hotshot lawyer been in town five years but with ties to that damn carpetbagger governor going all the way back to their fathers' fraternity."

"Yes, sir."

"Walking Lawton Chiles," the old judge said in a tone of admiration. "I'll tell you what, that's the last Florida governor to actually be a Floridian. Walked the whole damn state when he was just a guy from Lakeland nobody'd heard about, running for the U.S. Senate, shaking hands with everybody he met and listening. Listening to them, by God."

"Yes, sir. I met him once, shook his hand. Of course, he was running for reelection as governor then and riding around in a big-ass car."

"His walking days, you were still in diapers."

We sighed together, as if on cue.

"You mark my words," the good judge said, "we'll live to rue the day we let the damn carpetbaggers take over."

· · ·

That night, still weary from the veggie baby hearing, in the nearly dead hallway of my law firm, I passed Jackson, who without greeting or breaking stride said, "Doll, now you got that continuance in the brain-damaged baby case, I've got another case for you."

"No, thank you," I said.

We stopped and stared at each other for a moment. I had never said no to this man before. My heart beat too fast and my mouth went dry.

"Doll, if you're overworked, give some of the low-billing files to that little orange-haired gal of yours." Having spoken, Jackson turned and started to walk away.

"Angela Harper. That's her name. Her name is not 'that little orange-haired gal.' And she is not, technically, my gal. She's an associate and she has her own caseload." I raised my voice, though I struggled for control. This man had dumped a killer veggie baby case on me at the last minute and hadn't even warned me about the pretrial and didn't say nice job for getting out of that, and now he wanted to dump more of his work on me. "No," I said, loudly and with an edge. "The brain-damaged baby case is quite enough of your work for one week."

His eyes narrowed into that eagle-eyed glint that Stonewall's face bore in the bigger-than-life-size portrait over Jackson's desk. "What?" he said, as if misunderstanding me.

"No. I'm not taking any more of your cases."

Jackson's eyes squinted another notch, so much so that I doubted he could focus on me.

"You didn't even warn me about the pretrial," I said shrilly.

Possibly in response to my sharp voice, little Ashton the Maniac stuck his head out of the conference-room door across from where I stood. He cleared his throat, and I glanced at him and saw that his girl-friend, Jennifer the Stairmaster wizard, was hanging over his shoulder, and I realized I was yelling and stopped.

When Ashton started clapping, Jackson made a loud, inarticulate noise and stomped down the hallway.

"Good girl," Ashton said. "Come in. Join us. We're relaxing."

"Relaxing" is a lawyer euphemism for drinking on the job. I slipped into the room and shut the door.

Ashton, whose irises were huge bowls of blue glass, grabbed me, hugged me, and gave me a big kiss, right on the lips. I kept my mouth tightly closed as I tugged away from him.

"Proud of you, babe. Telling the big guy off. Told him not to give you that brain-damaged baby case." Ashton then twirled me around as if we were square-dancing.

I spun and came to rest in front of Ashton and rolled my eyes at Jennifer.

"Oh, don't worry about Jenn. I told her all about us." Ashton grinned.

Huh? Ashton and me? An "us"? He told Jennifer what? *Caray!* There is no "us," as in Ashton and me, and that was about the last rumor I needed.

"What do you mean, 'us'?" I narrowed my eyes in a plausible imitation of Jackson and looked into Ashton's as he took a swig of his drink.

"Oh, don't worry," Jennifer sang. "He said you had this big, you know, schoolgirl, like, crush thing and all, because he was your, ah, mentor, but he, you know, didn't want to mess up how you worked together. That was all before he met me, anyway." Jennifer smiled the confident smile of a pretty blonde with big tits. "Martini?" she asked and held up a shaker.

"With vodka," I said, and eyed Ashton again. "Us?"

"Ah, babe, come on, you're gorgeous and all, so don't take it personal, but you're an Amazon, not my type. I told Jenn we never consummated it."

"Here you go, Lilly." Jennifer handed me a glass and winked at me.

I sipped, and I simmered, and I wondered if it was safe for Ashton to drink when his dilated eyes suggested other mind-altering substances were already afloat in his system.

"You were *sooo* cool out there," Jennifer said.

I sipped, and sipped again, and I mellowed.

Jennifer, in my unstudied opinion, was a dingbat of the highest order. But the girl knew how to make a martini. There is, of course, a hidden bar in the credenza in every conference room in the firm, and in most of the lawyers' offices, and soon I felt the warm, fuzzy feeling of hard liquor running down my throat. I also felt the warm, fuzzy feelings of a friendship beginning as Jennifer continued to ooh and ah over me as if I had single-handedly ended male dominance of the female sex.

"They just won't ever respect us," Jennifer said, shaking her martini and her Barbie-doll breasts, which were, naturally, generously displayed.

"Un-huh," I said, wondering if Jennifer understood about irony.

"Why, I had this boss once, when I worked at a big bank, and he, no matter what I did, that man just never gave me credit for having any sense."

"Un-huh," I said, sipping my drink and losing interest.

"You were *sooo* wonderful to stand up for yourself and that other woman," Jennifer cooed. "I showed that banker boss a thing or two, like you, and I taught him about respecting women."

"Yeah? Did you tie him to the bed and read him Betty Friedman?" Ashton asked.

"Who's that?" Jennifer responded.

Yup. I had definitely lost interest.

"That squat woman with the big hats. You know, that feminist congresswoman," Ashton said.

Swallowing my vodka martini, I started to correct him, plus educate Jennifer, and then I thought, You can't teach a pig to sing, and I took another sip.

"No, what I did was I bought out a bait shop full of crickets and put them in his house, and then I spray painted his car windows—he had a Mercedes, a huge, black one, and it had just about the best speakers, had 'em special installed—Bose, I think—and that car rocked, and the leather seats, those leather seats . . ." Jennifer glazed over for a minute. "That car, I . . . those leather seats. Then I . . ." Jennifer seemed to have lost her place. I know I had.

"Baby," Ashton said in a soft tone, almost endearing.

"Anyway," she said, suddenly beaming her baby blues across at me with a quick-change giddiness that made me suspect psychogenic drugs, "you are just so cool, and Ashton's always telling me how smart you are, how you don't miss a trick."

I was so this and so that, she continued, winning back my interest. The vodka teased my brain into believing her. I might forgive her for being blond, blue-eyed, and stacked.

But I wasn't sure I would forgive Ashton for spreading a tale that I'd had the hots for him.

Chapter 9

Bonita knocked on my door and stuck her head in to tell me that Newly was on the phone. So, okay, I thought, and waited for the maternal postscript I could tell was coming.

"Don't you break that man's heart again," she said, and closed the door gently behind her. Because Newly had represented her in litigation after her husband's fatal encounter with an orange juice bottling machine and didn't charge her a dime, letting his office eat even the expenses, Bonita had a special affection for Newly. "My five children have a college trust fund, thanks to that man," she had told Jackson to his face once when he was thunderously cursing Newly for some sleight-of-hand nonsense in a case.

Notwithstanding Bonita's rare regard for Newly, I thought, Break his heart, my ass—he's a pretty tough guy—and I picked up the phone. That morning I'd asked him to find out what was going on with the Trusdale investigation. But Newly's sources in the police department apparently were more attuned to auto wrecks and industrial accidents and didn't have a clue as to why Sam Santuri might be investigating me in connection with Dr. Trusdale's death.

So I called the hunky detective, not to ask him that directly, but to ask about the autopsy.

Before he answered my question, he asked me how the Trusdale malpractice case was coming along, now that my client was dead.

"Settled it," I told him and lied when he asked, "How much?" Frankly, I was embarrassed that the figure was so high, and maybe just a bit afraid the amount might make him think I was in cahoots with the bum-knee guy's attorney or something.

You know how paranoid you get driving in traffic when a police car pulls in behind you? It doesn't matter if you're going the speed limit, seat belt fastened, and no illegal contraband or not—a cop on your tail makes you nervous. Basic human nature.

So, yeah, I lied to Detective Santuri because I was paranoid.

But he let it go and told me what he'd learned from the autopsy.

Dr. Trusdale had died of smoking the highly toxic but common flowering oleander. There were dried oleander leaves in the joint, along with some skunk-hybrid marijuana, a green marijuana particularly adapted for growing in the South, the detective explained, of a color that would blend with the oleander leaves.

"Damn," I said, not owning up for a moment that I knew what skunk sativa was, had weeded, watered, and fertilized plots of the stuff myself for summer work between my freshman and sophomore years in high school. Moderately mold resistant, with a kick-ass high. But not mixed with oleander leaves. "That would have been an ugly way to go."

Yes, Detective Santuri agreed it would be.

And all those kids at college laughed at me because the only marijuana I'd ever smoke was that which my one outlaw brother grew in his back forty, strictly organic skunk-hybrid, a rural southwest Georgia "u-pick" with a modest row of opium poppies blooming red and beautiful in the bright southern sun. But he was taken by religion and became a Pentecostal, and though his u-pick business continued to grow, he had started speaking in tongues, and he proselyted, so I gave up going around until he calmed down, only he never did. By the time I was used to his speaking in tongues, I was in law school and too busy memorizing the penumbras of the Constitution to smoke dope. I never did touch the poppies.

Poisoned marijuana. Damn. I thanked Sam for the information and, feeling queasy, was about to hang up.

"Did you know Dr. Trusdale had two other malpractice judgments against him? One in Texas and another in Florida."

"No." I felt sweat break out on my face. How had Henry and I missed this? I had done the standard search through LEXIS and Westlaw for judgments against Dr. Trusdale, plus looked through the guard-dog consumer sites that list lawsuits against doctors, and had found nothing. Our firm's private investigator had done a background search on the good doctor but hadn't listed any prior suits. And, of course, Henry was supposed to prowl the extensive resources and databases available to insurance companies and find out about other suits before he even assigned the case to me. And, naturally, I'd asked Dr. Trusdale about this too. Damn doctor had lied straight-faced to me. A con made that much easier by a system that helps doctors hide malpractice judgments by a simple change of location and carefully worded language in the settlements. I said another quick prayer of thanks to the cosmic forces that the bum-knee guy's attorney apparently hadn't known about these prior hits either.

Then I wondered, if I hadn't been able to find this out, how in the world Sam had.

"How'd you find out about the other lawsuits?"

"His wife told us."

Oh, research the old-fashioned way.

"Got any details?"

"Not yet. The wife didn't know, but she's trying to find his papers. That's coming."

"Let me know when you do, please?"

We said our pleases and thank-yous and hung up. I was still shaking off the sense of the narrow escape when Fred O'Leary, partner number two and husband of Olivia, aka the bird lady, knocked on my door and opened it at the same time.

"Come in," I offered, though technically it was too late to issue the invitation.

"Puppies," Fred said, and lit a cigarette right under the No Smoking sign on my wall.

"Ooh," I murmured, not, I realized, unlike a girl, something I try to minimize around Smith, O'Leary, and Stanley, P.A. "Puppies. When? How many?"

"Three. Last night. Olivia says to come over after work and see them. One female. Olivia says she's got your name on her."

"Oooh, puppies," I repeated, drawing Bonita into the office with my cooing. Little bundles of black and brown Rottweiler, tiny tots of blind dependency, with their sweet, soft skin and mewing little mouths. "I'll stop on the way home and see them."

"You too, Bonita. Bring your children for a peek," Fred said, and left, trailing smoke down the hallway of our "smoke-free" building. He's the only partner who ever socializes with the support staff. In fact, he was the only partner to socialize with me when I was a mere associate, and at the end of my first terrifying day he had taken me home with him, where Olivia mothered and fed me fresh vegetables sauteed in secondhand cigarette smoke.

After Fred left, I leaned back in my chair and closed my eyes and had visions of puppies running over me, their little tongues licking and tickling, and that sweet puppy smell they have. "Ahh, puppies."

"That's how you're supposed to feel about babies," Bonita said.

So, okay, spank me, my maternal instincts had been diverted from babies to puppies.

Bonita sighed and left my office, leaving the door cracked.

. . .

Technically I was supposed to be doing the final edits on an appellate brief, but my mind wandered back to Dr. Trusdale and my mugging and Sam and Newly and just about everything except the appellate brief. So when Bonita knocked on my door and asked if I had a minute for Detective Santuri, I was actually glad.

"Twice in one day," I said, smiling, as he walked into my office.

He nodded, which I assumed was Strong-and-Silent for hello.

"Let's go outside," he said.

"Sure." I was game and led him out the back door by my office.

"This is where you were mugged, isn't it?" he asked.

"Yes."

"Did you know the code on the lock was changed the day before you were mugged?"

Lock codes, I thought, trying to remember but mostly noticing the way the sun lit up his chocolate eyes. "Yeah, sure. We changed it after we fired one of the bookkeepers."

"Did you already know the new code, or did you have it written down, have to get it out of your purse?"

"No, I knew the code. I memorize numbers easily."

"Talk me through the mugging again," he ordered.

I complied. Leaving out, I realized, that I'd stomped on the mugger's foot and then screamed. "Did I mention I fought back?" I didn't want Sam thinking I was a sissy.

"Yes. You struggled, you said. But walk me through it again."

My not-so-latent fondness for theatrics—another fine trait for a trial attorney—came out as I acted out the stomping, the scream, and the knock upside the head.

"He hit you when you screamed?"

"Yes. With something hard. In his hand."

"You didn't mention this before."

An accusation from Sam? That I was making it up? Or not cooperating by leaving out details?

The best defense is a good offense is a trial strategy I had frequently followed to mixed results but still favored. So I said, sounding, even to myself, a bit snippy, "I did too."

"Not to me." Very sure of himself, I saw.

Dodge on my part. "Why is that possibly relevant?"

"I'll show you. Where did the mugger come from?"

"Beats me," I said. Thin air? Hell? The karma of a misspent adolescence?

"You walked through the alley, right?" Sam nodded toward the alley beside the law firm.

I nodded.

"So you would have noticed somebody in the alley?"

"One would hope," I offered, unsure.

"You would have seen him if he'd been standing here, by the door?"

"One would think so, yes."

"So he must have been here, behind the stairs." Sam pointed to the stairs that led to the door on the second floor, the stairs used primarily by the smokers as a hangout during the workday, where they inhaled carcinogenics and avoided work.

"So," Sam said, "it must have been like this."

With the "this," Sam turned me toward the door, positioned my right hand on the lock, stepped back by the stairs, then advanced on me, put his arm around my neck and lightly tugged, pulling me closer against him.

Hmm, I thought, feeling his body heat through our clothes, this is kind of nice.

"Had you already punched in the access code?" he asked.

"Maybe."

"Was the door opened?"

"I don't know." He still had his arm around my neck, though this seemed unnecessary by now. I inhaled, and he pressed up against me, his chest coming neatly and tightly up against my back.

I held my breath. He dipped his face into my hair.

"Gardenias," he said, and sighed, and paused. "Now, scream. Like you did that night with the mugger."

Wondering if this might be some kind of turn-on for Sam, I faked a modest scream and his left hand came up with the speed of a demon and clamped over my mouth, shutting me up. I tried to bite his hand, but his grip was too strong. Then he dropped his hand from my mouth and his arm from around my neck and stepped back.

"That's why it doesn't make sense that a mugger would let go of your neck and hit you to shut you up."

"Oh." Well, yeah. Sam did have a point.

"What I'm thinking is that we've got somebody who is a rank amateur. It doesn't seem like the mugger was trying to kill you. And he didn't steal your purse. So what was he after?"

"Why do you say he wasn't trying to kill me?"

"He had you by surprise. You were unarmed and a clear target under the security light. If he wanted to kill you, you'd be dead. He'd have shot you, or used a knife. Unless he's a total idiot."

"He was trying to choke me."

"A choke hold isn't designed to kill someone, but to subdue them. And despite what television might show, it's hard to kill somebody with your bare hands. Especially someone tall and fit like you."

Ah, "fit." So he had noticed. "And the guy was, ah, small, I'd guess you'd say. Or, short—maybe not small," I said. The image was fuzzy in my brain. I'd gotten only a dizzy, air-deprived glance as he'd run away: jeans, jean jacket, baseball hat. He must have been hot as hell.

"You know, could've been a stoned junkie who didn't know what he was doing, and it doesn't mean a thing," Sam said.

"It wasn't a rank amateur who killed Dr. Trusdale, was it?"

"Probably not."

"Why do you think there is a connection between Dr. Trusdale's death and my mugging? Couldn't it just be coincidence?"

"Maybe. But it bothers me—the timing, the connections. You get mugged. Next day Dr. Trusdale visits you and dies."

All business again, Sam made his good-byes and left me standing in the back parking lot, watching him drive off and wondering what that clutch-and-scream reenactment was *really* about.

Chapter 10

Though I was earnestly trying to finish the damn appellate brief, I kept remembering both Sam's body pressed against mine and what he had said (or not said) about Dr. Trusdale. Such a hideous way to die, and Sam wouldn't even commit to whether it was or wasn't murder.

Murder or not, I decided to call a pathologist I'd worked with before in a couple of med mal cases. She's a kind of paleo-hippie. She and Olivia would be a good match on that score, I thought. Once, when I sat with her at a Kiwanis luncheon, I noticed one of the pathologist's dangling earrings was a fancy roach clip and the other a silver and jade dragonfly. I get a kick out of her, Dr. Annie Watts, and if we were seven-year-old kids I would have asked her to ride bikes to the lake and share my Fudgesicle, but I wasn't sure how grown-up women initiated friendships.

Despite my habit of calling on her only when I needed information, Dr. Watts acted glad to see me and welcomed me into her overstuffed office. I shifted and fidgeted in my chair during our small talk as her jars and files and journals pressed in on me. After we caught up, I got out the basic story about Dr. Trusdale, whom I identified as a client. She knew him, slightly, and had read the story in the paper. Though the newspaper still had not mentioned the poisoned marijuana, she'd already heard about the pot from someone in the medical examiner's office.

"Oleander—that's what the detective told me," I said.

"Extremely toxic plants, oleanders contain both the toxin oleandrin and nerioside." Dr. Watts pulled a cigarette from a half-filled pack, tapped the cigarette on her desk, and then put it, unlit, in her mouth. She sucked air through it with a notable gurgle that distracted me momentarily from the towering stacks of books not two feet from my chair.

"These toxins are like those found in foxglove—they work on the heart. One leaf can kill a child and thirty leaves will kill a horse. All those people planting hedges of oleanders don't appreciate its danger. Water drunk from glasses where cut oleander flowers have been can make people sick. Even honey made by bees visiting the flowers has produced toxic results."

I nodded, remembering that the real estate agent had warned me about the one clump on the corner of my lot when I bought my house, telling me never to burn the trimmings when the oleanders were pruned because even the smoke was dangerous. To this day, I tread a wide berth around my pink oleanders and hope the bush will die on its own. But they are tough plants, one of the reasons the highway department likes to plant them in the right-of-ways.

Still, they are pretty. I said so.

"Sure. But so are coral snakes. Beautiful creatures. But are you going to raise a few for pets?"

"Point taken."

Annie tapped the unlit cigarette in an ashtray and then put it back in her mouth. "Clinical symptoms develop rapidly and can include death without warning. Other symptoms can include gastrointestinal distress, vomiting, bloody diarrhea, and abdominal pain. The toxins in oleanders can also cause irregular heart rates and rhythms."

"Not a pretty way to go, eh?"

"No. Not a good way to die."

"So whoever did this, I mean, assuming somebody deliberately laced his pot with oleander trimmings, was pretty up on plants, and also mean."

"It's mean, and it's imprecise, so if someone knew enough to lace the pot with oleanders, they were also taking a chance that the deceased would smoke enough. Not a good plan. Not a plan you could count on." The pathologist tapped her cigarette again. "Not a plan somebody with good sense would use." Tap, tap with the cigarette.

"You want a light?" I offered, eyeing a box of matches on her desk, easy reach from me.

"Hell, no, I don't want a light. I quit smoking. Two years ago. Nasty habit. You ever see the lungs of a smoker?"

"Nope. Missed that one."

"I could show you."

"Nope, that's all right."

"Well, you change your mind, you let me know. In fact, we're doing an autopsy in just a little while on a man who died of lung cancer. You could stand in."

Though I had some other questions for the doctor, I was seized with an acute desire to leave, so I headed out to Fred and Olivia's house to see the puppies.

After a curse-evoking drive down the Tamiami Trail, a highway that gives all highways a bad name for tacky and traffic, I arrived at Fred and Olivia's house and pounded their front door. Olivia answered, arched her brows, and waved a lit cigarette at me by way of greeting. Fred came around the corner, smiled, and held up his drink, and I nodded. Olivia led me to the nursery, where one of their female Rottweilers was nursing three little squeaky furballs.

"You can't pick them up yet. Matilla is still protective," Fred said, joining us and handing me a vodka, which I immediately sipped. Absolut. Bless his heart, he remembered my brand.

Matilla growled at me as I leaned over her, admiring her children.

Olivia reached over and picked up one, and Matilla didn't so much as prick up her ears. "Knows the boss," Olivia said.

She handed me the puppy. "It's the girl. She's yours, say the word."

I went through the usual protestations—I was rarely home, working long days and weekends, and traveling for hearings, trials, depositions. It wouldn't be fair to the dog, I said.

But when I retire, I thought but didn't say, I was taking at least two, maybe three of Olivia's prize Rottweilers to my new home. Nobody knew my five-year plan. Which, of course, had been a seven-year plan when I'd first bought the 180 acres of apple orchards and woods in north Georgia two years ago. Farmer Dave, the man who had taught my brother Delvon and me about loyalty and farming, was my current caretaker, hiding out as he was on a few dozen felony warrants. I pay down the mortgage and visit when I can, and Farmer Dave keeps the orchard green, happy, and mowed.

Thinking how a Rottweiler would be just the dog for Farmer Dave and the 180 acres, I said, "When I'm ready."

"When you're ready," Olivia repeated, and I pressed the puppy to my chest, where it tried to nurse on a button on my blouse. I hugged the puppy ever so gently, mentally named her Emily, and rocked her against me.

"You know who's doing well in her obedience training with a Rottweiler?" Fred asked, lighting his cigarette off Olivia's.

"Yeah, and it's not even one of our Rotts," Olivia said.

"Who?"

"Jennifer, that nitwit girlfriend of Ashton's," Fred said. "Olivia's been working with her and her dog."

"Yeah, a female, named Bearess. At first, I wouldn't have bet two plugged nickels that girl would ever even housebreak the dog, but she's doing pretty darn good with it."

"Dog must be pretty smart," I added, and thought, *Bearess?*

"Well, yes." Olivia nodded. "But I'll tell you what, Jennifer is not nearly as dumb as we all think she is."

"Nor," Fred added, sipping his vodka, "as smart as Ashton wants us to think she is."

"She's pixilated for sure, but she's not totally stupid. You should see her work with that dog," Olivia said.

"You teaching them obedience training?" I asked.

"They've been taking a class at the vo-tech, but Ashton asked me to work some with them on the weekends. It's not bad. They're kind of fun to work with."

Trust Olivia to find a word like *pixilated* when the rest of us were using words like *dumb* and *dingbat* and *nitwit*. But I was quickly tired of talking about Jennifer, who might or might not be as stupid as most of us in the Smith, O'Leary, and Stanley family were apt to think she was.

"How goes the Save the Scrub Jay campaign?" I asked, thinking to change the subject and learn how it was progressing.

"Those letters and petitions you and Bonita worked on will help. Thank you. Told you, I think, your Dr. Trusdale was the ringleader of the physicians who want to develop that land for a south-county medical arts building."

I nodded, and Emily the still-blind puppy mewed and then tried to nurse from my little finger.

"But Dr. Trusdale's getting killed off didn't help any. Another physician—this one's an obstetrician—has taken over the reins of the physicians' group. Putting a lot of pressure on the county planning board for approval."

"They wouldn't even know a scrub jay if one landed on them," Fred said.

I was focusing on what Olivia had said, that Dr. Trusdale's getting killed "didn't help any."

Olivia had sounded so wholly without sympathy.

Had she thought Dr. Trusdale's death would help save the scrub jays from the physicians' plans for developing the jay habitats into a medical arts building?

On the way out the door, I glanced around in their yard and spotted the oleanders growing in a pink and white clump at the front corner, far out of reach of the large fenced backyard full of big dogs.

It didn't mean a thing, I told myself. Almost everybody with a yard in Sarasota has a clump of oleanders somewhere on his or her property. Florida oleanders were as ubiquitous as the poison ivy of my native childhood, though more toxic.

Newly brought home steaks and asked me to cook them and didn't get it at all when I reacted with anger. "I'm a vegetarian," I blurted out. Not to mention I don't take domestic orders from my lovers.

"Since when are you a vegetarian?"

Well, all right. I'd converted, I admitted, since we had last been together. But hadn't he noticed I never touched the plastic chicken or the rubber-gravied alleged steak at the weekly Kiwanis meetings, where we'd been sitting together for years so we could make fun of the speakers?

"Converted, like a religion? So, can I cook a steak for me to eat," he asked, "or would that defile the temple?"

Snip, snap, snarl. After we crackled at each other some more, I excused myself to wash up and change before supper, which he promised would include a salad and a baked potato for me.

The salad he made was ordinary iceberg lettuce, not the organic romaine I use, and imported Mexican tomatoes wholly without taste but laden I suspected with pesticides, and he hadn't washed any of it. Eyeing the toxic tomatoes, already sliced and beyond washing now, I told him I had a headache and wasn't hungry, though I picked at the baked potato, and asked him to sleep in the guest room.

Having Newly living with me was wearing thin already.

The next night I came home and he had hung two paintings on my white, real plaster walls bearing the delicate swirls of a true plasterer in his prime. Not the kind of walls you can find in the half-mil and up condos, with their mass-market Sheetrock.

"Look, hon. Original art, by local guys. This one is by Ted Morris and this one is by A. J. Metzgar."

I looked at my formerly blank, clean, white walls, where Newly had hung a painting of a bobcat in a lush Florida hammock, the sharp blades of a palmetto thicket shading the cat, and a second painting, a surreal, ethereal painting of what might have been a waterfall in what might have been a dream.

Yes, I agreed, they were nice paintings. They were. I liked them.

He'd had to pay Karen the Vindictive, his soon-to-be ex-wife, for them before she'd let him take them out of the house that she had a temporary court order banning him from entering, but he'd presented the sale receipts and paid her full value plus interest. And now they were mine, he said. For me.

But Newly didn't understand that my walls, like my floors, and my bookcases, and my dresser tops, were all clean, clear, and white for a reason. To cope.

I didn't know how to explain it to him.

"I just can't stand stuff around me, clutter," I said, remembering the piles of magazines, paperbacks, dirty clothes, and garbage in the house of my childhood.

"This is like when you have to wash each piece of lettuce about fifty times, isn't it?"

"Yes, perhaps. Sort of."

"Don't they have medicine for that?" Newly asked, looking concerned.

"Yes. Paxil. It made me tired. I couldn't take it and be a lawyer." That Newly understood, because stamina is perhaps the universal attribute of every successful trial lawyer.

Therapy had helped, I told him. In fact, I assured him, I was perfectly functional and under the general impression that an obsessive-compulsive disorder benefited a trial attorney, so long as it was controlled.

Newly didn't understand just how much better I was. I didn't have to rush home at noon every day and take a shower anymore. I could eat out in restaurants—good ones that would let me inspect their kitchens, that is. Though I had yet to meet a salad bar I could force myself to eat from, I could eat the packaged salads from the Granary after a tour of their kitchen, and I had learned self-hypnosis and visualization techniques, and I knew how to go to a cool, safe place in my mind. My waterfall, as I explained to Newly.

"A waterfall like this one?" Newly looked at the Metzgar painting he had hung on my wall.

"Yes," I said. Just like that one—cool, green, blue, and aqua, and soft, and safe, as much dreamscape as waterfall.

"My baby," he said, and held me gently until I felt him press against my stomach and we ended up in the shower together, where we discovered that the warm and tingling sensations of pure peppermint soap when rubbed expertly into sensitive spots had a rather electrifying result.

Long after we'd tumbled into the bed, I realized Newly never did take the paintings down.

Chapter 11

When I stumbled into my office through the back door, still tingly from Newly's inventive morning devotional involving copious amounts of Dr. Bronner's peppermint soap, Detective Santuri was already sitting in my office, waiting. Bonita shrugged when I glared first at Sam and then at her.

We all grumped something that might have passed for good morning, and I left my door cracked so Bonita could overhear from her office without straining.

"So what do you know about those other malpractice lawsuits against Trusdale?" I jumped in and asked before Sam could get started.

Sam protested that he still didn't have the particulars on the other lawsuits, only that one was in Miami, one in Dallas, both had settled, and the records were sealed, he said. "Mrs. Trusdale can't find any of the settlement papers. She thinks he destroyed them."

"See if Mrs. Trusdale remembers the names of the attorneys," I said, thinking, Sealed, my ass. "I'll take it from there."

If Henry couldn't dig out the facts from his insurance networks of rats, spies, and databases, one of those attorneys would brag the details if I approached him or her lawyer to lawyer. And if Mrs. Trusdale didn't remember the attorneys' names, now that I knew the cities I could eventually get copies of the complaints out of Miami and Dallas, as those are public records. But I was a lot more interested, now that my role in defending Dr. Trusdale was over, in making either Henry or Sam do the work.

While I glowered, Sam admitted, more or less, that he had no leads about where the marijuana laced with oleanders might have come from. If Dr. Trusdale was a pothead, he hadn't left a track.

"Could someone have forced him to smoke it?" I asked, envisioning someone with a gun pointed at him, not telling him the joint was laced with poison.

Sam shrugged.

He asked me about the mugging again. He asked me about Dr. Trusdale's file, his liability policy, the settlement, the opposing counsel, and what I knew about the doctor, which I admitted was fundamentally nothing. After all, it was Sam who had told me about the prior two malpractice hits on Dr. Trusdale. This version of twenty questions was just a warm-up though, I soon learned.

"Why'd he write you a prescription for Percocet?" Sam asked, blowing me away.

Act calm, I told myself. It isn't a crime and he isn't after me. Is he?

"Remember, I'd been mugged," I said. "My neck was a mess. I hurt. He saw I was in pain and offered me that prescription." Yeah, after I belabored my pain and bluntly asked, but who could dispute my version now?

"Shouldn't you have gone to your own doctor?"

"Sure, if I'd had time, which I didn't."

"Hmm," he said, and wrote something down in his notebook.

"What has that got to do with anything?"

"I don't know. You want to tell me?"

This time I shrugged.

"You smoke marijuana?"

Oh, yeah, as if I'd admit it to a cop if I did. "No. Not since a little experimentation in high school." Leaving out my brother's patch and my liberal college use of Delvon's pure and clean homegrown. "I don't do street drugs."

Too late, I caught the implication of this last statement in the overall context—no street drugs, just pharmaceuticals, like the ones the good, but dead, Dr. Trusdale had prescribed for me. True, I'd given up marijuana more than a decade ago for the FDA-assured purity, and the legality, of the occasional prescription with a bang, and I kept a careful rein over even that, but none of this was information I wanted a Sarasota police detective to know.

To try to edit what I had said would be to highlight the mistake. I kept silent, and then I noticed the dark hair on Sam's arms, and his hands, noticed the big, long fingers, the strong-looking hands, big hands. I raised my eyes up to study his face, his shoulders, and I was acutely and physically aware of this man in my office just a few feet away from me. He was, as Bonita had first pointed out to me, a real hunk.

"Why do you think his death has some connection to me?" I asked, distracted by Sam's physical presence into forgetting that the first rule about holes is to stop digging.

"I don't. Do you?"

I heard Bonita's phone ringing and then, through my slightly opened door, her voice, and then she knocked on my door.

"I need to go to the hospital. Carmen jumped off the roof and Benicio thinks she might have cracked a bone in her arm. He's driving her to the hospital, but I need to meet them there."

Bonita's house, like my own, was a squat, concrete-block style known as a Florida ranch for some reason having nothing to do with cows. It was a low-to-the-ground house, but I still wouldn't want to jump off of it.

"Why was she jumping off the roof?" I asked.

"She's a five-year-old," Bonita said, with that oddly peaceful look of resignation. "They don't need reasons."

Apparently Benicio, the oldest and the summer version of family day care for the other children, was a better driver at fourteen than he was a babysitter, I thought.

"Go. But call me and let me know how she is."

Bonita waved, and I let that be the excuse to run Sam off.

With Sam gone, I pulled Dr. Trusdale's liability policy out of the file drawer to see who had approved coverage for him. Damn doctor, I thought, lying straight-faced to me, denying prior malpractice suits. And lying on his application for malpractice insurance, I noticed as I scanned it. Damn Henry, I thought, when I saw that Henry himself had approved the policy. I had to question Henry's promotion to claims adjuster after seeing this big a screwup. Henry's company would not have issued the liability policy if it had any notice that Dr. Trusdale's subspecialty was getting sued. And Henry, as the policy's point man, was not supposed to just take the doctor's word for it; he was supposed to dig out the truth from insurance company databases that rival those of the FBI. I punched in Henry's number on my phone and after the usual delays got his happy-sounding little bleat.

"Henry, you screwed up," I said. Who needs hello when you're on a mission.

"What?"

"Trusdale—you approved his policy application. He had two prior malpractice suits, both settled. You didn't catch that? You're supposed to investigate, aren't you, to find that out?"

I listened to Henry breathe.

"What difference does that make now?" he finally retorted, a bit sharp for Henry.

"Don't get sloppy on me," I snapped back.

"But you didn't know either," he said.

"Henry, I just told you."

Henry breathed some more, and then he asked what else I knew about the suits. I admitted that Detective Santuri had uncovered that uncomfortable little fact, and Henry bleated and agreed to dig around.

"Yeah, you do that."

"Does Detective Santuri think these other suits have anything to do with the doctor's death?" Henry asked.

"I don't think he knows," I said and made my good-byes.

Bonita returned just after six to declare that her five-year-old was fine, just a little bruised, thanks be to God, and that the little girl's aunt had come by to stay with the kids now so she could work late to catch up for the hours she'd missed that afternoon.

After expressing my own relief that her child was all right, I told Bonita that everything could wait for tomorrow, as I was just studying Jackson's discovery files in the veggie baby case.

"Would you please stop calling it that?" Bonita's usually calm voice had a sharp tone that I didn't often hear.

"Calling it what?"

"The veggie baby. That child has a name. It has a soul. It is a child of God, and you disrespect it by what you call it."

Well, of course I disrespected it. I was trying to prevent a jury from giving the veggie baby's parents millions of dollars because of it. A jury in Mississippi gave a family $25 million for a brain-damaged baby last year. If I lost a $25 million case, I'd be back to waiting tables and weeding pot for a living. I could hardly allow myself to become attached to the child, could I? Besides, the black humor of attorneys on both sides of personal injury cases—like ER nurses, paramedics, cops, and firemen—was a system of emotional self-defense. We saw a lot of truly crapped-up, hurt, disabled, and painfully broken people, and humor, however callous, was the way we coped with it. Well, that and the good wine, the vodka, or the substance abuse of one's choice.

"I didn't mean to upset you," I said, aware that of all the people at Smith, O'Leary, and Stanley, Bonita was the one person whose respect I most wanted to have.

Bonita nodded. I resolved to be careful not to call it the veggie baby in her presence anymore.

But Bonita's anger at me dug in deeper than she might have intended.

I was ashamed.

Something that happens more often than I will admit to anyone and try not to admit to myself—this shame.

Poor Dr. Trusdale was dead, and it was not a good death at all.

In typically lawyer fashion, I had reacted to the news of Dr. Trusdale's death in terms of what this meant to my case: that is, how I could wrestle a good result from the paper in Dr. Trusdale's file, even though Dr. Trusdale was presumably past caring.

Well, actually, technically, my first thought had been to wonder about the prescription he had written me, and I had some shame over that too.

When I have these episodes of morose, introspective hand-wringing, I am apt to drive down the full length of Longboat Key and Anna Maria Island and trespass through the yards of the rich folk in the pink stucco monster houses on the tip of Anna Maria and sit on the beach, which is still technically open to the public along the shoreline, though there is no public access within miles. My habit, or perhaps solace, is to sit and watch the reflected sunset over the yellow arch of the Sunshine Skyway bridge. The bridge is like an incredibly large piece of avant-garde jewelry in the water, a geometric display of modern engineering, a high-rise double-span bridge, with a bright yellow mast that crosses Tampa Bay. It is beautiful. It is a particular favorite for suicides. I have seen both dolphins and sharks swimming under its pilings, and once, when I was a kid, I saw eternity off the edge, beyond the girders, in the vast, deep expanse of water.

That moment, be it hallucination or divine gift, draws me periodically back to stare at the bridge, as if the flash of immortality I felt that time more than two decades ago might return and impart some wisdom, or peace.

The most scenic, but not the quickest, route to the best point of land to view the Skyway from my side of Tampa Bay is down the islands. This long drive meanders down Longboat and Anna Maria, two shifting sands of barrier islands washed on the western shore by the Gulf of Mexico and on the eastern shore by brackish bay waters filtered through a few remaining mangroves. As I drove, I listened to the folk music on WMNS and contemplated the evils in my soul.

Such contemplation while driving was possible because the winter hordes of seasonal visitors, snowbirds in the local jargon, had gone back to their cool native habitats, finally died, or else were summering in Highlands, North Carolina. Snowbirds are typically ancient people who originated up north and have bad reflexes and bad vision. These tribes of ancients attempt to make up for these shortcomings by driving very big automobiles at very slow rates of speed and keeping their left blinkers on at all times. They are particularly fond of engaging in long, slow winter parades on the two-lane road that runs down Longboat and Anna Maria. But in the summer, the ancient ones are replaced by younger and poorer tourists from the neighboring Deep South states with battered pickups and minivans full of rambunctious and sunburned children. They have to stay in Manatee County because Sarasota has zoned out anyone who is other than a millionaire, unless that person provides a service that the rich retirees need, like cardiologist, lawyer, CPA, New Age healer, upscale jeweler, plastic surgeon, and undertaker. Say what you will about these summer tourists with their raucous kids; they at least know how to drive and can still see.

Keeping pace with a van with an Alabama tag and a red-faced kid leaning out the window and yelling at the sky, I watched the Gulf of Mexico in the breaks between the condos as I drove and introspected.

Then I parked by a No Parking sign at the northern tip of Anna Maria Island and walked past the No Public Access and No Trespassing signs.

Technically criminal, yeah, but I'm basically of the opinion that since I'm an articulate, well-dressed person with a job in an air-conditioned office, no one will actually *arrest* me for trespassing.

Once I was safely on the public beach without encountering any irate private landowners, I walked. The sun was going down over the Gulf, and the reflected colors were a baroque delight as they tripped through the clouds over the Sunshine Skyway.

After dragging somebody else's lawn chair down to the point, I sat and stared at the Skyway, and I said to myself: "I am not always a nice person." I resolved to be better. I resolved to care the next time a client got killed. I resolved to become a Big Sister, to adopt an ugly mutt from the brink of the Humane Society's gas chamber, to go to Mass with Bonita the next time she asked, and to quit bitching about my United Way contribution, which is a mandatory component of life at Smith, O'Leary, and Stanley because Jackson's wife is perennially either a chair, co-chair, vice chair, chief nag, or face person of the annual fund drive.

Kicking off my shoes, I rubbed my bare toes in the warm, wet sand and studied the Skyway. This was the new bridge. The spring of 1980, a cargo ship captain rammed his empty ship into one of the pilings under the 150-foot southbound span that was designed to let tugs and ships pass unheeded into the port in Tampa. When the boat hit, the whole damn section of the highest span of the bridge shuddered, then crashed into the stormy waters below. Fortunately, the separate, northbound span survived. Unfortunately, at the time the southbound bridge collapsed, a Greyhound bus full of tired travelers and a few cars were crossing its span. Thirty-five people followed the wreckage of the bridge into the dark, deep waters of Tampa Bay to their deaths. One old coot in a pickup survived the fall into Davy Jones's locker.

Why the cargo ship captain had driven into the piling was explained variously by the bad weather, his undisclosed multiple sclerosis, allegations of alcohol, and the demon bad luck. Of course, when the wrongful death lawsuits started, one of the key allegations was that the Florida Department of Transportation had designed the bridge wrong, allegations prompted largely because the State of Florida had way more money than the hapless captain or his employer.

Even in south Georgia, the news of the Skyway's collapse was played big-time on television and in the newspapers, and the photographs of the crumpled bridge were awesome.

My brother Delvon, though technically not old enough to have a driver's license, had his first car, bought from wages earned helping Farmer Dave cultivate marijuana on Dave's back forty acres. Delvon needed to get out of town for a while, and I wasn't fussy about skipping school. So we hit the road to see this collapsed bridge. I don't think either of my parents actually noticed that at fifteen Delvon owned and drove a car, without a license and without insurance, or if they noticed they let it slide. Like most things.

In Delvon's 1965 Chrysler Newport, it was a six-hour drive from our house to the wrecked bridge, which he measured by beer and joints, and I, by Moon Pies and Tootsie Rolls. We were loopy by the time we reached the causeway and drove out slowly on the remaining bridge. At the highest point of the surviving northbound span, where all traffic had been routed, we stopped the Newport, which was no big deal because everybody else was also parking and checking out the devastation below. Delvon and I, flatlanders all of our lives, were hit with vertigo as we crept out of the Newport and stood on the high, high metal grid and held on to the railings and looked at the crumpled pieces of bridge still dangling over the water across from us on the doomed second span of the Skyway and the garbage below it. Wreckage that still contained unrecovered corpses. Once it was certain that there were no more survivors, recovery operations had been abandoned until the storm abated, and the high, cold wind blew right through our T-shirts.

Delvon thought we should do something to commemorate the dead, and he ducked out of the wind into the front seat of the Newport and lit a joint. He passed it around a small crowd of gawkers. Delvon and I, our median age being thirteen, naturally had left the car radio playing as loud as it could play. Out of the mixed bag of Top 40 rock, as we stood there swaying on the surviving span of the Skyway and passing a joint with strangers, Simon and Garfunkel's "Bridge over Troubled Waters" played.

Something about the song totally freaked me, and I almost jumped or fell, tumbling willy-nilly against and partway over the railings as if called by a ghost in the murky waters below me. Delvon had grabbed me, and perfect strangers gathered to soothe and reassure me and offer benign banalities about the Greyhound bus and its dead, still trapped in the rough black waves below us.

As Delvon held me, I looked out over the railing and into the waters of Tampa Bay, and for a moment I saw eternity, right there, on that bridge, in the cold wind of the fading storm.

Years later, as a summer law clerk in Sarasota with one year of law school behind me, I had worked on one of the last Skyway lawsuits still churning in the court systems of Florida and the federal system. Well, "worked on" might be too generous a term. Mostly I had photocopied reams of paper in the discovery process, a proper use of my first-year law school skills, especially since I worked cheaper and knew far less than the secretaries. I learned the nuances and complexities of running a photocopy machine, which was far more useful than what I had learned in law school during the previous nine months and on an even par for boredom. Delvon, on the lam, had come south with me, and we rented a duplex on the northern tip of Anna Maria. Delvon worked construction and made three times what I earned, plus he got to take his shirt off, listen to Lynyrd Skynyrd, and smoke dope while he worked.

When nobody was watching that summer, I actually read the documents I was copying. No detail was too grisly, and most theories of blame hoisted against the various defendants struck me as just plain silly. The cargo ship captain, the only one to blame, it seemed to me, was not a defendant because he didn't have any money. The "deep pocket" theory of liability, in which a wounded plaintiff sues not the party actually responsible for the mishap but the next closest party with the most money, struck me as patently unfair. Thus, a defense attorney was born.

And although technically the new bridge with its yellow mast wasn't the same bridge on which I had stood as a kid and seen eternity in the whitecaps over a sea of the recently dead, the new bridge was still my talisman.

With the bridge fading into a purple night, I sat there in somebody else's lawn chair and contemplated my soul and struggled to find that glimpse of eternity again, until the sand fleas and no-see-ums got to be too much, and then I drove home down the Tamiami Trail.

Newly was nearly asleep, and I watched him with the same puzzlement I've felt studying indignant clients who don't understand why they should pay for their own stupidity, as if "But I didn't mean to hurt him" took away their culpability. "Why did you take that whiplash case?"

"Hmm," he muttered, rolling over to face me and reaching out his hand toward my stomach.

"You know, the kayak whiplash?"

"You know why I took that case?" he asked, as if he'd introduced the topic.

"Yeah, because you advertise on buses and daytime TV and take every case that walks in your door."

Newly looked a bit wounded when he looked up at me.

"No, I took that case because I felt sorry for that woman."

"Because she was fat and stupid?"

"No, because in her whole life nothing had happened to her that was interesting. I mean, at parties, this woman didn't have anything to talk about except television shows."

"You took her case because she was boring?" I couldn't believe that.

"No. Because she didn't have any stories to tell. Now she's got one. She's got a great story about her lawsuit, and her lawyer, and being on the witness stand, and how she was screwed out of a just verdict by a cruel legal system and a foxy defense attorney. Her own three days of *L.A. Law*. And it's her story."

I looked at Newly a little differently for a moment, remembering the migrant workers he'd taken on against the tomato conglomerate. He'd lost a wife in the process, but he had helped those people. A rush of tenderness flooded over me, and I looked down at Newly's sweet, rough face, dark against my pillow, and for a moment I thought we might just make this work out.

"Then again, it was a cheap case to try, and you never know—right jury, feeling sorry for her, I might have hit a jackpot."

Chapter 12

Someone had been rifling through my veggie baby case files. I could tell at once.

Most of the files were still in the storage room upstairs, where, box by box, I was reading through them. But the most important ones—the medical depositions and the patient's medical records—were in my office, where I had been studying them between working on other cases.

"Bonita," I said, making her get up from her computer and come into my office, a quizzical look on her pretty face.

"You been going through these files?"

"No."

"Anybody else been in here?"

"Not while I was here."

"The medical records on the plaintiff, the mother, I started through them last evening. Somebody's gone through the file with her records— the file clasps holding the pages together are not aligned evenly."

Bonita sighed. "I'll straighten them out, but first I have to finish those notices of deposition and get the interrogatories in the Windjammer case ready, and—can't you just let the clasps be crooked for a little while?"

"That wasn't my point." I hadn't finished reviewing the plaintiff's medical records last night because I had reached a point at which I could no longer focus, and now I realized somebody could have taken something out of the file and I wouldn't know. "Somebody's been messing with my files."

"Now why, *chica,* would anybody want to do that? Not a person in this law firm wants a thing to do with that case."

The phone rang before I could retort, and Bonita picked it up, spoke a word or two of greeting in her professional voice, then smiled at the phone as if it were a person and whispered something, and laughed sweetly at the response. Hmm, I thought, reading the whisper and laughter as a hint of romance and wondering if someone was finally giving the ghost husband a shove. Then she handed the phone to me. "Henry," she said as I took it.

"What'd you pull up on Dr. Trusdale's other suits?" I didn't bother with hello because Bonita had already given him a good enough greeting for both of us.

"I got the reports from his prior insurers. He didn't list either of them on his application with us. Guy had a talent for covering his tracks. You wouldn't believe what I've had to do to find this out. Why, it took me over three days just to—"

"Yeah, yeah, Henry, life's hard. Now what'd you find?"

"Suit in Texas was nothing, really, a bit of an infection, apparently cured right up with superantibiotics. No permanent damage, so it settled for nuisance value. But the one in Miami was different. Kind of a sad story."

Yeah, as if I'd never heard a sad story before. "Define nuisance value in Texas first," I said.

"Twenty thousand."

Nothing, I thought. "Okay, what about Miami?"

"Guy getting a hip replacement picked up a nasty staph infection."

Well, that was sounding familiar. What was Dr. Trusdale, the Typhoid Mary of staph? Maybe he *did* go to the bathroom and not wash his hands. I wondered if anybody had ever scraped his nails or tongue to see if he was a carrier.

"Infection got into the patient's heart," Henry continued. "He needed a heart transplant after the staph ate up his heart muscle, but his HMO wouldn't authorize it."

"Oh, and that'd be new," I said.

"Guy was just a regular joe, not rich enough for a heart transplant, so bottom line was he died. His widow sued Dr. Trusdale, the HMO, the hospital, and just about everybody else."

"What was her name?"

"Elaine Sanford Jobloski."

"How'd it play out?"

"Court dismissed the suit against the HMO. Trusdale's insurer settled for a quarter of a million and the hospital fought back until the widow cracked and went into a mental institution. Her attorney let the hospital suit drop."

"Henry, write me up a file memo of everybody's names and addresses and get it to me soon as you can. Bring it over—don't mail or fax it."

"But our case is over. No harm done. I mean, I didn't catch those prior lawsuits before, but it didn't hurt you. Or the company." His voice almost squeaked. "I mean, yes, if I'd caught those prior suits before, we'd never have issued the policy to him in the first place, but, look, nobody was hurt by that . . . that oversight."

"Henry, I'm not after you. I just thought Detective Santuri should know this."

"Oh," Henry bleated.

"Look," I said, "we're buds, okay? We watch each other's back. Don't worry."

But when I hung up the phone, I thought, Man, Henry had screwed up big-time in not finding out about those suits during the insurance application process. If Henry and I had learned about those prior staph cases for the first time at trial, it would not have been pretty.

Only the fortuitous event of Dr. Trusdale's death and my quick settlement had saved us both from being cut off at the knees in front of a jury.

I looked up from that thought and said, "So?" to Bonita.

She smiled and shut my door on the way out.

That night, I was telling Newly that somebody was screwing around with one of my files, that Henry was getting sloppy and defensive on me, and the other highlights of my day.

Newly was painting my toenails while he listened, and he said, "You think there is some connection?"

I stopped doodling my fingers in his chest hair to wipe up the drop of Radical Red he had spilled on my leg, and said, "Between what?"

"Well, you got mugged. Your client had a history of staph suits that he was covering up, and he got killed. Now somebody is snooping in your files."

"They don't even know if Dr. Trusdale was actually murdered," I said, missing the point as Newly finished my toes, put the nail polish away, and started brushing my hair.

He was wearing my pink satin tap pants again.

"Haven't you done your laundry yet?" I asked, leaning my head back as he pulled the brush through my long black hair in smooth, even strokes. This laundry question was a test—if he even hinted that I should do his laundry, he was out. Right then. On the curb.

But Newly didn't get trapped that easily. "Sure, hon, I've done a couple of loads. Great washing machine. Folded my stuff, put it up in the guest room. In that empty chest, just like you told me."

What I had told him was not even to think about putting any of his stuff in my room.

"So, why . . .?" I pulled up the laced hem of the satin panties.

"Because they feel so much better than mine. Much softer. You don't mind, do you?"

Making himself right at home, I thought, but then forgot about it when he slapped the brush lightly across his hand and asked, "Want me to tie you and spank you? We've never tried that. Or you could do me if you want."

Chapter 13

If I had known that I would end up getting shot at and ruining one of my favorite suits, the blue seersucker from Nello's that cost a ton of money but fit like a tailor-made, all in all, I would have skipped what was primarily just a courtesy meeting in the veggie baby case with the good doctor, my new client, the obstetrician Dr. Winston Calvin Randolph the Second. His name alone told me I was going to have problems. Juries tend to hate physicians with snooty names as this reinforces the image of the aloof, arrogant money-grubber. But it was probably too late to have him legally change his name, and so, wholly unprepared for the *mierda* storm that would follow, I'd begun my business day by trying to actually get through on the telephone to Dr. Randolph to set up a face to face.

In my innocence, I'd tried calling his office, only to speak to four different women, each snottier in turn as I repeated my simple request to have the doctor call me. No, I wasn't a patient, I wasn't in labor, I wasn't selling anything, and, no, I didn't have free drug samples. Obviously they were not going to take a message without my identifying myself as his lawyer, so I did, fully aware this often pisses off doctor clients who suffer from the notions that 1) the support staff doesn't already know they've been sued and 2) anybody cares unless his or her own ass was on the line.

Yeah, he was pissed when he got back to me. He was busy, and he was pissed, and he was arrogant, and he didn't know why Jackson had assigned the case to me. But he finally agreed to come by my office and meet with me at six-thirty P.M. "First chance I've got, only chance all week. Busy, busy," he insisted. What did I care? I routinely work past seven anyway.

Before I had my hand out and my smile fixed in place, Dr. Randolph's first words to me were "Where's Jackson?"

"Hello. I'm Lilly Cleary. I'm taking over your case from Jackson."

He started bitching. Why was his case reassigned to a younger attorney, a woman attorney, an attorney in midstream, with the lawsuit pending for over a year and getting near a trial date? Where was Jackson? Was a woman tough enough to try a case like this? He didn't want some affirmative-action hire handling his case. Et cetera.

Oh, for crying out loud, I thought. Get over it. Girls get to practice law now. It's in one of the penumbras of the Constitution.

Instead of pointing that out, I decided to match arrogance for arrogance.

"What you need to know, Dr. Randolph, is that I'm a board-certified trial attorney (this is true) and I graduated second in my law class (this is not true, but it sounds good) and I've represented count-less physicians in countless malpractice suits with favorable results (this is more or less true). You haven't been abandoned."

"So, you're a good attorney?"

"No, Dr. Randolph. I'm not a *good* attorney. I'm an excellent attorney. Now, please, make yourself comfortable."

"Second in your law school?"

"Yes," I said, carving the lie into stone. I mean, who checks? Technically I was ranked seventh in a class of 187 students, which is pretty darn good, but I've learned over the years that this doesn't seem to impress people. Telling clients that I graduated number one sounds like a lie. But second, hey, that sounds true and it triggers the "tries harder" image of the second-place winner. Now, just don't ask what law school, I thought.

The doctor took a seat at the head of the rosewood conference-room table and grunted as he eased into the chair. "I've been to some malpractice seminars, you know. And what you need to do is file a motion for summary judgment on proximate cause."

Oh, frigging great.

It took me a good half hour to get him off of that one, pointing out repeatedly that we had already done that and lost, and then he was right back to bitching about Jackson abandoning him to me, a mere female, and I'd had it up to here. I said, "Look, first thing we're going to have to do is coach you on your attitude."

"My attitude?"

"Yes. Juries hate arrogant pricks."

Yes. We were learning to work together well, weren't we?

The upshot of this exchange was that Dr. Randolph insisted on seeing Jackson, right then, and so I snapped something passably rude at him and said I would take him to Jackson "right then" and led him out the back door into the parking lot, which was by then largely deserted. My plan was to drive him to Jackson's house, where Jackson and his wife were no doubt enjoying a good wine over a low-fat dessert, probably some exotic, expensive fruit. Dr. Randolph instinctively headed toward Ashton's Lexus, and I said, "Nope, the Honda."

"This runs?" he asked, snidely.

I had opened my mouth to say, "Like a little baby jet," when a whisking, popping noise went off nearby. The good doc and I looked at each other, and then looked around us. Another noise, like a backfire, went off, but this time something tore through the sleeve of my blue seersucker suit. *"Chingalo,"* I yelled, a word Bonita's son Benicio had taught me so I wouldn't sound crude and cheap by saying it in English, and I was thinking that I'd paid three hundred dollars for the jacket alone when I noticed Dr. Randolph had disappeared from sight.

Dr. Randolph recognized gunshots for what they were. I reflected later, loudly and repetitively for his and everyone else's benefit, that he didn't think to warn me, or to knock me down and cover my body with his, or any of those chivalrous things a man is supposed to do when being shot at in the company of a woman.

What he did was drop like a rock and crawl under my aged Honda.

When the next bullet took out the window of my poor car and shattered shards of glass over me in a spray, I got it. I dropped, pulled out my cell phone, hit 911, and screeched into the ear of the poor woman answering the call that I was being shot at in the parking lot behind the law firm of Smith, O'Leary, and Stanley, but before I gave the actual address, my cell phone exploded into tiny pieces of plastic, clueing me in that ducking was insufficient protection. I rolled under the car, collided in a thunk with the shaking Dr. Randolph and ruined the lovely matching seersucker skirt.

Almost immediately, I heard the sound of sirens and I finally exhaled. The police department was only three blocks away.

Half an hour later, we were stomping around with the uniformed police officers, trading versions—mine the truth, the good doctor's a version in which he miraculously saved me by throwing himself over me and pushing me under the car—when I began to feel the need to do a girl-like thing.

But I held the urge to cry in check because Ashton was standing around, and one never cries in front of any of the big three partners.

However, when Sam Santuri arrived on the scene, I didn't think, then, to question why he was there, as technically nobody was dead and he was a homicide detective. Instead, I rushed into his arms and burst into tears.

He held me and patted me, putting his arms protectively about me, and when my need to cry evaporated, as it did in seconds, I thought,

Hmm, this is nice. He had good, strong arms and a good, strong chest, and he smelled clean, like sunshine on the beach. Though I felt safe and comfortable in his arms, I slowly became confused about what was going on and wondered why exactly we were holding on to each other. As I started to pull out of his grip, his arms seemed to tighten around me, and maybe he pressed his chest against mine. It was hard to say, given the yelling that had broken out between Ashton and Dr. Randolph, who was, excuse me, now officially on my *mierda* list.

When the yelling stopped—Randolph had threatened to sue the law firm because he'd been shot at in our lot, and Ashton had not reacted well—Sam took me inside, into the cool of my own, safe office, where I sat and breathed for a few minutes while he waited.

"Now, tell me what happened."

I did. Then I excused myself, went to the ladies' room, washed my face and hands in my special tea-tree soap, and took a double hit of kava, a south-seas herb touted as a safe, natural alternative to Valium.

When I got back to my office, Newly was there, his face stricken, and he said, "Oh, hon," and he took me in his arms and held me so tight I didn't think I could breathe, and then kissed me, a bit too passionately, I thought, given my near-death experience. When I saw Jackson and Bonita hovering in the growing crowd, I guessed Newly and I were out of the closet as a couple. I also saw the way Sam was taking in this tender display between Newly and me.

Of course, Sam had an hour's worth of more questions, and he wore me out before finally the overprotective Newly drove me home in his gold Lexus, the only thing of financial worth that Karen the Vindictive, the couldn't-be-ex-quick-enough-wife, hadn't persuaded the divorce judge to enjoin Newly from touching. Already my little Honda had been yellow-taped with official crime-scene streamers and would be impounded, Sam had explained, while the crime-scene technicians looked for bullets and such things that might shed some light on who was trying to murder either me or Dr. Randolph, or both of us.

Chapter 14

There was great consternation about my bodily safety among the Smith, O'Leary, and Stanley firm and my small but devoted personal circle.

Jackson called our insurer and doubled the amount on my life insurance key man policy, the proceeds of which went to the firm to help them survive the loss of me, a key man, in the event of any untimely and tacky demise on my part. Newly had his secretary cancel all his appointments and sent his harried partner to his hearings so he could personally escort me everywhere. Bonita had her priest come and pray over me, and she herself pressed a silver saint of somebody on a chain—the saint of endangered lawyers, I guessed—into my hands. Ashton and Jennifer invited me to stay with them at Ashton's house. Fred and Olivia invited me to stay at their house, where a wall of Rottweilers would surely protect me from anything short of the Antichrist or a meltdown at the Crystal River nuclear power plant just upwind from Sarasota.

Sam Santuri did not invite me to stay with him, though I saw him checking out Newly again and looking at me in a sort of "What do you see in him?" way while he finished up the investigating police thing with me. He did, however, offer to assign a patrol car to watch my house. I resisted the urge to point out the obvious—that no one was shooting at my house—as I've learned the hard way that men don't usually like a smart-alecky retort at their own expense.

The night after the shooting, Fred and Olivia brought over one of their big male Rottweilers, Jack the Bear. Olivia had him sniff me and gave him explicit instructions on protecting me, and Fred and Olivia eyed Newly but didn't say anything. We all had a round of Absolut vodka, and I furtively popped a kava capsule in the bathroom. Only after Fred and Olivia left did we discover that Jack wouldn't let Newly get within five feet of me.

Jack the Bear slept that night on the floor by my bed and didn't, I might add, snore at all. Newly complained, but he slept on the futon in the guest room, his door open in case I called out in peril.

Despite all this outpouring of concern over the days that followed and the constant companionship of Jack the Bear, there was, as Sam Santuri pointed out during a follow-up visit, still some question as to who was the target of the shooting spree.

"The sniper didn't have good aim," Sam said.

"Thank goodness," I said.

"The whole thing doesn't make much sense."

"And I was hoping you could explain it to me," I said, forcing my face into a girl simper.

"From the damage to your car and your clothing and the broken glass, we can account for the four shots you heard. We were lucky and recovered a projectile in your car. It's a twenty-two-caliber bullet, but it's badly deformed and I doubt the lab will be able to match it to a particular firearm. If you don't already know, a twenty-two can be fired from a revolver, a semiautomatic pistol, or a rifle. We didn't find any ejected cartridges. This suggests a twenty-two-caliber revolver. There used to be about eight million of them floating around. Some pretty good, the rest just junk like the ones that were put together in Miami.

Nowadays, since all the gun-control stuff, cops'll get shot at with a MacTen or an Uzi instead of a Saturday-night special. But that's what the evidence at the scene suggests. That you and the doctor were shot at with a Saturday-night special. They're notoriously inaccurate."

Wow, I thought, that was the most Sam had ever said at one time. I let the meaning sift in. "So somebody shot at us with a notoriously inaccurate gun?"

"Maybe," Sam queried, "somebody just wanted to scare Dr. Randolph? Or you?"

Worked pretty darn well, I thought, noting privately that my herbal kava quota was getting up there into liver-damage-alert territory.

But somebody needed to e-mail or call or fax and tell me exactly what I was being warned off of because, as I repeatedly explained to Sam, I personally did not have a clue.

In the meantime, I had filed another motion for a continuance in the veggie baby case, even though a new trial date had not yet been set. Getting shot at along with the defendant ought to be worth at least another couple of months' delay before the trial date was reset.

Continuances aside, and as if I didn't have enough crap to cope with, Dr. Randolph was campaigning to have me fired as his attorney, despite the provision in his liability insurance contract that says the insurance company—that is, Henry, as the claims adjuster—picks the defense attorney. Dr. Randolph had it in his head that everything that sucked in his life was my fault, and he didn't want a girl lawyer even if she didn't get shot at. Naturally, he bitched to Henry and Jackson both about replacing me as his trial attorney. Jackson, fed up with the many mutual bitching phone sessions between Henry, himself, and the irritatingly snide doctor about kicking me off the case, scheduled a lunch meeting at his favorite eating place, the Ivy Club. "We're going to settle this, once and for all," he barked.

Naturally, the Ivy Club, which charged a monthly fee so its members wouldn't have to eat with riffraff—as if the prices at most Sarasota lunch spots didn't take care of that on their own—took a dim view of Jack the Bear, my guard dog.

Jackson and Henry took a dim view of Newly, my guard man.

So there I was, totally unprotected, the only woman, sitting at a table in a swank and over-air-conditioned private eating establishment, surrounded by Jackson, who I feared was still mad at me for raising my voice at him in front of Ashton; Dr. Randolph, who for inexplicable reasons thought I was responsible for his being shot at; and Henry, sweet, affable, malleable Henry.

Henry was my only ally, I thought. A man I could outtalk, outmaneuver, terrorize, and probably physically beat up even on a day when I was wearing a pink sweater and feeling demure.

In other words, I was strictly on my own.

While the waiter tried to coax us into commiting to the daily special (allegedly fresh trout with new potatoes and a salad of mixed greens), Dr. Randolph made clear for the hundredth time that he personally couldn't stand me, and that Henry, as the claims handler for his malpractice liability policy, must hire him another attorney and another law firm, as apparently his distaste for me now flowed over toward Jackson.

Henry bleated and peeped a bit in the early rounds, signifying nothing.

"By God, I trained that girl myself," Jackson thundered.

At thirty-four, I thought I qualified as a woman, but I had better sense than to interrupt Jackson on a tear.

"And don't give me that girls-can't-try-cases crap." Jackson pounded his water glass into the table. "Lilly's as tough as either of you."

Okay, damning by faint praise on the "tough" issue.

Unswayed, Dr. Randolph threatened Henry with a bad-faith suit if he didn't authorize replacing me with a "real attorney." I decided not to explain to Dr. Randolph that what he meant was a breach of contract case, that bad faith technically referred to a liability insurer's failure to negotiate a settlement in good faith, but I was going to take him on over the "real attorney" phrase.

But then, before I could swallow my coffee and speak, Henry, my alleged ally, surprised me by saying that perhaps, maybe, possibly, since Dr. Randolph and I obviously had a personality conflict, I should withdraw and that the insurance company could hire Dr. Randolph another attorney and another law firm.

Jackson slapped Henry across the hand with his napkin, and the waiter, apparently at a loss for getting any of us to order anything, simply brought a round of bread to go with our coffee and left us to our bickering.

Henry, rather forcibly for him, again said to the table at large that the company should hire another attorney and, given my "obvious inability to work well with Dr. Randolph," I should surrender the file. This, he said, would be cheaper than defending a bad-faith suit, a misnomer that Henry knew better than to repeat, but I was too indignant that Henry wanted to paint me as the one with the "obvious inability" to point this mistake out. Weren't Henry and I friends? Buddies from way back. What in the world was troubling Henry that he wanted to pry the Randolph file out of my hands and give it to a perfect stranger?

Jackson, slitting his eyes into that had-enough look, suddenly jumped up from his chair. "Lilly Cleary's the best damn trial attorney in Sarasota. If I'd had a company of men in 'Nam who could think and move as fast as Lilly can, I'd've taken the whole damn country. She's the only lawyer I know who can pull your sorry butt out of the fire. You want to set the record for the biggest judgment in Florida against a doctor, you go get somebody else. Otherwise, you'd better get on your knees and give thanks she's agreed to take your case."

Nobody said a word.

Everybody in the Ivy Club was looking at Jackson.

The waiter ran over, and Jackson sat down, looked at me, and roared, "Now, Lilly, order something normal."

I ordered the daily special for all of us and felt a blush of pleasure glowing across my face.

Jackson thought I was a good trial attorney.

He believed in me.

Henry and Dr. Randolph became deeply intrigued by their butter and rolls and didn't speak or make eye contact with Jackson, or me. Fine, I thought, you little worms. Eat your cow fat and white bread. But I wanted to get up and dance around the table. And here I'd thought Jackson was still mad at me.

While he surely understood that he'd won, as he usually did, by the force of his own conviction, Jackson iced his cake by explaining his own girl-factor theory to Dr. Randolph. As a woman of childbearing age, with the ability to look and act sweet and sympathetic, I would be a gentle touch for cross-examining the plaintiff good-mother (which would have to be done with white kid gloves, Jackson explained, to avoid looking as if we were picking on her and pissing off the jury) and conducting the direct examination of Dr. Randolph on the stand, and my obviously sympathetic, sweet, feminine, demure, ladylike, maternal, trusting, even charming girl factor would, thus, convey to the jury that Dr. Randolph was a man a woman could absolutely trust; that is, he didn't screw up in delivering the baby. Quite a burden to lay on my estrogen.

The nervous waiter was hovering again, placing plates of the main course more or less in front of us, and Jackson shooed him away as soon as the plates touched the table.

As I pretended to eat my food, I realized that Jackson had sucked me in deeper. Before his stand-up routine on my behalf, I hadn't cared two whits whether Dr. Randolph got a new attorney or not. I didn't particularly want to try the case, but it wouldn't have been the first time a client and I hissed and spat at each other during a trial. But now I was on fire to try this case, to win it, to live up to Jackson's faith in me.

"Stop messing with your food, Lilly," Jackson said. "Just eat it."

After our luncheon, I spun my wheels and churned my files and agitated the rest of the afternoon, while Bonita went quietly about the important tasks. That night, at my invitation, Olivia came over to teach Jack the Bear that Newly was allowed to get near me, even touch me.

Olivia greeted Newly by asserting, "I remember you."

Her tone of voice revealed nothing about whether this was a good memory or a bad one.

"Sure," Newly said, extending his hand and smiling, "the other night, at Lilly's office."

Jack the Bear growled at Newly as he reached his hand toward Olivia, and she tapped the dog on the noise lightly and took Newly's hand.

"No, the petitions, in 'ninety-eight, to persuade the county planning department to deny the variance granting Wal-Mart the right to build on the property next to Oscar Scherer."

"Oh, sure, you're the scrub jay lady."

Turned out Newly had been a big help to her, rounding up a whole crew of his clients to testify before the planning committee about the value of that acreage to them personally, as it was the nesting and breeding ground for the scrub jays and gopher turtles that pulled them into Oscar Scherer State Park on a regular basis.

"I love the way those little birds will come and sit right smack on top of you," Newly said, and I wondered how all this had happened without my knowing it, but 1998 was the year I was off busy being in love with the dermatologist who eventually broke my heart. A great many things had slipped past me that year.

"Could use your help again," Olivia said, and she and Newly went into the kitchen, Jack the Bear in tow and growling still, and they sat and discussed saving the scrub jays from the evil doctors' plans of putting up the medical arts building.

I made green tea for all of us and pretended to listen, but I was caught up in replaying the mysterious tape in my head of who killed Dr. Trusdale, and why, and what could that possibly have to do with Dr. Randolph, and (or?) me.

An hour after Olivia left, having vented her spleen about the evil doctors who would put a profitable location of a building ahead of little bluebirds, Newly and I discovered that Jack the Bear still wouldn't let him near me.

Later that night I dreamed of the Sunshine Skyway Bridge. I was standing on its girders, and then suddenly they were falling, crashing into the murky black waters of Tampa Bay, with me, a small, clinging person on the crumpling metal and concrete, hurtling toward sure death.

Before I crashed into the water, I came awake with a start and a small cry.

Jack the Bear leaped into the bed, nuzzled my face, licked my cheek, and put a protective paw on my shoulder. I petted the big dog's broad head and contemplated popping a kava capsule, but the health food stores don't sell these herbs cheap and I didn't want to waste it if I was going back to sleep anyway.

From the guest room, Newly's snores continued unabated. So much for his sentry duty. Jack snuggled against me, and I put an arm around his wide black shoulders, closed my eyes, and hoped for sleep.

Chapter 15

Watching my back was getting old.

Even Newly's protective presence had been tempered, as he had been forced to go back to work to earn money for all the ex-wives and for Karen the Vindictive, who got temporary support pending the divorce.

Leaving me even more vulnerable, Jack the Bear's attention and enthusiasm for protecting me had clearly fallen off in the last few days, so much so that I had Bonita take him to the vet on her lunch hour. I paid a royal ransom to learn he was probably just depressed over the change in his environment and I should see he got more exercise. As I plowed unprotected through the minutia in the discovery files in Dr. Randolph's case and made lists of information we still needed, Jack moped on the carpet near me, a melancholy sigh occasionally slipping out of his otherwise inert black and tan dog body.

There was still no trial date in the Dr. Randolph case, my deadline to amend the witness list was clicking closer and closer, and I'd yet to actually nail down a new expert witness.

Our expert witness—that is, our hired physician—would be critical in this case because there were compelling and obvious facts against us. The mother seemed like a nice, normal woman, and she was actually married, and her husband seemed like a nice, normal person. During labor, the mother had developed problems delivering, and the prevailing evidence in the depositions I'd reviewed indicated that Dr. Randolph should have performed a Cesarean. The monitors showed fetal distress consistent with a lack of oxygen, and a lack of oxygen during labor is a known cause of brain damage in an infant.

So our expert witness would be vital in establishing, beyond a reasonable medical degree of probability, that the infant's brain damage had not occurred as a result of oxygen deprivation during a prolonged and traumatic delivery, but rather was a result of a failure of the infant's brain to properly develop in the womb, probably because the mother had contracted CMV, a virus known to cause precisely the type of brain damage this infant had, especially the small-head thing.

Our expert had to be good enough to overcome sympathetic plaintiffs and facts that tended to condemn the defendant. Such as all that deposition testimony about HMO incentives paid to the doctor to avoid surgeries like Cesareans.

Our expert had to be a compelling enough witness to explain technical, boring, medical, and scientific information to a jury whose collective minds were probably made up against Dr. Randolph the moment they saw the spastic movements and vacant stare of the child, dressed as cute as a Gerber baby and sitting right there in his mother's loving arms.

Divorce work suddenly looked good.

Deep in my losing veggie baby files, I was nearly as morose as Jack the Bear when Detective Santuri dropped by. Bonita led him into my office while they discussed how her five-year-old, astonishingly, had not been in the least hurt by her jump off the roof. Jack the Bear disdained to growl at Sam but did at least open his eyes and stare at him. Naturally,

I was sitting unglamorously on the floor, shoes off, reading depositions and aligning interrogatories in categories, to be memorized later.

"Nice photo," he said, coming around my desk and looking at a snapshot of my apple orchard that Delvon had mailed me the previous week after his visit with Farmer Dave at my request to make sure Dave wasn't doing anything illegal on the property that would allow the government to confiscate the orchard. "Looks peaceful."

"It is."

"That dog okay?" he asked, stepping over the prone body of Jack the Bear, my guard dog.

"Yes. The vet says he is in great shape, just depressed." Me too, but I didn't say that.

"I had a Rottweiler once. Great dog."

"What'd you call him?"

"Bear."

"Oh, well, what else?"

"I'd like to have another Rottweiler someday."

"I know where you can get a wonderful puppy, great lines," I offered, thinking of Emily and her brothers playing at Fred and Olivia's house.

"Not home enough."

"Any wife? Kids? You know, to take care of a dog?" Oh, subtle, I thought, and wanted to kick myself.

"No." But Sam, I saw, watched the way that information landed on my face.

"You run down anything on that widow, Elaine Jobloski?" I asked, feeling a blush creep over my cheeks as Sam stared at me.

"Yes. Thanks again for that report you sent me. It helped. We got a history on Mrs. Jobloski now. She had a classic nervous breakdown, what with the stress of losing her husband and the lawsuits. Some of her settlement money went toward an expensive residential counseling program. She got out of that program after six months, but then there was an involuntary commitment into a second institution. When she got out of that, she apparently fled the state. We're trying to find her. There's a trail to California."

"California. That'd be a long drive to spike the good orthopod's marijuana, wouldn't it?"

Sam nodded.

"And nothing to connect her to Dr. Randolph's shooting, right?"

Sam nodded.

"And there'd be no reason for her to mug me, right?"

And no reason for Widow Jobloski to rifle through my files, I thought, as Sam nodded.

Okay, so I wasn't being original. But I wasn't the homicide detective.

"We're trying to get a photo. You can take a look. See if she looks familiar."

This time I nodded.

There didn't seem to be any reason at all for Sam to have dropped by. A point I made to Bonita after he left.

"Man's got his eye on you," she said, without pausing in her typing.

I wasn't sure if she meant he wanted a date or considered me a suspect.

Chapter 16

Jennifer the Stairmaster wizard was my new best friend, and, as with Newly's moving in, I didn't remember giving her an invitation either.

Standing in my kitchen, she was playing twenty questions about my work, telling me that Ashton says I am "so, so" smart. I was slicing carrots for a tray to take out to Newly and Ashton, who were eyeing each other like two fully racked bucks, circling for the charge to see which alpha male would win the doe herd.

When I brought the tray out, with dip made from soy sour cream we had to stop specially for at the Granary because Jennifer didn't "do dairy," Newly's look seemed to ask why these people were in my house.

Frankly, I didn't know. It was late Saturday afternoon. Ashton and I should be at the law firm, working, and we had been, but he'd dropped into my office and Jennifer had beamed in from the ladies' room and chat, chat, chat, and now here they were.

Before they'd descended on my office, I had been working my way through the veggie baby file, my medical dictionary strapped to my hip, reading through the scientific literature on CMV. I was so frigging tired of this case.

But at least I had a potential expert now, a Dr. William Jamieson. Such a great, American-sounding name. Not only had he published the most definitive of the medical articles on CMV and brain-damaged babies, he maintained both an active practice and a place on the medical faculty at Emory. Dr. Jamieson had sounded great over the phone, and he was willing to meet with me and review the file. And, "Get this," I had told Ashton as he and Jennifer pretended they cared, "this man has never been an expert witness before in his life."

"A virgin," Ashton had stated, a touch of envy in his voice.

Jennifer had giggled at that.

So it looked as if I had a pure, untainted doctor, one that the veggie babe's good-parents' attorney could not paint as some doctor whore who regularly supplemented his already outrageous income by testifying to anything he was paid to testify about.

All I had to do now was fly to Atlanta and meet him, check him out for visible defects, and grill him for composure. Of course, I would have done this already but for his own busy, busy schedule. Seems this potential expert was off summering at important conferences in Hawaii, and though I was chewing at the bit to meet him, it would be awhile before his schedule allowed a meeting in Atlanta. Thank goodness for my cumulative motions for continuances.

So, all in all, things had been reasonably tolerable that Saturday afternoon when Ashton and Jennifer had come into my office, and we moved to my house, where we were now munching carrot sticks, straining for conversation, and staring off into my backyard during the awkward silences while Jack the Bear curled morosely in a corner.

After one silence, Jennifer looked at my big live oak and said, "You know, if you took that tree out, you'd have room for a swimming pool."

I let that pass.

"Ashton, here"—she reached over and patted his knee as if I didn't know who Ashton was—"he has a very big swimming pool." Extra emphasis on *very big*.

"Good for Ashton," Newly said, and in his voice I heard the faint tremor of stamping hooves on the ground.

"Jenn, here," Ashton said, and reached over and patted not her knee, I swear, but one of her huge breasts, as if that identified to me who Jennifer was, "is an ace swimmer. She went to college on a diving scholarship and did competitive swimming."

"Oh, a P.E. major?" Newly quipped, and I thought, Well, that would explain a great deal. I'm sure her breasts float, and that must help in the competitive swimming, whatever that was.

Jennifer took a bite of a carrot stick and then dipped it back in the soy sour cream, teeth marks plainly visible on the end that went into the dip.

"Oh, no, not P.E. I was a public relations major. But I never actually graduated."

Well, no duh, I thought, and made a mental note to throw out the dip at the first opportunity and certainly not to take another bite of it.

"Tell her what you do now, babe," Ashton said, and poked her breast with a carrot stick.

"Oh, later, sweetie, that's so *bor-oor-ring*. Why don't we all go over to your house, sweetie, and go swimming? I can show everyone my dance series of dives."

And, I thought, your cute little Stairmaster-toned butt and breasts by modern science. Out of the corner of my eye, I saw Newly sit up and suck in his stomach, and I wondered if he was embarrassed to appear in swim trunks in front of Jennifer and Ashton. This from a man who'd been cavorting around my house in a pair of ladies' pink tap pants.

"No, tell us," I asked, curious about what Jennifer did do. I had assumed, apparently incorrectly, that she was simply a professional blonde and that Ashton supported her.

"Oh, it is so *bo-oor-ring,*" she repeated.

"Tell us," Newly said, and I thought, Oh, great, now we're begging her to tell us what she does for a living.

"Oh, okay. But I warned you. I work for a service that does medical transcriptions and billings for doctors."

Yep, right, boring, I thought.

"That's how we met," Ashton said. "I was deposing her boss in a case. Just background stuff, but Jennifer helped me understand the procedures."

"You see, we do a lot of work for different doctors. Sometimes it's overflow, you know, stuff that their regular staff can't handle, and sometimes we do all the transcriptions and billings for the doctors. See, that way, the doctor doesn't have to pay all our, you know, benefits and salary and stuff and fool with all that paperwork of hiring staff. Instead they just pay us a fee."

Okay, boring, I thought. Stop.

None of us said anything.

"Well, told you," she said, and grinned. "So, let's go to Ashton's and go swimming in his big pool."

"Sounds fine," I said.

"First, though, where's your powder room?" Jennifer asked. "I can't hold it any longer."

A huge, rowdy Rottweiler jumped all over Jennifer when we first stepped into Ashton's overly air-conditioned house. Why do people who live in the subtropics set their air conditioners at thirty degrees? Why don't they just move to North Dakota?

Jennifer and the dog had a love fiesta with each other, cooing and licking and petting and romping, while Ashton said, "This is Bearess, her dog." You know, *Bear* but with the *ess,* like *actress.*" Even Ashton seemed sheepish about explaining that.

"Does Jennifer live here?" I asked.

"No, just stays over on the weekends. Her and the dog."

"Her and the dog" were about done demonstrating their undying devotion to each other, and yes, it was sweet, but a bit overdone, and we followed Ashton inside, where he pointed out a changing room for Newly and me.

Ten minutes later, we were all suited up, gathered in the screened porch of Ashton's big pink stucco monster house, ready to dive into the very big swimming pool. Jennifer oooed a bit and then went into the kitchen to bring us wine, giving Newly a good view of her perfect butt, which I noticed he noticed even though he was turning blue from holding in his stomach. Bearess followed her mistress into the kitchen in a perfect show of doggy devotion.

Ashton was fuddling around, waving his arms, and being just way, way too manic even for him. I noticed his pupils were like full moons over the Gulf. He had not been that way at my house, but then he had taken a long time to change into his swimsuit, which I suspected had been chosen by Jennifer, as the average man of Ashton's age, even if he did do the YMCA with the rest of us, would rarely choose a suit that way, way too brief. Unless he was European, which Ashton, the native Floridian, was not.

His little swimsuit left few secrets, but that didn't particularly interest me beyond a quick assessment to see if he was falling apart since the last time I'd seen his body on display. I'd seen Ashton completely naked at a resort in Boca Grande, during a late-night drinking contest that ended up in the pool, much to the dismay of the management of that old, genteel plantation inn. Needless to say, the law firm of Smith, O'Leary, and Stanley went elsewhere now for our yearly firm retreats.

After noting that Ashton was holding up remarkably well for a man duking it out with his fifties and with questionable substance-abuse habits, I studied the pool in his backyard and checked out the new diving board. A bit high for my taste. Personally, I like to tiptoe into a pool, one inch at a time.

Jennifer came back into the screened porch wearing a pair of white jeans over her bikini bottoms, Bearess following in a tippy-toe fashion and looking oddly whimsical for such a big dog. "I'm so sorry," she said, purring, "but we are just *sooo* completely out of wine. I need to run down to the ABC Store and get some more. Won't be but a sec."

We made the usual protestations that we didn't need wine, but she was going to be a good hostess whether we wanted her to be or not, and she left. Ashton and Bearess followed her to the door.

Not two minutes later, Ashton came back out onto the porch. Bearess came with him, but she seemed all out of energy and mopey. Ashton had changed into a polo and jeans and said he needed to run out for refreshments too.

After an exchange of euphemisms, I basically figured out that he needed to run out to score some coke. I didn't need any, thank you, I told him, emphasizing that I didn't do street drugs, and Newly was non-committal, no doubt trying to get a read on whether he'd get in trouble with me for snorting a line (he would!), but Ashton was adamant.

Poof—like little bunnies down a hole, our host and hostess were gone. Only Bearess, the oddly named Rottweiler, was left to keep us company.

"Pretty weird, huh?" I said. "They invite us over and then, one at a time, they leave us."

All by ourselves. Except for the dog, who looked pretty permissive.

Not a hall monitor in sight. Kicking around in our bathing suits in the shallow end of a truly enormous blue-tiled pool. I felt a tingling rush start running up and down my legs, then heat gathering at the fulcrum of the rushes.

Newly, apparently thinking along the same lines, reached over and fingered the elastic in the top of my bikini bottoms, then tickled my flat stomach, which I kept that way by working like a son of a bitch on the evil crunch machine at the Y.

"You work out like you do for the job, to keep your stamina up? Or because you're afraid of getting old?" Pretty serious questions for Newly. But then he grinned. "Or just to look drop-dead in a bikini?"

"Because I'm afraid of being weak," I said.

"Yeah, me too."

Um, things are getting too heavy, I thought.

As if he read my mind, Newly grinned again and added, "And to catch young chicks like you." Then he tickled my belly again, ran his fingers down low on my stomach and circled, not too low, but low enough to get me thinking about whether you could make love in a big blue pool and not drown.

"Skinny-dipping, anyone?" I said, and giggled, pulling away from Newly. I swam out to the center of the pool and floated, my face up to the security light overhead and my hair drifting out behind me like a dark veil on the water. Then I flipped over and dove under, my not-too-shabby butt pointed up in the air for a moment until I submerged and pulled my bikini bottoms off. Breaking the surface of the water, I threw my bottoms toward Newly, who missed them but definitely caught the spirit of things. A minute later his trunks were floating on the water, drifting toward the drain in what passed for a current in the pool, and Bearess jumped in, grabbed the trunks, shook the dickens out of them, and jumped back on the tile floor. She began to do that growly shake, rattle, and roll thing dogs like to do with your clothes.

We didn't care two whits about the dog and Newly's trunks. He wasn't going to be needing them for the next few minutes.

Newly started swimming toward me as if he were trying out for the Olympic swim team. I dove for the bottom. When I surfaced in front of him, he caught me and kissed my mouth and then my breasts, which were still modestly in the little bikini top.

The water made me buoyant as Newly rubbed against me, and then I remembered my safe-sex rule. "Condom," I screamed. From the edge of the pool, Bearess stopped killing Newly's swim trunks and started watching us.

"Aw, hon," Newly said. "Just this once won't hurt."

The national anthem of the teenage pregnancy roster. No way I fell for that.

"Condom," I said, pinching his nipples extra hard in frustration.

Newly swam to the edge of the pool and vaulted up on the tile next to Bearess, who jumped up and wagged her tail. Newly turned back and said, "Hon, I didn't bring any."

"Look in Ashton's bedroom," I shouted, and Newly ran off, trailing pool water through Ashton's house as Bearess ran after him. Good thing she was an affable dog.

He was gone so long I was about to lose interest. But when he came running back out, Bearess still running and wagging after him, he said, "Hon, you would not believe what all that man has in his nightstand. Want to try a French tickler?"

I convinced Newly that an ordinary Trojan would do fine, thank you, and to hurry it up. He complied and jumped back into the pool and swam over to me. On the side of the pool, on the wet tile floor, Bearess picked up his trunks again and started eating them.

Soon, I forgot to worry about the impact of nylon on the digestive track of a Rottweiler, as Newly revived my interest.

At my house the next morning, Newly raised the ante and asked the dreaded C question.

Children.

Technically, "it depends" is about the most honest and accurate answer a person can offer to most questions.

So when Newly had casually sipped his coffee, safely across the kitchen from me, with Jack the Bear playing chaperone, and then asked, "How do you feel about children?" I answered: "It depends."

It depends on whose children, and how soon they go home.

Of course, Benicio, Bonita's firstborn, who had practically grown up in my office, was a pretty cool fourteen-year-old, and had taught me the dirty words in Spanish like *caray, chingalo,* and *mierda,* and Bonita's other children were not without their accident-prone charm. Even my brother Dan's children were not wholly without appeal, though I saw them twice a year for about an hour when they visited before they rushed off to the beach to get sunburned and jellyfish-stung.

What, of course, Newly was asking was whether I wanted to have children.

No, I was saving up my mess tolerance for a puppy, a Rottweiler like Emily, from Fred and Olivia. Children did not figure into the equation.

I was going to have to do something about Newly, and soon.

Chapter 17

I make lists. I make memoranda to the files that contain detailed lists. I photocopy my lists and take copies of the most important ones home in case the law firm burns and I have to document my actions in a legal malpractice suit or during a partnership investigation of my work. Once I've memorized these memos, I store them in large plastic boxes in a climate-controlled, fire-protected (meaning sprinklers and an extra charge) storage unit, for which I pay a monthly sum to avoid collecting plastic boxes of paper in my own house.

This list-making is neither a genetic nor an environmental trait, as neither my brothers nor my parents were list makers, nor did they ever draft a memo to a file.

Oh, yeah, my mother's list would be "Open Coke bottle. Drink. Take pill. Open next bottle."

My outlaw Pentecostal brother's list would be "Fertilize the pot. Pray in tongues. Save a heathen." Delvon might have been three decades late for the Jesus Freak movement, but he fundamentally believed Jesus was the first great peace-and-love hippie who didn't object to pot smoking so long as you loved your neighbors.

My other brother's list would be "Go to work. Fill vending machines all day. Come home." Proving the fruit doesn't fall far from the tree, my brother Dan drives a Coca-Cola delivery truck and starts off each week by delivering two cases to our mother, who won't let him in the house and never pays him. Dan had joined the Marines after graduating from high school, triggering identical cries of outrage from Delvon and me. But affable, shallow-thinking Dan had gone into the Marines and come out again still affable and shallow-thinking. Except he had seen enough of the world to satisfy him, and he had saved his money to put a down payment on a red-brick three-two, split design, and married his high school sweetheart, another affable, shallow thinker who reads *TV Guide* and *Dear Abby* and absolutely nothing else. They had two tow-headed kids who appear, so far, to be perfectly normal.

My father's list would be "Get up. Walk to dock. Sit down." In his days as an attorney, my father was a disorganized, somewhat disheveled professional who skated on thin ice and would never have survived in either a city law firm or the modern legal environment. But he was scrupulously honest and unfailingly polite, and he never let the paint peel on the outside of the house, and in our small town that made him a success, notwithstanding his dearth of lists and file memos.

My own lists and file memoranda transcend the mere to-do lists and cover your ass memos of the average attorney and approach Russian novels in their scale and proportion and incomprehensibility.

It was while boxing up the lists and memoranda I had collected in my house for the now closed Dr. Trusdale file that I realized someone had gone through that modest collection—modest because I had had the file only five weeks before he was killed and I had settled the case.

The papers were not perfectly straight across the top, and one page had been returned to the folder out of numerical order.

Newly, of course, became the lead suspect. Newly, who for some reason was still living in my house. Newly, who had no obvious reason to snoop in a closed file but was the only person with full access to the files in my house.

I discovered my misaligned and soon-to-be-stored papers on a Sunday and went to the television room to accuse Newly as he drafted a complaint in a rear-end collision case on a yellow legal pad balanced on his knees, sipped a beer, and cheered on the Marlins. Jack the Bear was a morose pudding of dog inertia at Newly's feet. I glanced at the Rottweiler and wondered if you could give a dog Prozac. Somebody did something on the television screen, and Newly cheered. Jack didn't even rise or growl or move.

"Don't you need to concentrate?" I asked, looking at the legal pad where Newly was scribbling something his secretary would have to decipher later.

"I can do this in my sleep, hon," he said, smiling at me. "What do you need?"

I needed him to get out of my house, I thought.

I needed him to explain why he was snooping.

But first, I realized, I needed him to fly with me to Atlanta when I met with Dr. Jamieson, the new expert witness I was going to hire in the veggie baby case unless he turned out to be an ugly, repulsive human that juries would inherently mistrust. I needed Newly to get me through the airport in Atlanta, given my dreaded airport phobia. It was bad enough that the doctor's own schedule was delaying my trip to Atlanta to interview him, but the thought of flying there without Newly to protect me was just too much to consider right now.

Newly had, of course, already agreed to go, taking a day off from work, for which I could not reimburse him.

So, as I watched him lounging on my couch, I decided I'd better wait until after the trip to Atlanta to pick a fight and kick him out. Marriages have been based on less.

Now that Jack was off duty, Newly and I ended up christening the couch, which for some reason was about the only piece of furniture we hadn't made love on or over, and then I showered and went back into my den for a few hours of work. Jack the Bear, looking like the poster child of depression, lay on the floor and refused to budge.

Chapter 18

Before I could even get to Atlanta to check out my potential expert witness, Stephen LaBlanc had hyperventilated himself and me back into an emergency hearing before Judge Goddard, demanding that I commit to an expert witness immediately and that we set a trial date promptly, and, of course, that the judge deny my second motion for a continuance, because Stephen's clients, the ever gentle good-parents, were simply unable to cope with the emotional blackmail of our stalling, plus they were under enormous financial strain, having to, you know, like, actually care for their own baby.

My associate, Angela, twisted a strand of orange hair around a finger into a tighter and tighter knot as she sat beside me. I had a migraine that had been gritting itself against my skull and my personal fortitude since morning. Dr. Randolph, despite his busy, busy schedule, had decided to come and listen in.

Worse than having the prick doctor, my own client, physically present, Stephen had brought the good-parents and the little veggie baby with him. That was a particularly gut-punch play, I thought, so maybe he was getting desperate, hoping the sight of the veggie baby would influence the judge.

I stared at the kid. This was my first up-front and in living color exposure to the plaintiffs and their own little darling. I tried to pretend the veggie kid didn't look so bad. By now, he was three, and at the rate I was going he'd be ready for kindergarten before we sat before a jury, unless today was the day Judge Goddard got pissed at me and set a date and made me try the case. Jason was the baby's name. Though, at three, I guess he wasn't really a baby anymore. He was blond and hazel-eyed, and his movements were difficult, stiff, and jerky. As I stared, trying to assess his impact on a jury, Jason's head circled in a random, uncontrolled way and his mother took both her hands and held his head until the child stilled. He cooed when she touched him.

Oh, frigging great, I thought, listening to the pathetic, and oddly moving, noises. Not unlike a mourning dove. Cooing and pathetic, but responsive to his mother. How did I beat that?

The parents, Mr. and Mrs. Jonathan Goodacre (née Nancy Bazinskyson) were the perfect candidates for sainthood, with their visual displays of attention to the child. They were attractive in a sort of unkempt, wardrobe-by-Wal-Mart sort of way. I remembered from my review of their depositions that she stayed home full-time with Jason and he had a perfectly normal job as a manager of a McDonald's. They had moved to Sarasota from Idaho to pursue a better life and because they were tired of the cold, and Nancy had been seven months pregnant at the time. She had not had any insurance when she became pregnant, and Jonathan didn't marry her until her fourth month. But his Idaho insurance, of course, wouldn't take her on, as she was already pregnant. Fortunately, the McDonald's where he started working offered an HMO that did not have any preexisting-condition exclusions, so after a modest employee probationary period, Nancy Goodacre became insured—at eight months and in the nick of time, though for all the good her husband's HMO ended up doing her.

Nancy had claimed, and her meager records supported this, that due to her lack of money (her boss had fired her the first time she threw up at work, in violation of all kinds of federal statutes, but then Nancy wasn't wise in the ways of employee rights) she'd had no prenatal care in Idaho except some very basic, cursory public health clinic workups. Henry, in a rare show of backbone, had refused to allow Jackson to travel back to Idaho to subject friends, coworkers, Nancy's public health obstetrician, and neighbors to depositions, and Jackson let it slide because he had already been to Idaho years before on a hunting trip and didn't want to go back. But the private eye Henry finally did authorize hadn't found out anything except that these were ordinary, young, somewhat boring people who had dated for a long time but waited until Nancy was well into her pregnancy before they married. No hidden records of child molestation or drug use. Too bad for Dr. Randolph. And, of course, we did have her medical records from her Idaho public health obstetrician, the result of the early work of subpoenas and aggressive discovery on Jackson's part, which showed that she had normal blood pressure and blood workups and no ultrasounds or amniocentesis.

So here we all were, face to face, the good-parents, the veggie baby, the prick doctor, the impatient judge, the never-to-be-underestimated Stephen, me, and the increasingly high-strung Angela.

Oh, frigging great.

With earnest tones, Stephen began to detail the costs and trauma facing the young good-parents in caring for a physically and mentally disadvantaged child. The good-parents needed to get the show on the road so they could collect some money from their lawsuit and hire somebody to take care of their kid because they were oh so tired. Naturally, I'm paraphrasing Stephen's argument. Mrs. Goodacre, née Nancy, I swear, actually began to cry, no doubt, I thought, as a warm-up for the jury trial; that is, if, in contrast to my current strategy, we ever actually got around to having a jury trial.

When it was my turn, I expressed my heartfelt sympathy for the parents and for Jason but pointed out that Stephen's argument on their behalf assumed the truth of the matter in dispute; that is, that my doctor was negligent and therefore the jury would award the parents a substantial amount of money. The essence, I argued, of Stephen's argument was that the doctor was a recalcitrant creditor who wouldn't pay his bills on time and the plaintiffs wanted the judge to force him to pay up now. Of course, I went through the usual lawyer double-talk, your honor, your discretion, it's his own fault for stealing our expert in the first place, et cetera, and I threw in enough big legal words to, I hoped, placate my client, the lurking doctor.

Ever alert to the rule that you end with a bang, not a whimper, I pointed out that Dr. Randolph and I had been shot at, a matter documented by the police report I had attached to my second motion for a continuance. Entirely aside from the normal disarray that this caused in our ability to prepare a defense, I argued, our new security measures had completely prevented me from traveling and meeting with my proposed new expert witness (this was only a small fib, as it was my potential expert's own summer travel schedule that was delaying my meeting him in Atlanta), and I certainly couldn't be expected to try a case like this without an expert witness. A little more of the your honors and your discretions, and I shut up.

Hard as it was not to keep staring at Jason, I kept eye contact with the judge, trying to read his face, and, of course, to avoid eye contact with the good-parents, who no doubt perceived me as in league with the Antichrist.

Judge Goddard's expression suggested that he didn't care to hear any more about any of it. But he gave Stephen enough rope on a rebuttal to my argument to see if he'd hang himself, and Stephen launched into a pedantic argument that I had not cited a single case, statute, law review article, provision in *The Florida Rules of Civil Procedure,* or any other legal support in which being shot at had been legally recognized as a valid basis for a second continuance in a case of this magnitude.

Judge Goddard blinked at me, a signal that I could respond, even though the usual hearing protocol didn't allow me to rebut a rebuttal.

I stood up. My head pounded.

"So what?" I said.

And I sat down. Judge Goddard was going to do whatever it was he was going to do, and nothing I said would make any difference.

Dr. Randolph made an audible hissing noise. Angela clicked her jaws, Nancy gasped, and Jason cooed. I wondered if Judy, the court reporter, noted all that in the record.

But Judge Goddard, known for his fondness of a concise argument, denied Stephen's motions to compel a witness list and set a trial date.

Dr. Randolph lambasted me all the way back to the law firm of Smith, O'Leary, and Stanley. Angela plucked at her hair. It was as hot as blue Hades. I was sorry the shooter had missed Dr. Randolph. But I was glad the speedy-trial provisions all pertained to criminal cases.

Back in the office, once assured it was unlikely that we would be trying the Goodacres' lawsuit against the prick doctor any time this month, or next, Bonita explained to me that her health insurance company had refused to pay for her daughter's trip to the emergency room when she jumped off the roof and hurt her arm because this did not constitute an emergency and she should have scheduled an appointment with the HMO doctor at his earliest convenience, which, of course, would have been at least two weeks.

I held out my hand and took the letter denying the claim, and I promised to do something about it.

Inside my office, I handed the letter to Angela and said, "Do something about this."

I had learned a lot from Jackson after all.

At home that night, the phone rang while Newly was puttering about in the shower, solo, as I was icing my migraine and contemplating whether it made sense to take any drugs for it if I was just going to bed soon anyway.

The ringing startled me, and I dropped my ice pack. I had an unlisted number, as do most lawyers, doctors, and law enforcement officers. It much improved the quality of life to keep as many barriers as possible in place for members of such usually scorned but always necessary professions, and only Jackson, Bonita, Angela, Ashton, Fred, and my brothers and Newly had the number.

And Newly wasn't calling from the shower, so this wasn't going to be good news. I picked up the phone. In my anxiety, I forgot to speak.

"Hello?" The voice, after my pause, was vaguely familiar.

"Hello," I said back, my phone manners replacing my fears that Delvon had been busted or one of Dan's children had emerged from their cocoon of normality and had done something requiring an attorney's assistance.

"Ah, is, ah, is Newton there?"

Newton? Nobody calls Newly "Newton," though technically that was the name he adopted when he legally changed his name from Lester Ledbetter.

"Who is this?" I snapped.

"Who is this?" the voice snapped back.

"Look, it's my phone and I asked first." Peevish, definitely.

"This is Roy Mac. Newton gave me this number."

"Roy, damn. This is Lilly." Roy was a process server and a genuinely nice, funny guy who loved to play cards and who threw great Christmas parties.

"Lilly? Man, you all right? I haven't seen you since, I don't know, last Christmas party. Man, you were dancing up a storm."

"Yeah, till somebody stepped on my hand."

"Man, you and Newton?"

I wasn't sure if I liked the incredulous tone of his voice when he paired me up with Newly. That ought to start some rumors, I thought.

When I didn't respond, Roy asked if he could speak with Newton.

"Newly's here, but he can't come to the phone now."

"Well, you gotta tell him to call me. About his ferret. My wife says it's got to go. Tonight. She's gonna make me lock him in the garage as soon as I get off the phone."

A ferret?

Like, a long weasel?

"Yeah, Roy, will do."

I wasn't sure which to throw at Newly first, that he was giving out my number and I didn't like it, or that Roy's wife had locked his ferret in the garage and wanted Newly to come get it.

That meant the ferret, which I understood to be a long, thin, weasel-like varmint, would soon be locked in my garage.

"Mierda," I said to the room. *"Chingalo."*

Newly had to go. First all his piles of junk and his smothering, next raising the C question, and now threatening to bring rodents into my house.

But what I had figured out over the last few weeks was that Newly had no place to go. Karen the Vindictive had his assets locked up and had an injunction against his even thinking about coming back into the house his hard-earned contingency fees had paid for. She hadn't managed to garnish his salary, but a heaping chunk of it went to cover her temporary alimony and the rest was carved up between the other ex-wives and the daily expenses of food, wine, dry-cleaning bills, gasoline, client entertainment, and the usual regular stuff like fancy coffee for everyone at the courthouse and flowers for the women in the police department who slipped him photocopies of things they were not supposed to slip him.

If I kicked him out, he might end up sleeping on his office couch or living in a cheap rent-by-the-day, -week, or -month efficiency. I wasn't ready to do that. Or was I?

Not knowing how close to the edge of the limb he was, Newly started shouting from the bathroom. "Hey, hon, want to come see what I've got for you?"

Chapter 19

I had pulled my duplicate set of Dr. Trusdale's files out of private storage, taken them to my office, and had been studying the papers again, trying to figure out what there might be in that file that could connect him, me, and Dr. Randolph.

Nobody tried to harm me as I read the fine print on a lot of paper, but my head rocked with the fact that someone had gone through two of my files, and not incidentally that the client attached to one of those files was dead and the other had been shot at by someone hiding in a bougainvillea jungle.

Was there something in those files worth killing over?

When I'd read tiny print until I couldn't focus anymore, I buzzed Angela, explained the situation to her, as if she hadn't stayed fully informed via the associate rumor mill, and set her to the task of finding some connection in the files.

An hour later she came back in and said, "You and Henry are the only connections that appear in those files."

Damn impressive. It had taken me days to come up with that. But an hour didn't give her time to study the huge vat of Dr. Randolph's files.

"Look deeper," I said.

"There is one other connection. Outside the files, I mean."

"Yes?"

"Both Dr. Trusdale and Dr. Randolph were part of a doctor group that's trying to buy this land down south and put up a medical arts building. They've been advocating before the county planning board."

I narrowed my eyes, frowned. "How do you know that?"

"Olivia told me."

"Olivia?"

"Sure. She's got that scrub jay thing, you know. And she's babysitting Crosby now, during the day, while I'm at work. Poor little fella is too frail to stay by himself now, and we, Olivia and I, talk."

Like Olivia and I used to talk. In the old days. When I had the time and the temperament. When Olivia had been like a mother. Like she was now with Angela.

I looked at Angela with a sudden understanding of her—lonely, overworked, anxious, out of her league, far from home, looking for an anchor.

Just as I had been eight years ago.

Except I'd had gorgeous hair, not an orange mop. I studied Angela carefully, perhaps for the first time, and registered her face. I mean, who noticed she had a nice nose, two perfectly fine green eyes, and a rosebud mouth that just needed more color. True, her eyelashes and eyebrows were pale to near invisibility, but that's why God made Maybelline.

"Got a couple of minutes?" I meant a couple of hours, but no young associate will admit to a partner that he or she has a spare hour, let alone two.

Angela nodded, but I could tell she was wary.

One frantic phone call later, Angela and I spun into a baroque hair salon with coveys of smartly dressed young men and women with individual customer rooms that was about as close to a French bordello as I was likely to get. We were there, over Angela's multifaceted excuses and protestations, for a color job with Brock the expert and a quickie with the salon's makeup man. Angela was going to be transformed into an auburn-haired beauty. My treat. After all, I maintained a tab with Brock, tithing over to him each month the cost of my own gorgeous hair and sanity brought about by his therapeutic listening skills and sage advice (summed up: "Screw 'em all but six"), not to mention the divine way he dressed. I had learned to dress from this man, and that, I noted, glancing at Angela's definitely not natural-fiber dress, one that fairly screamed sale rack, was something else Brock could do for my little orange-haired mouse.

"But my hair's always been this color," she protested.

"All the more reason to change it, sugar," Brock purred, as he rolled his eyes at me behind Angela's head and began pulling out bottles and tubes and things.

While Brock worked his magic and his charm, I wondered if Olivia would kill a human to save the scrub jays.

Once Angela's hair was too doused with wet, perfumy gels to allow her to leap from Brock's chair, I excused myself. I drove to Olivia's house and was glad when she invited me in. She had a playpen in the middle of the living room, filled with blankets and pillows and dog toys, and in one corner of it curled Crosby, the ancient and going-downhill little dog.

"Is he going to make it?" I asked.

"No. None of us are 'going to make it,' are we?" she said, smiling sadly to deflect the words.

"I mean, will he make it until Christmas? So Angela can take him home and bury him under the pecan trees. With the others." Christmas was the only time the law firm of Smith, O'Leary, and Stanley shut down for four days, four *paid* holiday days off, with an uncharacteristic generosity in granting leave time before or after those four days. Nobody did any work that close to Christmas anyway. All this Olivia knew, of course. I repeated, "Will Crosby make it until then?"

"Doubt it. He's pretty frail."

We leaned over the playpen, and the little dog opened his eyes and took about half an hour to stand up on wobbly legs and come over to us, where we petted and ooed and ahhed, and he licked us both once, wagged his tail, and wobbled back to his corner and folded up into a knot of gray fur and put his head down.

"Maybe I can ask the executive committee to give Angela a compassionate leave. Kind of an open-ended one that she can take when she needs to." The executive committee was the big three—Jackson, Fred, and Ashton. Compassionate leave meant Angela would get paid and nobody would hold it against her or think she didn't have enough work to do. In contrast, a vacation would be without pay, as she'd taken her week in May to participate in a multigenerational gaggle of kinfolk at some Mississippi river town. The partners also perceived any vacation longer than a three-day weekend to mean that the associate did not have enough work and was not serious about a career with Smith, O'Leary, and Stanley.

Olivia understood the distinction between a compassionate leave and a vacation. Doubtless, by now Angela did too, as she'd come back from her weeklong family reunion to find every partner in the place had dumped extra work on her desk.

"Compassionate leave, huh. That'd be good," Olivia said. "Count on Fred's vote."

"I'll set it up, then." I paused awkwardly and wondered how I should ask a friend if she had, by chance, just maybe, possibly, killed one of my clients. "I can't stay long." As if that would work as a segue into "By the way, did you poison Dr. Trusdale?"

"Want to see the puppies?" Olivia asked.

Yes, puppies might be the antidote to the sadness I felt while looking at Crosby.

While Olivia and I sat outside in the afternoon heat and humidity, the three puppies tumbled about us and Emily peed on my foot.

"That's it, then," Olivia said. "She's marked you. You're her person."

"Olivia, would you kill a person to save the scrub jays?"

Without looking at me, or answering, Olivia went into the kitchen and came back with paper towels for my wet shoe, fortunately just a pair of flats I didn't care about, and she sat back down and appeared to be thinking.

"Do I get more facts?" she asked. "Like, if I just kill one person it saves all the scrub jays forever, or what?"

"Ah . . . I . . . er, I don't know."

"This is about that dead doctor, isn't it?

"Ah . . . er, yes."

"Don't hem and haw with me. Ask me what you mean."

"Olivia, did you kill Dr. Trusdale and shoot at Dr. Randolph because they were trying to get that land and ruin the scrub jays' habitat?"

"No. I didn't. It wouldn't do any good. Another doctor would just spring up, and if I killed all the doctors, then it would be lawyers, or a Wal-Mart, or an Eckerd's, or another damn mall. I know I can't win this. But I couldn't live with myself if I didn't try. So, no, I didn't kill anybody."

I leaned over and wiped the puppy piss off my shoe, asked to wash my hands, thanked her, and left.

Olivia wasn't a liar. I believed her. And damned if I was going to be the one to point out to Sam Santuri that Dr. Trusdale and Dr. Randolph had something besides me in common—their leadership role in trying to kill off one of the last remaining flocks of scrub jays on the southwest coast of Florida. Such a tip would have led right back to Olivia, and she had enough to do as it was.

Driving away, I decided that since I was already so far behind in my work, what with my unscheduled side trips to Brock's and Olivia's, another procrastination wouldn't matter. So I stopped at my house to change shoes and to check on Johnny Winter, the newest member of my household.

Johnny was chittering in his cage when I peeked into the guest room. I refilled his food dish, checked on his water, and fluffed some fresh cedar chips in the cage.

Johnny Winter kicked the fresh cedar out onto the floor and knocked over his food.

"Hon," Newly had previously explained, "he's not used to being locked up in his cage. I used to let him have the run of the house. Honest, he's litter-box trained, like a cat."

Despite that reassurance, the first thing Johnny had done the night we rescued him from Roy Mac's garage, that is, after he bit me, was run through my house spraying like a tomcat.

"Hon," Newly had explained, "he's a boy. He's just got to mark his territory. Honest, he's litter-box trained."

After that, Newly and I had reached a compromise, which I considered far more than fair. I wouldn't kill Johnny Winter, and Newly would keep him in his cage. Even after Newly had cleaned up with vinegar and baking soda, a faint scent of tomcat piss still hovered throughout my house.

"Hon," Newly had said, looking wistfully at the caged ferret, "that cage thing is just for the time being. Till you and Johnny get used to each other."

I didn't think Johnny Winter would be staying that long.

The ferret was an albino, with long white hair, pink, malevolent eyes, incessant chittering, and a long tail.

"Hon," Newly had explained, "he's named after Johnny Winters."

"Who?"

"You know, Johnny Winters, the rock singer. The one with the long white hair. Great guitar. Awesome. You know him."

"No, I don't. That's why I said 'Who?'" Sometimes that decade gap between our ages did make a difference, as Newly and I had definitely not grown up listening to the same rock stars.

"Aw, hon," Newly had said, "wait till Karen lets me get my CDs, and I'll play you some of his stuff."

Further discussion of listening to the real Johnny Winters playing awesome guitar ended when Johnny Winter the ferret hurled himself against the side of his cage and squealed like a banshee.

"Just let me let him out for a little bit," Newly had said. "I'll stay here with him and see he doesn't tear anything up."

From that first week with Johnny, things had not improved. I kicked the cedar chips back at him. "Little weasel, your days are numbered," I said, and headed back to the law firm.

Shoving the thoughts of Newly and his damn weasel out of my head, I plowed through the back door into my own office. Bonita followed me in. "You need to be nicer to Henry," she said, plunking a basket of red peppers and tomatoes on my desk.

"What are these?"

"Red peppers and tomatoes," she replied, her face blank, though she fingered her gold cross necklace.

So, okay, she'd be a great witness, wry and never giving more information than asked for. "What I meant was, why are you giving these to me? Where'd they come from?"

"From Henry's greenhouse. He grows them organically. He is an amateur botanist, a good gardener, and a very fine cook."

"And he is sending them to me?"

"Yes. He brought them by while you were out."

"Why?"

"Henry thinks you're mad at him. Because he didn't catch the Trusdale prior malpractice suits. Of course, you didn't catch them either. And then, because he tried to get you out of the Randolph case that day at the Ivy Club. He thought you wanted off the case and was trying to help you."

I sighed. I could tell that between making over Angela and visiting Olivia and checking on Johnny Winter and now soothing both Bonita and Henry, this wasn't going to be the day I billed those twenty deficit hours I needed to beat the firm's monthly billing average. "Shut the door, sit," I said, and started my personal pot of filtered Zephyrhills spring water boiling for the French press. "Coffee?"

"Please."

"So, spill," I said.

"Henry is a nice man. You should be nicer to him."

Too many *nices* in one conversation for my taste. "Look, he screwed up," I said, overlooking the import of Bonita's observation that I too had missed the prior malpractice suits against the good, though thoroughly dead, doctor. "If Dr. Trusdale hadn't died, we'd have been hit big at the trial. I would have been sideswiped big-time with those other lawsuits, and I would have looked bad, really bad. Henry is supposed to investigate, all right?"

"Yes." Bonita looked serene. "Still, you need to be nicer to him."

Without talking further, I did my thing with the French press and my ten-dollars-a-pound organic coffee that I don't share with just anyone, and then poured each of us a cup. Bonita drinks hers black, so I tried to do likewise.

"So, you and Henry are dating?" This was far more interesting to me than pursuing a theory that I should be nicer to the man who sold a malpractice policy to a staph-carrier surgeon with two prior hits and a possible substance-abuse problem, and who had blamed me for my "obvious inability" to get along with the doctor on the Randolph case.

"Not dating. But seeing each other. He likes the children."

While I sipped caffeine and contemplated pursuing the difference between dating and seeing each other, Angela burst into the room, teetering on high heels and looking like a petite, traffic-stopping starlet. Her hair was a perfect Veronica Lake pageboy, only in a delicious shade of auburn with absolutely gold golden highlights. For a moment, I wondered if I wanted to go red. Brock, bless his heart, was a genius.

"Belleza," Bonita said, rising from her chair to greet Angela. "So beautiful. Your sweet little face. And your hair—*magnifico."*

Sounding like a mother, I thought.

"I can't walk in these shoes. And my lips feel all waxy. And the guys in the library, all the clerks, they're . . . they're teasing me." Angela kicked off the shoes.

"They're flirting," I said, beaming. "But you're right—ditch the shoes. Did Brock take you shopping too?" My idea about high heel shoes is that they are weapons, to be used as such, and therefore not worn every day. Besides, even in spikes, Angela was still short, so short was a look that was going to have to work for her, and she might as well be comfortable, which you cannot be in the type of shoes Brock had apparently persuaded her to try. Also, in those kind of heels she'd never be able to keep up with me and carry my extra briefcase.

I poured the newly minted Angela a cup of coffee, loaded it with milk from my minifridge and sugar, topped mine off with milk, and grinned. I had a trophy protégée of my own creation.

Only later that night did it occur to me that Angela now looked better than I did.

Chapter 20

And lawyers wonder why nobody likes them?

Once a year, in a spirit of exclusivity, the members of the Sarasota County Bar Association have a picnic. It's an all-day affair, with any kind of liquor a lawyer could want. With no exceptions, no one but members of the Sarasota County Bar are allowed. It's a whole treed and green grass spread on one of the few undeveloped plots of land in the county, packed full of lawyers and judges, drinking heavily on the county bar's tab.

I've often wondered who they got to do the work before women joined the bar.

The events are dreadful. But most of the lawyers in town go. Not to go is to invite suspicion and gossip.

The main food is dead cow. The main topic is some version of "I'm smarter than you; mine is bigger; I have more money" or "I'm a trial attorney and you're a wussy, gutless estate planner." Testosterone and beer are the drugs of choice, though whiskey runs a close third. Estrogen isn't even in the running.

I had Jack the Bear with me on a leash, and Newly was there too,

though I told him in no uncertain terms he was not to hover about me.
The man was absolutely driving me crazy. He was smothering me. He
had my house a mess. And he had dared to raise the specter of children
and all that implied.

If Newly's bugging the crap out of me wasn't enough, Jack the Bear,
during his ultra-watchdog phase, had ended my sexual inebriation with
Newly by making sure we didn't get close enough to touch. Sleeping in
my big bed with a depressed Rottweiler, I saw Newly and me for what
we were: painfully mismatched and doomed. And then there was the
not-so-small matter of Johnny Winter, the albino ferret that now lived
in the den and chittered constantly for Newly's attentions.

But there he was, a shadow under the tree. Newly the ever watchful,
as if someone would willingly enter into a crowd of drinking lawyers in
full brag and attempt to do me harm.

Turning my back to Newly, I smiled in pretend attention as Angela,
who had drawn quite a few "ahs" that morning in her newly madeover
glamour, and an attorney named Jill discussed the proper diet for old
dogs such as Crosby.

While I waited for an opportunity to jump ship to a better chat, one
of the imminently exchangeable young lawyers from our firm, a first-year
associate whose name I might have remembered if my life depended on
it, came up and put his arm around Angela and greeted her with a
drunken attempt at wit.

I saw Angela flinch, as if to dislodge his arm from her shoulder. At
my feet, Jack the Bear rose, the hair on the back of his huge neck a bris-
tle of warning in a rare showing of something other than his doggy
depression. The clueless associate offered some inane banter.

As a partner with at least technically some authority over this associate, I opened my mouth to tell him to leave, but before I spoke he
grabbed Angela's right breast.

Acting on what must have been sheer instinct, Angela hooked his jaw with enough clout that he spun off, collided with the beer keg, and knocked it down against a concrete picnic table, sending beer spurting everywhere. As the associate crumpled on the ground, moaning and bleeding at the corner of his mouth, Jack the Bear lunged, dragging me with him at the other end of his leash. Dog and I collapsed on top of the associate, and beer rained down on us.

Only the quick command of Fred, fortunately nearby, saved the now bloody associate from a trip to the emergency room.

Once we had pulled the dog off of the drunk associate, I was quick to stand beside Angela, ready to defend her if the men took the old-school "boys will be boys, why overreact?" response.

Fred, holding Jack's leash, said to a very red-faced Angela, "Good for you."

To the associate on the ground, he said, "You're fired. Get up and get out. Now."

Jackson and Ashton had materialized from a congregation of judges and agreed. "We don't tolerate that kind of boorish behavior," Jackson said, though he might well have been referring to the young man's inability to hold his liquor rather than his pawing of a fellow associate.

Missing entirely the opportunity to leave bad enough alone, the now ex-associate stood up—nobody helped him—and began to threaten Angela and me with a lawsuit for assault, negligent infliction of emotional harm, wrongful termination, and dog-bite damages.

Judge Goddard, who had sized up the situation in a hurry, put his grizzled Florida cracker face an inch from the young man's and said, "Boy, every judge in the circuit saw you grab that girl. Now you tell her you're sorry and you get out of here. And don't let me see your face in my court."

Suddenly understanding and outwardly repentant, the man apologized to Angela.

As he limped off, I asked her, "Where'd you learn to hit like that?"

"I was the only redhead in school and I have six brothers and I grew up in Lumberton, Mississippi."

Ah, that explained a lot. Though whatever had possessed her to think of herself as a redhead when her hair had clearly been orange before Brock converted it to auburn was a matter I didn't pursue.

Newly, who had been hovering close in case of assassination attempts, inched in closer to Angela, and I saw his eyes twinkling, and he said, "Good right hook."

Angela blushed and ran her fingers through her newly normal-looking hair. She thanked him and twinkled back at him with her green eyes.

Hmm, I thought, Newly and Angela. Now, that might be a way to get rid of Newly without hurting him.

Leaving Angela and Newly to their flirt, I decided to bug out on the picnic. Especially since I was sticky with sprayed beer and humidity. Newly was so busy doing his Sir Galahad thing with Angela that he didn't seem to notice me as I left.

Clammy and ignored, I crawled into my Honda, fresh from the police impound with a black garbage bag taped over the window that had been shot out in the parking lot of Smith, O'Leary, and Stanley. The morose Jack the Bear drooped down in the bucket seat beside me.

Ashton and Jackson had both chastised me for driving the Honda with the garbage bag over the busted window, as this didn't set the right tone for our law firm's parking lot, but my auto insurance claims manager had taken the unenlightened attitude that having my window shot out was not covered by my insurance. The policy would pay for necessary repairs for incidents "arising from the use and enjoyment of the covered automobile," but getting shot at was not "arising from the use and enjoyment" of my Honda according to my claims manager.

Well, technically, he was right. Unless, of course, you lived in

Miami, where getting shot at most certainly arose frequently from the use and enjoyment of one's car.

And a window doesn't cost that much to replace.

But what the hell good was a law degree and a junior partnership at Sarasota's biggest and best defense law firm if I couldn't bully a mere mortal claims manager into forking over coverage for the damaged window?

Until the matter was resolved, I was just going to drive around with the black bag in place. It doesn't rain in Sarasota anymore anyway, the result, Olivia said, of overdevelopment and something about the air currents being disrupted by concrete and that global warming thing she's always talking about.

Under my musings about Angela, my auto claim, and Newly, a series of relentless thoughts were plaguing me—like when you turn on an oldies radio station and it's playing "Sugar Sugar," and you don't hit the button quick enough to go to the next station, and for the next hours or days, the annoying chorus of "Sugar Sugar" plays in your brain. Just like "Sugar Sugar" would drive you nuts, this was driving me nuts: "Who had killed Dr. Trusdale? Did that person also try to mug me? Had that person, or persons unknown, tried to warn or kill me, or Dr. Randolph, or both of us? And what did my rifled med mal files have to do with any of this?

Was Sam next in line to replace Newly, or did Sam think I had something to do with all this? Did he know I was withholding information? Was that stare he gave me one of professional interest, romantic, sexual interest, or just suspicion?

There was only one thing to do—go sit on the beach at the end of Anna Maria Island and stare at the yellow arch of the Sunshine Skyway, watching the sun go down and thinking on my sins. Maybe, I thought, romping on the sand and playing in the Gulf of Mexico would perk up poor down-at-the-snout Jack the Bear some.

As was my habit, I drove down Longboat Key and Anna Maria to the northern tip of Anna Maria Island, parked by the No Parking sign and walked past the No Public Access and No Trespassing signs to the public right-of-way along the shore. Jack the Bear moped along beside me until we sat down directly in the sand.

I rubbed Jack's ears, and he put his big head in my lap and sighed. I sighed.

While I might work in chaos, neither my brain chemistry nor my physical constitution was designed to live in chaos at my own house.

My head was so jumbled, I decided, because my house was so jumbled. Jumbled with Newly's stuff. Jumbled with Jack's toys and Jack's mat and Jack's drinking dish and Jack's pillow. But mostly jumbled with Newly's stuff. And Newly's ferret.

Newly needed to leave my house. The ferret too. I'd just have to get someone else to go to Atlanta with me, that is, if my potential expert witness ever lighted in the city long enough for me to actually interview him. If he didn't soon, despite my various continuances, I'd have to track the expert to one of his many seminars and conferences and interview him between his presentations.

So, Atlanta trip or not, Newly had to go. Jack probably had to go too. It didn't seem like anybody was trying to kill me anymore, if anyone ever had been.

Rubbing Jack's ears again, I asked him: "Do you want to go home to Olivia's?"

At the word *Olivia,* Jack jumped up and pranced around and started running back to the car, past the No Trespassing signs. I guess that was Rottweiler for "Take me home to Mama." So I did.

Not being an attorney, Olivia wasn't allowed at the picnic and she answered the door. Jack leaped at her with unabashed dog joy.

"He misses his mama," I said, "so I've brought him home."

Squeals came from the backyard.

"I've got my grandkids here. Playing with the puppies. Come on back."

With Jack prancing at her side, we walked through the disarray of her house and into the backyard. Two girls, maybe six and eight or near to it, were doing crooked cartwheels in the cropped Bahia grass of the backyard while three puppies whirled after them.

"Where's Crosby?" I asked, looking around for the playpen.

"Oh, he's upstairs, away from the kids. He's doing all right today, but those kids'll wear out a puppy, let alone an old fella. Want to see him?"

"No, I'll take your word for it."

"Not that there's any urgency—at least, I don't think so—but that compassionate leave thing, have you talked to Jackson about it yet?" Olivia asked. "It'll give Angela some peace of mind to know she can go without penalty when she needs to."

The littlest girl ran up to us. "Can you do cartwheels, Grandmom?" she shouted.

Olivia shrugged, then we traded looks and grinned.

What, after all, had all those yoga classes and gym work-outs been about, if not for this? Well, okay, technically all that exercise had been about how we'd look in bathing suits, white jeans, or naked. Olivia might have been of the generation that danced half-naked at Woodstock, but she was still buff.

When Fred came home a half hour later, Olivia and I and the Rotts and the grandkids were doing cartwheels, none of us too grand at it, and Jack the Bear was spinning with glee, while upstairs in a playpen the ancient little rat dog slept.

Only later, when I was leaving and followed Olivia into her garage to rinse off some of the grass and dirt, did I smell something familiar. I couldn't place it right off, but I knew it.

"What's that smell?" I asked.

Olivia picked up a blue bottle and handed it to me. "This?"

"Yes." A perfumy, chemical smell. Familiar, but at the same time not familiar.

"Flea spray. I get it at the Granary. They special order it for me. It's got way too much perfume in it, trying to cover up the smell of the tea-tree oil and the pyrethrins. But it works, and it's mostly natural."

Olivia said she didn't completely trust those new systemic flea and tick preventatives, so she stuck with this spray, perfume and all.

Smell has a long memory, as well as a way of triggering the mind to remember.

I hadn't gotten to my Honda before it came back to me: the night I was mugged, the night before Dr. Trusdale was killed, the smell of the mugger's hands. A strong, perfumy, chemical smell. Like the flea spray.

Now, why would Olivia have tried to mug me?

Chapter 21

At my insistence, the executive committee convened in Ashton's office the Monday evening after the bar picnic.

After the usual macho crap that passes for camaraderie among the big three had run its course, I launched in. "Angela needs a week's compassionate leave. Sometime soon, but no exact date yet."

"Why?" Jackson thundered.

"Her, er, her dog is pretty old, and when he gets near the end, she needs to take him home to Mississippi. Name's Crosby, he weighs about four pounds, and he *is* family."

"She needs a week to take a dead dog to Mississippi?" Jackson thundered again.

"No, he's not dead. But he's practically ancient, and fragile. She wants to take him home while he is still alive, let him see the rest of her family, let everybody say good-bye, and then bury him." Realizing how nuts this already sounded, I left off the part about "under the pecan trees with the others," still uncertain if the "others" were more dead dogs, dead members of the human family, or something straight out of a southern gothic that defied polite discussion.

Nobody said anything. I had the distinct impression Jackson and Ashton were waiting for the punch line.

"She was going to take him at Christmas, leave him with her brothers, but it doesn't look like he is going to last that long." From the looks on their faces, my explanation didn't help.

"Not but four pounds? Why can't she just put the dog in the freezer, wrap it up in tinfoil until Christmas, take it home then?" Ashton said.

"Damn, Ashton," Fred said, exhaling his cigarette smoke in a kind of cough toward Ashton, who prissily waved his hand in the air as if to ward off plague germs. This from a man who snorted things purchased from strangers on street corners in the bad parts of town.

Jackson slitted his eyes at me, looked me up and down. "You're not pregnant, are you?"

Leave it to Jackson to view common human decency as a peculiar state of female hormones.

"Look," I said, not even bothering to deny the pregnancy thing, "Angela works her butt off for all of us. She's a mule who works hard all day and doesn't eat much hay. Give her the week to take when she needs it, and don't dump on her when she gets back."

"I absolutely agree," Fred said, and lit up a second cigarette from the butt of the last one.

To my surprise, Ashton agreed too. Perhaps he was latently ashamed of having suggested Angela freeze-dry Crosby in tinfoil.

Jackson asked, "Does she need to go right now?"

"No. Crosby probably can hang on awhile longer. I just figured we'd leave it up to Angela to know when to go."

"All right, then. But Angela's working on an appellate brief for me, and she can't go until she's done, you hear?"

"I'll finish the brief if she needs to go before it's completed," I said, overlooking for the moment that since Angela was my associate, I was the only partner who was supposed to be assigning work to her.

"It's an antitrust thing," Jackson said. "Nobody but Angela understands it. Horizontal market shares. Do you know what a horizontal market share is?"

Of course I didn't. Antitrust was an eight A.M. elective in law school, so I'd skipped it. But damned if I'd admit that to Jackson. "It's okay. Angela can go over the case with me."

"Doll, it's got complex math and charts. By the time she explains it to you, she could have written the brief. She finishes that brief, she can take her dog home anytime she needs to. But you do her other work while she's gone and don't complain, you hear me?"

"Deal," I said, and I headed back to my own office.

Light came from under Angela's closed office door as I walked by. But I was tired. It was late. Tomorrow would be soon enough to tell her that when she decided it was time, she could have a week to take Crosby home to die, so long as she had finished Jackson's work by then.

Back in my own office, I gathered up my newest file—a man who made a living counseling rich women on Longboat Key who'd been kidnapped by space aliens had been sued for malpractice, and I was to defend him. I wondered how in the hell I'd find an expert witness for that narrow subspecialty.

At home, Newly was spread all over the couch in the living room with Johnny Winter, the albino ferret, draped around his neck like a scarf. The CD player was blasting out some kind of rock music that sounded like the stuff Delvon liked to listen to before he found the Holy Spirit and switched to Amy Grant. Apparently neither Newly nor Johnny Winter heard me come in. Newly jumped up, and the look of a teenage boy caught by his mother with his hands on his dick flashed across his face.

"Ah, hon," he started, but Johnny Winter squealed and launched himself off Newly's shoulders, and like a flying squirrel, or a spirit from the netherworld, he spun out through the air and then leaped from couch to chair to table to floor and then down the hallway, stopping once to spray my bedroom door, and then he disappeared.

Newly's expression went from caught to panic, and he launched himself down the hallway after the albino ferret, who obviously returned my sentiments.

Leaving Newly to the ferret, I cleaned up and headed for the kitchen. By the time I had finished stir-frying some tofu and making a salad of mixed greens, heavy with arugula and parsley, Johnny Winter had been corralled and returned to his cage. Newly had washed down my bedroom door with vinegar and vacuumed off the couch. I told myself to get used to this because a Rottweiler puppy would make messes too. But I was solid in my resolve to ask Newly to leave, even if he couldn't afford to rent a decent place.

While I wondered where Newly would go after he left here, we ate our salads without speaking. I served the tofu over brown rice and watched Newly eye it suspiciously. He took a bite and chewed slowly.

"Needs tamari," I said, chewing mine, and I passed him the bottle after sprinkling a few drops of the salty soy sauce on mine. It also needed some toasted sesame oil, but that was still in the refrigerator and I was too tired to get up. I was falling behind at the gym and in my wind sprints, and my rising fatigue was the first sign I needed to get back to my exercise. But who had time, between cleaning up after Jackson at the office and cleaning up after Newly and his beast from hell at home.

Newly took another bite. "Hon, what exactly is this?"

"Tofu."

"Huh? Heard of it." He sprinkled a great deal more tamari on it than was either necessary or healthy and ate another bite.

"Exactly what is tofu?" he asked.

"It's soybean curd."

Newly put his fork down and gave me a pained look. "You want me to move out, just say so."

My lips were forming themselves around the phrase "As a matter of fact" when the phone rang.

On the phone, Angela was all atwitter about Bonita's health insurance company and the things she had found out while looking into its denial of Bonita's ER claim for her five-year-old. She was talking in a nonstop, word-tumbling way that was more typical of me than her, but I gathered she now shared my view that health insurance companies were the right hand of the Antichrist.

"Whoa," I said.

"Those scumbags."

A mild rebuke for the Antichrist, I thought. Tired as I was, I started to tell her to hold it until morning. Then I looked over at Newly and saw him trying to spit the tofu into my cloth napkin. He winced sheepishly when he realized I'd caught him.

I remembered how smitten he had been over Angela when she punched out the drunk associate at the bar picnic.

I remembered how smitten Angela had been over Newly as he tenderly wiped off the beer that had sprayed all over her. Me, he didn't even hand a napkin to.

An idea crossed my mind.

"Angela"—I made my voice sound sweet—"why don't you bring over what you have and we'll talk. I have some Fuji apples and some decent Riesling wine we can have for dessert after we've talked it over."

I hoped Crosby would not mind sharing his last days with Johnny Winter, the evil albino ferret, because already I was moving Newly out and into Angela's crummy apartment.

In hardly any time at all Angela and Newly were sending off pheromones I couldn't help but pick up, trapped as I was between the two of them on my couch, where the faint scent of something reminiscent of tomcat wee-wee had defied the all-natural orange-peel pet odor cleanup spray the man at the Granary had assured me would neutralize ferret wiz. I intended to ask for my money back. He could come sniff the couch if he didn't believe me.

Angela had a ream of computer printouts from Bonita's HMO, printouts showing that for the preceding six months all of the emergency-room claims filed in Florida had been denied as not constituting emergencies.

"And look at this," she said, her normally pale face flushed. "Fully one half of *all* the claims for the last month were denied for insufficiency of information on the claims' forms."

"Apparently the company has a couple of new cost-containment techniques in place," I said, not at all surprised. But I took the computer printouts and started scanning them. Newly took the sheets as I finished.

Some of the denied ER claims didn't really sound like true emergencies, I agreed. But some of the claims listed on the printouts certainly sounded like classic emergencies. Out loud, I mused that the HMO probably counted on most people giving up right away, while others would write letters and take appeals before they gave up. But only a minority—such as Bonita and the few who'd been in head-on collisions at high rates of speed and managed to survive so they could fight with their HMO as part of an increasingly common postaccident therapy—would consult a lawyer. No doubt, those people would eventually be paid, at least in part. But even on the claims finally paid, the delay allowed the HMO to hold its money in interest-bearing accounts that much longer.

"Nice trick," I murmured, flipping through the printouts as Angela and Newly covertly sniffed each other.

Denying or delaying the ER claims was probably worse, but the denial of half of all claims for the last month for insufficient information hit a chord with me. My own last claim for a routine office visit had been denied because of insufficient information. The denial letter explained that the insurance company did not have my current address in its computer. Yet that letter had been mailed to my current address, and I didn't even have an HMO but a real policy. It took me three months and an increasingly shrill approach to straighten that out. In the process, I had learned one of the health insurers' dirty little tricks.

"I know what's going on," I said.

"Me too," Newly said.

"What?" Angela the Naive said.

"Florida, like most states, has a prompt-pay act on the books that requires a health insurance company to promptly pay the claims submitted to it," I said.

"But, there's a hole in the statute," Newly continued, running his fingers through his hair and leaning around me toward Angela.

"What?" Angela said, leaning around me toward Newly. "What's the hole?"

"If the insurer doesn't have the right information, that is, the right code, address, whatever, it can deny the claim until it gets the right information," Newly said.

I leaned back, out of their way.

"Why delay payment?" Angela asked Newly.

Oh, Angie, I thought, wake up. No way I was that naive at her age.

"Same reason they deny the ER claims. Save money. Sure, they will eventually have to pay some, maybe most, of those denied claims, but if they delay payment for a few months, that's a few more months that their money sits around earning interest. On a small scale, it doesn't seem like it would matter. But consider that we are talking about thousands and thousands of dollars delayed each day, collecting interest, and it adds up."

"Then they are violating the spirit of the statute, if not the actual statute," Angela said.

"Precisely. It sounds like a perfect class-action suit to me," Newly said, and he practically stood up and danced, he was so pleased.

Ever the wicked stepmother for details, I said, "Where'd you get these computer printouts?"

A very good question, and one Newly or I should have asked immediately. The insurance company certainly wasn't going to hand these out.

"Ah, I . . ."Angela paused, and her face turned red again.

"Spit it out," I said.

"You can trust us," Newly said, in his most perfect "trust me, I'm your lawyer" tone of voice. No wonder he had such a high seduction success rate, as he made "trust me" sound so darn good.

"My brother works for the company." She ducked her head a moment. "But you can't tell anyone. He'd get fired."

Angie, sweetheart, he'd get killed, I thought, but kept that to myself.

"Is he a claims adjuster, or what?" Newly asked.

"No, he's one of their big computer gurus. He works in Atlanta, home office for the southern region. He's not supposed to have access to this kind of data, but you know those computer geniuses—you can't really keep anything from them if they put their minds to accessing a file."

"And you asked him to, ah, access the files?" I was surprised, this from a girl who wouldn't even push a yellow light on the Tamiami Trail.

"Yes, I asked Ronny to help me." Angela's look was innocent, as if she had not perceived her potential breach of law, ethics, and privity. "The HMO people I spoke with about Bonita's claim were so damn irritating. Smug. Way too smug. The manager told me he ate lawyers like me for lunch."

"So," I said, beginning to understand something of this woman's psychological makeup, "you figured you'd show them."

"Exactly." Angela smiled, the smile of the benevolent to the outward eye, but the smile of sweet revenge in actuality. This woman had the makings of a trial attorney after all, I thought.

"The problem is how to get this information on the up and up and then start collecting the class members," Newly said. "It's one thing to know something, it's another to prove it in a court of law. And these printouts would be inadmissible, given that your brother more or less stole them. We can't subpoena these records unless we have a lawsuit, and we don't have a lawsuit until we have some evidence to support the suit."

"Newly." I couldn't resist. "Angela is an attorney. She knows that."

"Ah, hon, just thinking out loud." Newly refused to be embarrassed as he plotted the class-action suit that would change the world and make him a rich man. The pheromones ground down as the attorney brain chemicals overtook them.

And all I'd had in mind when I handed the letter denying Bonita's claim to Angela was a simple, well-placed phone call. Usually insurance companies will capitulate on the small stuff once they realize that there's a whole law firm ready to fight with them over nickels and dimes. Wasn't that exactly why my auto insurance company finally forked over the cost of a new paint job and new window for my ancient Honda after the still-at-large bad-aim shooter took out the window? Too bad for this HMO that it had not followed the usual course of capitulation on a relatively minor claim by a mother backed by a whole law firm. Now the wrath of Angela and the ambitions of Newly were at play in the field of the class action, and no telling where this would go.

Where the class action might end, I couldn't say. But as I watched Angela's eyes get greener and Newly's hands snake toward her, I knew where they would end up.

Chapter 22

Sam had been looking particularly fetching to me as he sat across from my desk, sipping my organic coffee, until what he had told me sank in like a dozen eggs splattering against my face.

"Say that again," I requested, hoping I was only suffering stress hallucinations.

"Dr. Randolph was the chair of the HMO's appeals review board that denied the heart transplant for Mr. Jobloski after Dr. Trusdale's surgery caused the staph infection that traveled to his heart. He voted against the transplant."

"So, like, there's a connection between Dr. Trusdale and Dr. Randolph on the Jobloski case?" Even as I said that, I thought, Like, no duh, girl, get it together. I should probably start actually sleeping again, I cautioned myself.

Then a couple more eggs went splat. "*Mierda,* it's the same HMO. I mean," I said, "Dr. Randolph was on the board of the same HMO that denied the heart transplant, and that's the same HMO for Dr. Trusdale's bum-knee guy and that paid Dr. Randolph financial incentives not to perform surgeries, like say, a Cesarian on the veg . . . the brain-damaged baby's mother."

Sam nodded. "We are definitely taking another look at the missing Mrs. Jobloski. For some reason Miami hasn't come up with a photo yet, but we're still trying. Maybe she blamed Dr. Trusdale for the infection and then blamed Dr. Randolph for upholding the HMO's decision to deny the heart transplant that might have saved her husband." Sam half smiled at me as if waiting for praise for finding a link between the dead orthopedic surgeon and the shot-at obstetrician that didn't actually involve me.

Okay, good for you, I thought. You've got a suspect and a motive. But I had a bigger pile of crap in the veggie baby case. Revenge, huh? Yeah, I understood that. I'd like to strangle Henry and Jackson for not knowing Dr. Randolph sat on the HMO review board of the same HMO involved in the veggie baby case. This wasn't likely to bode well for my defense of Dr. Randolph.

"Is Dr. Randolph still on the review board?" I asked, desperately hoping the answer was no.

"Yes."

"Does he get paid for this?" I asked, desperately hoping the answer was no.

"Yes. Big bucks."

I closed my eyes at the thought of Stephen LeBlanc's smirk as he danced this out for the jury: Dr. Randolph was paid big bucks to sit on the review board of the same HMO that paid all its doctors, including Dr. Randolph, yearly bonuses for cost-containment measures such as, you know, not providing health care. The bonus thing was bad enough, but paying Dr. Randolph to sanctify similar financially based denials of care was icing on evil. To even a dim jury, that would smell nasty.

Sam said something, but I couldn't hear him over the roar in my head.

How in the hell did Henry do a preliminary investigation of Dr. Randolph and not know this?

How in the hell did Jackson spend a year doing discovery that filled a room with interrogations and deposition transcripts and not know this?

More important, how was I going to keep these facts from a jury?

While I fretted over the ramifications of Sam's tidbits, he quieted. Assuming Sam's silence meant he'd said what he had to say, and in a huff of generalized anxiety, I pushed him out the door. Only later I hoped I hadn't been rude.

I was still reeling from Sam's new information when Newly brought me a framed canvas of a girl with a scrub jay on her shoulder, another painting by the local artist Ted Morris.

Standing in the doorway to my office, he said, "Hon, this is for you."

I knew it was over and that Newly would be leaving me now for Angela.

After he left, Bonita came into my office and studied the painting.

"It's very beautiful," she said, and sighed. "And here I thought you were going to break *his* heart."

She closed the door behind her on the way out.

I stared at the painting and plotted my next move. The ferret was gone, and that meant a new wiz-free couch was in order. Thinking I could hang the scrub jay painting in my office, I called up Brock the Hairdresser-Therapist and asked if he could go to the Women's Exchange and other quality used-furniture shops with me on Saturday. The man had impeccable taste. Sarasota, having such an abundance of the truly rich, who apparently replace their couches like most of us change the oil in our cars, has an incredible array of really fine used-furniture to chose from.

"Why furniture shopping again so soon?" Brock asked.

"Because a weasel pissed on my couch and I can't get the smell out."

"Oh, sugar, haven't I been telling you to date from the deeper end of the gene pool?"

Now that Newly had officially moved out of my house and into Angela's apartment, Angela naturally tried to avoid me, which was difficult given that I was her supervising attorney and needed her to keep me from getting even further behind on my exponentially expanding workload. That Angela would take to hiding from me was a side effect of my engineering her and Newly as a couple that I hadn't anticipated—like the way people in the hallways looked at me with a kind of pity now that the story of Angela snaking Newly away was out. I remembered the same curious signs of pity—overly solicitous behavior or avoidance being the dominant ones—from when my dermatologist lover, the one who officially broke my heart, had left me. Everything had been grand between us, I had thought, until one day, as we were walking on the beach, he reached over and touched my face.

Tenderly, I had thought.

Then he stretched the skin under his fingers just a bit. "I could make you look twenty-one again," he said.

"Why would I want to look twenty-one again?" I had asked, and meant it, then at the relatively young age (so I thought) of twenty-nine.

Sure enough, he left me for a twenty-one-year-old office nurse. Blonde. Big knockers. The night of the big breakup, Olivia and Bonita and I shared a bottle of Jack Daniel's to steady my resolve to keep living. Though Bonita had later survived the death of her husband on the strength of prayer and by overworking, to help me through my heartbreak that night she had broken with her strict hold on morality to get perfectly drunk with Olivia and me, and we had officially formed the "Death to Blondes" sisterhood. Though technically Olivia was about as blond as one could be, the Black Jack helped us overlook that in her case. Now, well after the fact, I wondered if the youth-hungry doctor had left his blond nurse for still another twenty-one-year-old now that the nurse would be four years shy of the dreaded thirty, or if she had submitted to his knife and laser.

Water under the bridge, I told myself, but I found myself looking again at my crow's-feet and laugh lines. The Retin-A definitely wasn't winding back the clock.

And now, in the eyes of the lawyers and staff of Smith, O'Leary, and Stanley, as well as the legal community of Sarasota, I had been dumped not once but twice for a younger woman.

Given that public interpretation, whenever my path and Angela's crossed, everyone stopped to watch, waiting to see if I would do the hissy-fit thing. No way. It was my idea to bring Newly and Angela together. I was cool with Angela. Totally.

To show how cool I was with the situation, I invited Angela to go with me to Atlanta on my trip at long last to scout out Dr. Jamieson in living color as our expert witness in defending Dr. Randolph in the Jason Goodacre (née the veggie baby) case, officially relieving Newly of that travel task, though he repeatedly assured me he would still go with me. No, I said to Newly, that would not be fair to Angela.

However, when I invited Angela to go with me instead of Newly, she seemed to view this as some kind of trap. Judging from the expression on her face, she must have thought I planned to get her far away from the protective eyes of her fellow associates and murder her.

"If you want to be a trial attorney, you're going to have to develop a better poker face," I said, and reissued the invitation with a logical, legal explanation that loosely translated into "We need to gang up on Dr. Jamieson to see if he can take the pressure of a cross-examination." Angela and I would go a few rounds in a pretend deposition, playing good lawyer/bad lawyer, to see how the doc handled himself under the pressure of intense questioning.

Conveniently, I left out that the real reason she needed to go with me was because I needed her to guide me through the tube, the concourse, the hordes of people, the luggage claim, and the cab ride in the Valium-and-vodka haze I knew from experience I would be in by the time we landed in Atlanta.

Still looking anxious, Angela made the usual lawyer excuses, plus she threw in Jackson's antitrust appellate brief and the care of little Crosby.

"Not even two days. Thirty hours. That's all I'm asking."

"But Jackson's brief—I need to edit it and—"

"Bring the damn brief. Edit on the plane," I said, thinking that any lawyer who couldn't simultaneously bill travel time to one client and preparation of a brief to another—a practice known technically as double billing and as common as gray suits in the profession—wouldn't make partner. "Olivia will babysit Crosby."

Of course Angela eventually, though warily, agreed. Olivia had assured Angela that she would keep Crosby, leaving Newly and Johnny Winter, the evil ferret, the run of Angela's apartment for a couple of nights.

Chapter 23

If there is a cab driver in Atlanta who speaks English, I've yet to encounter him.

The one who Angela had flagged down spoke a language I did not recognize, and he smelled of tuna and marijuana, but he grinned at me and winked at Angela as he lifted our luggage into the cab. I slumped in the back, woozy with the stress of walking through hundreds of strangers, many of whom no doubt were carrying spores of a new and particularly virulent strain of Ebola or some similar deadly virus, my heart pounding and my hands sweating. Angela, using a combination of talking loudly and pointing at Emory on the napkin-size map of Atlanta she'd snaked from a car rental booth, persuaded the cabby to deliver us to Emory Medical Center. Dr. Jamieson was expecting us there in about an hour.

Naturally, I would have preferred a shower, a nap, and a stiff belt of espresso before meeting the doctor, though, as Angela repeatedly and rather annoyingly kept pointing out, the flight from Sarasota to Atlanta was only two hours long and it wasn't as if we were flying to Africa. We settled for a good hand-washing in an Emory café bathroom, plus copious espresso.

More or less, I was functional when we tapped on Dr. Jamieson's faculty office door at the appointed time.

Please don't let him be ugly or fat, or stutter, I prayed to the cosmic forces. Juries tend to best believe tall, thin, good-looking men who speak like Dan Rather, this according to jury studies by the Institute of Something Ostentatious that had charged us over a hundred dollars for software that told the lawyers in the firm of Smith, O'Leary, and Stanley such things. Any attorney at the firm could have told anyone that for free.

The man who opened the door made me hold my breath in fear he was a stress-overload hallucination.

He looked like Robert Redford.

Angela fluffed her hair and smiled.

When Dr. Redford shook my hand and his hand was real, and firm, and warm, I exhaled. For the first time since Jackson had dumped the veggie baby case on my desk, I thought I had a chance at winning the sucker.

Angela had insisted we stay with her brother Ronny, the computer genius who had filched computer data for his baby sister. But Ronny lived in one of those hell's little ten acres somewhere in the next county over from Atlanta, and his general standards of household cleanliness were unknown to me, so staying with him was wholly out of the question. Instead of our staying with him, I convinced Angela that he should stay with us at the Ritz-Carlton in Atlanta. That was not a tough sell. The real tough sell would be explaining the third hotel room on the bill to Henry, guardian of the liability insurance company's expenses, but if Henry denied reimbursement I was sure the Smith,

O'Leary, and Stanley executive committee would pick up the tab. I certainly wasn't going to.

And, of course, if one stayed at the Ritz, then one should eat there too. On the insurance company's tab, of course. So, there we were: Dr. Jamieson, the Robert Redford look-alike, who was drawing stares; Ronny, who had orange hair and thick glasses and wore high-heeled cowboy boots that made him substantially taller than me, drawing a few stares of his own; and Angela and me, slinky in our little black dresses and drawing a few stares too. Quite the foursome, dining out at the Ritz. Dr. Jamieson was not married, as it turned out, though I doubted he spent many Saturday nights alone, and Angela and I had already done the first round of quiz, quiz, flirt, flirt, on him, his qualifications, his research, his articles, his medical practice. We knew he could wow a jury. Tomorrow we would do the hard-core questions and answers on the actual case. Tonight was purely for the pleasure of eating expensive food in a fine restaurant with a good-looking man and having somebody else pay for it all.

Angela and Ronny had their heads together, playing catch-up and remember-when and talking about people with names straight out of Tennessee Williams. Dr. Redford, a.k.a. Dr. Jamieson, and I were somewhat ignoring them, intent as we were on flirting with each other.

About the time Dr. Jamieson was tilted just right to look down my little black dress, Ronny finished his monologue on the Lumberton High School graduating class of whatever and leaned into me, eyeing the pale skin at the top of my black silk. "You and Angie need to come out tomorrow and see my new house. It's a beaut. Brick, two stories, got a porch all the way around it."

Angela explained to Ronny that we had tickets for the late-afternoon commuter special back to Sarasota tomorrow and would need to spend the day with Dr. Jamieson, but maybe she and I could come visit another time. I nodded, studying the man's orange hair, which he wore in a kind of retro Afro frizz, and I thought he would be good-looking with normal hair and a better pair of eyeglass frames. What gene pool did they come from where orange frizzy hair was their lot? And why had neither of them thought to do anything about it?

Angela steered the conversation back to one of Ronny's old girl-friends, whom apparently Angela had not liked much, and I lost interest and returned my full attention to Dr. Jamieson, or William, as he had invited us to call him.

Flipping my hair and tilting my chin, I continued flirting with William while sharing a second bottle of truly awesome wine, eating an elegant, wholly vegetarian Middle Eastern meal and pretending to discuss CMV and Jason Goodacre.

There was a God—Delvon was right—and I was in high form, happy. With the airport-return trauma many hours away, I was troubled only by the vague question of whether, now that I was a single, unattached girl again, it would be too slutty to go to bed with my expert witness should William press his advantage, which I was certain he would.

Then Dr. Redford pushed the down-you-go button on the roller coaster and said, "You know what the two big problems with your case really are, don't you?"

Yeah, I thought, I have an arrogant prick for a client and at trial I'll have Mr. and Mrs. Good-Parents sitting at the plaintiffs' table with a cooing child whose head won't stay still unless his mother holds it.

"No," I cooed myself. "Please tell me."

"From the medical records you've shown me, you can't prove Mrs. Goodacre had CMV during her pregnancy. After the child was born, she was tested and came up with a positive on the CMV. But she could have had the infection when she was a child and would have tested positive. To hurt the fetus, the infection must be active during the pregnancy."

"Really," I murmured. Too buzzed on the expensive wine and the square jaw and perfect blue eyes of this man next to me to care, or absorb, his sentence of doom to my existing defense.

"Too bad she didn't have amniocentesis. Take a clear sample, four to six weeks after the symptoms, and CMV can be identified by a polymerase chain reaction in the amniotic fluid."

Oooh, I thought, talk dirty to me.

"The other problem you have is that even if you could prove that the mother had a primary CMV infection during the pregnancy, the fetal monitor strips showed fetal distress and oxygen deprivation. That could have added to the child's condition. It probably didn't cause the initial cerebral palsy or mental retardation if she really did have a primary CMV infection in the first or second trimester, but it most certainly could have made it worse. In fact, the birth trauma could have caused the Horner's syndrome."

The falsely dormant muscle spasm at the back of my neck pulsed alive.

"I believe you lawyers like to call it concurrent cause, and if I remember my malpractice seminars, that will support a jury verdict too." William finished destroying my life and then leaned back and sipped his good wine.

Yes, unfortunately, concurrent cause would indeed support a jury's verdict awarding Mr. and Mrs. Good-Parents a sizable chunk of money. Concurrent cause was just another legal buzzword that appellate lawyers liked to argue about, but the root concept was simple enough: For any one injury, there could be more than one cause.

So, let's see: a CMV infection as cause one (assuming I could prove the active case during the pregnancy), Dr. Randolph's alleged negligence as cause two, and a child whose lifetime therapy and care could cost millions, not to mention the emotional distress, pain and suffering, mental anguish, and all that stuff of the good-parents. And the jury could, and probably would, calculate CMV at one percent causation (at the most), the doctor the rest. Ninety-nine percent of, say, twenty million was still a loss, a big loss. I saw my career sliding away from me down the slippery slope of concurrent cause.

"*Mierda,*" I said, louder than I should have.

Angela's head jerked up, and she stared at the doctor and me.

My whole right shoulder was in a muscle spasm now, and I looked into those blue eyes, and I said to the doctor, "You wouldn't have to testify to that, would you? I mean, with a little wordsmithing"—this being a lawyer term for lying—"couldn't you still testify that the CMV caused the birth defects to a reasonable degree of medical certainty? Ignore the possibility of a concurrent cause as too remote."

Angela gasped. "You can't lie under oath," she said.

Oh, Angie, sweetheart, people do it all the time. Some professional expert witnesses do it for a living, I thought.

"It wouldn't be lying," I started to explain, but Dr. Jamieson cut me off.

"Of course, if I'm asked, I would have to answer honestly. Regardless of whether the infant suffered brain damage as a result of his mother's primary CMV infection during gestation, a primary infection that you haven't yet proved, the obstetrician's negligence in failing to alleviate the fetal distress and the oxygen deprivation could well have worsened the infant's overall condition. If there had been an ultrasound showing, say, the typical ascites, then this would be different."

"Ascites?" Ronny asked.

"Fluid buildup," Angela and I answered together like a cued Greek chorus.

"If an ultrasound showed that, or other signs of CMV damage, then you could establish that CMV was more than likely the sole, proximate cause. But without something like that, the best I can testify to is the possibility of concurrent cause."

So, okay, now I knew why he had never been a paid expert witness before, as a strict adherence to the absolute black and white truth usually precluded a paid witness's popularity among trial lawyers. And I also knew that I was back to square one in the search for an expert witness.

By the time dessert came, I had a migraine and couldn't imagine why I had even vaguely entertained the notion of romance with this man.

Chapter 24

Back in the green-marbled splendor of my Ritz-Carlton room, I gave wholly over to despair. The migraine clobbered my head and churned my stomach. I would lose millions on this case. My legal career was over. I had no sex life anymore and I missed Newly, and Sam didn't talk to me about anything except his damn investigations. My stomach lurched.

I mean, my life was so in the toilet—why shouldn't my head be too?

Eyeing the declining balance of the Percocet from the late Dr. Trusdale's last prescription, I considered my pharmacological alternatives as my brain banged painfully against my skull. I could take a Percocet and go to bed and hope I slept and didn't die of the mixture of that particular drug and alcohol or from pain. Or I could take an outrageously expensive oral triptan, a wonderful migraine pill that if it doesn't constrict your blood vessels into a stroke will miraculously ease a migraine. At twenty bucks for each single pill and with the risk of cardiac disaster, described in the patient information literature as "serious adverse cardiac events, . . . including death," I try to err on the side of caution in taking these little miracle pills.

Death as a possible side effect or not, I peeled back the bubble pack for the triptan, said a quick prayer my heart wouldn't explode, and swallowed it. I was done in by the combination of wine and the stress of the airport and watching my perfect expert witness disappear into the smoke cloud of his own self-righteous and steadfast refusal to testify to what I was paying him to testify to.

Wondering about the quality and purity of Atlanta's tap water, I filled and drank a glass of it.

Then, for good measure, I took a Percocet anyway, and I showered and I crawled into bed and waited for either drug-induced sleep, triptan relief of pain, or death. At that moment, I had no particular favorite among those options. Either, whatever.

Somewhere in the never-never land of dreaming while awake, a narcotic trick I'm particularly fond of, the phone rang. I rolled toward it in my big, lonely king-size bed.

My stomach did a free-fall dive, my brain shifted and collided with my skull and set off fireworks of pain, and I concluded that if I had in fact died, I had not made it to heaven.

I picked up the phone but forgot to talk. After a moment of silence, a male voice said, "May I speak to Lilly Cleary?"

"Sam? Lieutenant Santuri?"

"This is Detective Santuri. Sam. I'm not a lieutenant."

Yeah, whatever. "I hope you're calling from the lobby."

Long pause. No endearing response.

Damn, down we go again, I thought through the daze of chemicals duking it out inside my body, including my own failing brain chemistry, which was refusing to produce whatever those little neurotransmitter things are that keep you from saying stupid things and getting depressed.

"No. I'm in Sarasota." A heavy, tired, masculine voice.

Ah, Sam, I thought. Whether he sounded worn out or not, I wanted his big, strong arms around me. "How soon can you get here?"

Pause.

Uh-oh, I thought. Straighten up, Lilly girl.

"Have you been drinking?"

Oh, Sam, sweetheart, that's the least of it, I thought, but said, "You woke me up. I was dreaming." Not directly responsive, but close enough to skate over my inappropriate phone manners so far.

"I got your location from Bonita," he said.

Big-time uh-oh, I thought.

"Who's dead?" Why bother with the little niceties like "How are you?" when a homicide detective gets your number from your secretary, who knows better than to give it out indiscriminately, and calls you in the wee hours?

"Nobody."

But I heard the sound of "yet" in the pause.

"But Dr. Randolph is in the ICU."

I struggled to clear my head. "Shot?" I asked.

"Poisoned."

My stomach lurched, seriously this time, and I said, "Excuse me, please," to Sam and put the phone down. One thing about hotels, even big swanky ones like the Ritz, is that you are never far from the toilet, where I went and threw up the very last of my expensive wine and awesome wholly vegetarian Middle Eastern dinner. I hoped the triptan pill had had enough time to fully digest into my system.

After washing my face and hands, I picked up an additional phone, which was oddly—at least to me and my class of people—located beside the toilet. Closing the lid on the toilet, I sat down and leaned sideways against the wall.

"Sam?"

"Still here. You okay?"

"Er, no. I mean, yeah. Tell me what happened."

"How soon can you get back here?"

"Got a five-thirty out tomorrow—ah, today, this afternoon." But then, it wasn't likely that I could convince Dr. Jamieson to abandon his moral fiber in one day, not after my most seductive pleadings over wine had already failed. "I can try and catch an earlier flight."

"Might be a good idea."

"Should I stick with bottled water and packaged foods with the seals still intact?"

"I don't know if you're a target or not. You and Angela be careful and get back here. We need to talk."

"I'll call the airport right now."

We ended on the obvious and I hung up. I drank two glasses of tap water on the theory that the would-be murderer probably hadn't had time to poison the whole Atlanta water system, and I picked up the phone by the toilet to call the airport. Instead, I called Angela's apartment. Having, as I mentioned, that ability to remember numbers and having called her more than once in the past, I dialed from memory and hoped Newly would answer.

He did.

"Oh, Newly," I said, surprised that I was crying. "My life sucks."

Okay, so here I was worried about me when Dr. Randolph was fighting for his life in the ICU after being poisoned. Tacky, sure. But I didn't like Dr. Randolph, and I am intimately involved with myself.

I let it all spill out for Newly's freshly awakened ears. In the background, I heard the chittering of Johnny Winter, the evil ferret, who no doubt had the run of the place in Angela's absence.

"Hon, I can get there in seven hours. I've driven it that fast before. Say the word."

"No, I'm booking the first flight out."

"Call me back and tell me when and I'll meet you at the airport."

Only later did I realize he hadn't said a thing about meeting Angela at the airport too.

The next task, I painfully reminded myself, was to actually get the quickest flight home. I couldn't stand the thought of booting up my laptop and doing Delta online, so I weaseled a Delta 800 number from the hotel switchboard and punched it in. After some annoying exchanges with an officious airline employee, I changed Angela and myself to a noon flight—the first available, so said this employee.

Then I called Angela to tell her what was going on. She was all for waking up Ronny and the two of them joining me in my hotel room to protect me on what now seemed like a bit of an off chance that I was a target of the would-be assassin too. But I assured Angela that the Ritz had impeccable locks on the doors, but in the event that someone did break in and kill me, she and Newly should be sure to sue the hotel on my behalf and donate the judgment to the Salvation Army.

Thinking of the postdeath donation, I wondered, Could you buy your way into heaven after the fact? I called my brother Delvon to ask him and woke him up. Delvon sounded stoned, even in his just-awakened state, but happy, and we had a long, wholly incoherent conversation about getting into heaven, a phone conversation that Dr. Randolph's liability insurance company would have to pay for under the guise of travel expenses pursuant to interviewing Dr. Jamieson.

Then I crashed out on the bed, eyeing the alarm clock suspiciously and hoping, more or less, to live to see the light of morning.

Naturally, I didn't sleep. What I did as my overpriced triptan pill began to constrict my swollen brain blood vessels and ease my pain was to begin the counteroffensive. Okay, so first I had to prove that Mrs. Goodacre had active CMV while she was pregnant. Then I had to find another expert, one who would testify that CMV was the sole cause of Jason's brain damage. One who would refuse to entertain even the remote possibility that anything my client had done or failed to do during the delivery of young Jason had in any way caused anything more than a large medical bill. Legal journals are full of advertisements from physicians who offer their expert opinions for a fee. Abandoning my dream of a virgin witness with impeccable credentials, I realized I'd be dialing up these professionals and taking bids.

Then in the last aura of the retreating migraine, I thought, So who says Mrs. Goodacre never had an ultrasound that would show the damages that CMV could cause to a developing fetus? So who says she never had prenatal care of any serious kind? So who says she didn't have amniocentesis?

Mrs. Goodacre alone had said she hadn't had these things.

We didn't know for sure because most of her pregnancy had taken place in Idaho, and, of course, Henry in the guise of cost containment had refused to authorize payment for any trips to Idaho for discovery purposes.

I wondered just how good Ronny really was at computer snooping, and I watched the illuminated dials on the alarm clock until it was late enough in the early morning to call his room.

Chapter 25

The big question of whether the sniper with the puny gun and the bad aim was trying to kill Dr. Randolph *and* me or just Dr. Randolph, while not put to rest, was at least given a new, interesting twist by his poisoning.

By the time I returned to Sarasota, where Newly and Sam were both waiting for me at the airport, the prick doctor was out of danger and had been moved from the ICU into a private suite. Sam told me this while Newly hugged me, whispering, "Oh, hon," in my ear before he let go and hugged Angela.

Sam was all business and offered to drive me back to his office. My head still hurt, though only in a somewhat ordinary way, and I hadn't had anything to eat or drink that didn't come out of a bottle, a can, or a previously unopened package, and I was tired.

"Couldn't I just go home?"

"Later," Sam said. "I'd like your permission to have the poison control people check the contents of your refrigerator. I already looked for signs of a break-in from the outside but would like to have the technicians check inside too."

"Sure," I said, thinking, Whatever. "But tell them to clean up after themselves."

As Angela and Newly went off arm in arm—though Newly looked back over his shoulder at me—I announced that I had to have food. The upshot was that Sam drove me to his house, where, he promised, he would feed me.

In the car, he gave me some particulars about Dr. Randolph. The prick doctor had come home from a busy day of looking up women's dresses and grabbed his usual glass of iced tea. Keeps a jug of it in the refrigerator. Sam explained that the doctor makes it himself, using peppermint and green tea and some other herbs, full of antioxidants and plant phyro-things that are healthy.

About half an hour later, Dr. Randolph felt himself flushing and realized his heart rate was up, Sam explained. When the doctor started having fairly mild (at least to begin with) hallucinations, he called 911. Paramedics found him ranting, his face bright red. His blood pressure and heart rate were off the charts, which they discovered when they were finally able to corral him.

"It was touch and go during the night," Sam said, pushing a yellow on the Tamiami Trail and weaving between cars in a way that made my stomach dip and tuck too. "ER doctor probably saved his life by recognizing right off what the problem was. By the time the paramedics caught him and got him to the hospital, he was in a coma, but from what they told the ER doctor—red face, hallucinations, all that—the doctor realized it was probably Jimsonweed. Or Datura."

"That's the stuff the witches used, isn't it? It's like a belladonna."

"Yes," Sam said, and looked over at me curiously, I thought, and then he flat out ran a red and turned off on a side street and was heading east of the Tamiami Trail, where the few ordinary people left in Sarasota lived in their overpriced, modest homes in the less desirable neighborhoods. "What witches? How'd you know that?"

"I read a lot," I said.

"It's a common weed, with large, white trumpet-shaped flowers. Down here, they bloom spring to early winter. It's the seeds that have the most toxins. Teenagers hear you can get high off the plant and the seeds and make tea out of it," Sam said. "That's how the ER doctor recognized the symptoms. He'd treated some teenagers for it last summer. Of course, he ran some tests on Randolph, but he saved a lot of time by knowing what tests to run."

Sam pulled into the driveway of a very modest, even shabby, older wood house with a shed and what looked like a quarter-acre or so of land around it. Lots of orange trees. The yard was mowed and clear of debris. Okay, so the yard's neat, I thought. But his place was still about two hinges and a screen door shy of a shack.

He hopped out and ran to my side of the car and opened my door, offering me his hand. "You'll feel better when you get some food and coffee in you."

"Toast. And coffee," I croaked. Coffee, yes, my head screamed. In a wholly irrational state that morning, I had been afraid to drink any coffee in case it was poisoned, and I had tried to get enough caffeine from drinking Coke, but this brought forth images of my mother, and, though the Coke itself tasted remarkably good, I couldn't finish it. "Got whole wheat?"

"I don't know. Got what was on sale at the Winn-Dixie last week."

Oh, frigging great. The good-health breads never go on sale. "I don't suppose the coffee is organic."

"Folgers, I think."

I calculated the greater evil: common grocery store coffee versus the delay of a trip to the Granary for the good stuff. Bird in hand won out.

Sam made the coffee first. As I sipped my coffee and felt my blood vessels constrict, my headache ease, and my thinking clear, I pumped Sam for more details.

175

In the end, all he really knew was that someone had broken into Dr. Randolph's house and spiked the man's tea with liberal dosages of Jimsonweed.

"How'd they get in?"

"The back door was broken into," Sam answered. "Somewhat obviously and amateurishly. If Randolph had gone in the back, he'd have seen it and probably called nine-one-one right off."

I sipped the coffee and nodded as hunger kicked me in the stomach.

"Want bacon and eggs?" Sam asked, sticking his head in his refrigerator.

Oh, please, dead pig soaked in cancer-causing nitrates?

But before I could answer, Sam studied the package of bacon and then threw it in the trash. "Eggs are probably all right."

"Toast will be fine," I said, thinking the man needed some serious domestic training.

While Sam made me toast, which I noted was Roman Meal, which is pretty good even if it's not the multigrain stuff I bought, I looked around the kitchen. Neat, clean, stark. Not a spice anywhere, unless you counted the blue cardboard container of salt. White walls. No curtains. I liked it. Nothing that suggested a woman had lived here in recent memory.

Politely, I asked about the bathroom, got directions, and snooped my way through the center of the house. Clean, neat, stark. No knick-knacks. As if I'd found a soul mate, I noted the wood floors without rugs or trash, the complete absence of any newspapers, other papers, or magazines anywhere, and the completely bare walls. And he liked Rottweilers. I calculated his age as mid- or possibly late forties, which meant he might be near to a twenty-five-year retirement point if he'd joined the force at twenty-one. I made a mental note to ask him how he felt about apple orchards and north Georgia in case I decided he should retire and head up there with me. The way the Jason Goodacre case was in the toilet, I figured I'd be heading up that way much sooner than I'd planned. Maybe with Sam and a couple of Rottweilers beside me in my 1987 Honda with the 187,000 miles on it and the new window and paint job.

Jason Goodacre case down the drain or not, I thought another near-death experience on Dr. Randolph's part should be worth a third continuance in his trial, and then I wondered if Stephen LaBlanc had actually filed his petition with the appellate court asking that Judge Goddard be ordered to set a trial date. I needed to talk with Bonita, but first I needed to sneak a peek at Sam's medicine cabinet, check the tub for stains and soap scum, and scope out his bedroom.

When I saw the bottle of Dr. Bronner's peppermint soap on the edge of a very clean tub, I felt better than I had since Dr. Jamieson ruined my life by pointing out that I couldn't even prove my own theory of the Jason Goodacre defense. Though, I admit, Sam's toothbrush in an empty Jack Daniel's pint gave me pause.

But I didn't let the potential relationship with Sam spoil my professional obligation to a client who had nearly died, and, of course, would sue my butt if I missed a trick in his defense. After my lunch of toast and Folgers, I made my long phone call to Bonita and got caught up on things. Then I looked up at Sam. "Guess you'd better take me home."

"Maybe you'd better stay here," he said, and didn't blink, didn't lose the poker face. "At least till we're done checking out your house for any break-ins or poison."

Hmm. Guess he knew about Angela and Newly, I figured, and I looked around, thinking I could be comfortable here after a trip to the Granary for the basics. Might as well start training Sam now. I nodded yes but wondered, Why this offer?

Sam studied me, and his look made me wonder if he wanted to keep me in his house to protect me or to keep me under surveillance as a suspect. But, I mean, how could I be a suspect, since I got shot at too?

Under that stare, and to divert any thoughts he might have about my being a suspect, I finally told Sam that someone had looked through my files on both the Dr. Trusdale and Dr. Randolph cases. Naturally, he berated me for not telling him sooner. Naturally, he demanded to look through the files himself, and when I began to explain about attorney-client and work-product privileges and client confidentiality and the whole nine yards, he cut me off.

"I'll get a subpoena," he said.

So much for romance. I wondered if I should ask for Jack the Bear back.

Then, for no apparent reason at all, I thought about Henry's red peppers and his greenhouse. Bonita had said he was an amateur botanist and a good gardener. He had screwed up both the Trusdale and the Randolph files by failing to do proper background searches. Trusdale's death had saved him from being canned after a big judgment against the doc, which Henry's insurance company would have had to pay. Was he aiming for two out of two? Was there a stand of oleanders in his yard and a flowering white Datura bush in his greenhouse?

Chapter 26

Angela was behaving more like a trial attorney every day.

That is to say, she was increasingly melodramatic.

That night she called me at Sam's because she had something "really, really important" to tell me about the Goodacre case, but she wouldn't tell me on the phone. I had to go back to the office, where she had arranged the proper audience. While on the one hand I appreciated the trial attorney instinct to be center stage, mostly I was irritated.

After all, the Jason Goodacre case was still technically my case, even if the defendant, the nearly dead Dr. Randolph, was still recuperating from his hallucinogenic trip through Datura land and my third and most recent motion for a continuance had been filed just before the courthouse door locked at the close of my first day back from Atlanta.

But my case or not, Angela convened Jackson, Henry, and me—and Newly. Sam had escorted me to the offices of Smith, O'Leary, and Stanley but was kept waiting outside the conference room. Newly, though, I noted, was allowed to sit in on Angela's conference.

"We need," she insisted over Jackson's roar of protest against

Newly, "the plaintiff attorney's point of view," and she wouldn't budge from her position.

What she needed Newly for, I figured, was moral support, but that was fine with me.

I just wanted to know what in the world Ronny, her computer-sleuth brother, had found out.

Acting again as the evil stepmother of details, albeit this time at Jackson's command, I drafted a hasty contract making Newly our "consultant" for a decent fee that with only a bleat or two of protest Henry approved on behalf of Dr. Randolph's insurance company. I had to type the contract myself, as Bonita was long at home and Angela, being the queen bee this round, couldn't be asked to do such a menial thing as type. This consultant contract bound Newly to the attorney-client and work-product privileges and confidentiality accords, and if that wasn't enough, Jackson promised to personally beat the crap out of him if he took a word of this outside the conference room.

Drumrolls were all that were missing when Angela pulled out a series of computer printouts from a folder.

"Nancy Goodacre had amniocentesis in her fifth month, and it showed positive for CMV. She had an active CMV infection during her pregnancy, and the fetus picked up the infection from her." Angela's announcement was made in the clear, controlled voice of a trial attorney. I liked this girl more and more. She was saving my life and my career, and her voice didn't quiver or squeak, not even a bit.

No one in her audience said a thing.

"She also had a series of ultrasounds that indicated the probability of microcephaly well before labor."

This time it was Henry who had to ask what that meant.

"Abnormally small head," I said. "One of the classic CMV birth defects."

"How do you know this? About the ultrasound and the amnio, I mean," Jackson said, for once his voice low, as if Stephen LaBlanc was hovering outside the conference room door.

"My brother, he's a computer guru at Mrs. Goodacre's HMO. He was checking out her records at the HMO for copies of anything from the Medical Information Bureau. MIB records show she had ultra-sounds and the amnio. My brother, he's not supposed to do this, you understand—I mean snoop in the HMO computer files. But we knew the HMO runs every applicant's name through the MIB to check for preexisting conditions, to see if the applicants are lying when they sign up for insurance. You know the drill."

Yeah, we knew the drill. You apply for health insurance and if you admit, for example, that you have diabetes, the company will either refuse to insure you or raise your rates and add a rider that denies coverage for any diabetic-related claims—and everything, including a broken leg, will be deemed related to your diabetes. So the average American does the average American thing and lies, indicating on the form that he doesn't have diabetes. He does this not knowing that the odds are that a summary of his health-care records and his prior insurance claims have been collected by the MIB, including all those records showing he is a diabetic, and that the MIB will sell those records to the insurance company. So the insurance company gets his application form, cashes his check, and runs the applicant's name through the MIB, discovering, of course, that he is a diabetic. The insurance company then can deny his application and return his payment or keep accepting the monthly checks until the hapless diabetic makes a claim that is larger than the company's profit margin off his premiums, and then it can deny the claim and revoke the policy for fraud and keep the premiums. It's a great system.

"But she wouldn't be in the MIB, because she didn't have insurance coverage," Jackson said. "Not until the eighth month, when her husband's HMO took her in on the family plan."

"The thing is," Angela said, "the amniocentesis and the ultra-sounds were done under her sister's insurance. My brother, he and I were piecing this together, but this is what we're pretty sure happened. See, when he ran the HMO's records and found it didn't have any MIB information on Mrs. Goodacre, he, ah, he . . . hacked into the MIB databases directly and ran a search."

What power, I thought, and made a mental memo to file: Sign up for a computer-hacking course. If the local community college didn't offer it, I'd pay Ronny handsomely to personally teach me.

Angela paused. Nobody said a word. Everybody looked right at her. I figured Ronny was already on the list of consultants that Smith, O'Leary, and Stanley kept on its tab.

"See, as Jackson and Lilly know, Mrs. Goodacre didn't have insurance when she got pregnant. She lost her job as a waitress once her morning sickness started, and even after she got married, they didn't have any money. That's why she explained that she didn't have any pre-natal care, except some at a public health clinic that was mostly blood pressure checks and vitamin samples."

Yeah, we all knew that from her deposition testimony.

"But her sister had insurance. Her sister lived right there in the same town in Idaho, in Pocatello, but Mrs. Goodacre went to a clinic in Boise, two hundred forty one miles away on I-84. Nobody knew either of them in Boise—that's what my brother and I figured. I mean, you think about it, you go to a new doctor, you show the office staff your insurance card, and they verify the coverage. But they don't ask to see a picture ID to prove you are the same person on the insurance card."

A good point, I thought, wondering at the good Samaritan implications of loaning out one's insurance card.

"So, it was easy. The Boise clinic accepted the sister's insurance card, and Mrs. Goodacre just pretended to be her sister. Mrs. Goodacre used her sister's insurance, and the MIB spit out those records nice as could be. Ronny—that's my brother—first told me there weren't any records for a Nancy Bazinskyson, but his descriptive word search did pick up a Bazinskyson, only it was a Nell Bazinskyson, hometown Pocatello, Idaho, with amniocentesis and ultrasound and prenatal claims right at the same times Nancy would have needed hers. We figured, I mean, how many pregnant Bazinskysons could there have been that year in Pocatello, Idaho?"

"Mierda," I said. Jackson glared at me. "If her maiden name was Johnson, we'd never have known this."

While I was reeling at the implications of this new information, Angela showed me her loyalty.

"And to be fair, Jackson and Henry, you both need to understand," Angela said, "that this was entirely Lilly's idea. She got to thinking about the amniocentesis when we were interviewing Dr. Jamieson, and she's the one who put Ronny up to it. I mean, looking into the MIB."

"But how do you know the sister wasn't pregnant too?" Henry asked.

"Well, we don't, not absolutely, but the MIB records don't show anything about any actual birth, nothing about a miscarriage. You know, it just didn't look like the sister was really pregnant. All the claims stopped right about the time Mrs. Goodacre and her husband moved to Sarasota. And, really, I mean, what are the odds that two sisters would be pregnant at exactly the same time and both have a CMV infection?"

"If the sister was really pregnant," I said, "maybe they were both exposed to the virus from the same source and did get a CMV infection at the same time, and after the amniocentesis, knowing the baby would have birth defects, the sister aborted?"

"Possibly, but then again, a medically necessary abortion like that probably would have shown up in the MIB, but that will be something we'll have to run down."

"Henry, you son of a bitch," Jackson said, "if you'd authorized the expenses for me to go to Idaho like I wanted, to investigate, we'd have known all this months ago. Damn it, I'm going to Idaho now and you're going to pay for it."

"No, you're not going to Idaho. It's my case," I said. "You passed it off to me. Angela and I will go to Idaho, won't we, Henry?"

Henry blushed. I took it for a yes.

"Then at least fire that private investigator you hired for not turning up any of this," Jackson said.

Sitting in my chair, I felt a wave of paranoid excitement spin through me.

We could win this veggie baby case. But we had to be careful.

Not only did we need to protect Ronny, but we needed to protect our ability to collect evidence of our new theory before records disappeared or witnesses moved. All we had right now was inadmissible and illegally obtained evidence that Mrs. Goodacre had pulled not only a fraud on her sister's insurance company but a fraud on the court by lying under oath in her deposition and withholding critical information in her lawsuit.

I wondered if Stephen LaBlanc knew about the amniocentesis.

If he did, The Florida Bar's ethics division would have a field day yanking his license. I'd file the complaint myself at the first hint that he knew his clients were lying their way up the slippery slope of the litigation lottery.

"You think they set this up, deliberately, to sue?" Henry asked. "I mean, after they knew the baby had contracted the CMV and would have birth defects."

"I don't see how. Really, how on earth could they possibly know that she'd get into trouble during delivery and the doctor wouldn't do a Cesarean?" I said.

"Right, I agree," Newly said. "This was purely an afterthought. I can imagine how it came about. You type in cerebral palsy as a descriptive word on an Internet search engine and you'll get a dozen hits for law firms advertising that they handle birth defect lawsuits for cerebral palsy. Plus, some attorneys pay hospital workers for tips about babies with bad birth defects. The hospital employees slip the attorneys copies of the records, and if they see something they call the parents, pay the employees for the tip."

"You don't do that, do you?" Angela asked.

"No, hon, you know I don't," Newly said.

Jackson made a loud, rude noise deep in his throat. Even I wasn't sure I believed Newly's denial.

"I've been researching ways that we can bring this evidence in—I mean, once we nail it down so it can't be traced back to Ronny," Angela said. "I've been studying the evidence code, and I think I see a way to introduce this as impeachment to Mrs. Goodacre, assuming she testifies she didn't have amniocentesis. So we don't have to put any witnesses like her sister or the people at the Boise clinic on the witness list, or disclose any evidence to Mr. LaBlanc. I mean, just think of the impact on the jury to catch her in such a big lie in the middle of the trial."

Well, there were some serious problems with that, I realized. I mean, why would the sister admit this scheme without a subpoena? And the medical staff at the Boise clinic couldn't divulge patient information without a subpoena, and as soon as we started issuing subpoenas and setting up depositions in Idaho, we'd have to notify Stephen LaBlanc.

But yes, as Angela pointed out, it would be great fun to drop this in the middle of cross-examining the teary good-mother during the trial.

Glancing toward Jackson, I saw a look of admiration on his face as he watched Angela turning into a trial attorney before our very eyes, and I felt my crown slipping off another notch.

"So, why'd she have all this postpartum stuff from Dr. Randolph?" Newly asked, as he flipped through the purloined computer printouts that Angela had handed him. "I mean, you'd think she wouldn't want the man to touch her again. Look at all these office visits. Damn, the man wasn't a pediatrician. Plus, why have two ultrasounds *after* the delivery?"

Not my problem, I thought. So, spank me for my narrow vision, but my job was to defend Dr. Randolph against allegations his negligence had caused Jason's brain damage during Mrs. Goodacre's labor and delivery. What transpired after young Jason entered the world of the living had nothing to do with my defense of the doctor.

Chapter 27

While I was busily violating all kinds of client-confidentiality, work-product, attorney-client privileges by spilling all this to Sam on the ride back to his house, my subconscious was spinning and churning.

By the time we were back at Sam's and I was draped over his couch while he poured the wine, which, of course, I'd had to buy since Sam's idea of good wine was basically Bud Light, my subconscious had spit out two ideas. Neither of which I liked.

First, Jackson, my beloved mentor, my ardent defender, and my personal god of thunder, had been negligent in handling the discovery phase of this case. Sure, he'd deposed half of the citizens of Sarasota County, but he had never gone to Idaho and deposed the people there, where young Jason had spent more than half of his gestation period. With an even half-assed investigation into the Idaho prenatal experiences of Mrs. Goodacre, Jackson stood a good chance of discovering what had gone on in Boise. And, as Jackson is anything but half-assed, he'd have deposed everybody with the remotest connection to Mrs. Goodacre and he would have found out the truth.

In other words, if Jackson had done what he was supposed to have done, this case would have ended many months and many thousands of dollars ago.

So, why hadn't Jackson done what he was supposed to do?

He would, of course, say he didn't go to Idaho because Henry, as the claims adjuster in charge of allowing or disallowing payment for litigation expenses, had refused to pay for any trips to Idaho.

So why had Henry done that?

Yeah, yeah, yeah, everybody in the malpractice insurance world is frothing at the mouth about cost containment. But wasn't that a pretty important step to refuse to authorize? Wasn't Henry saving pennies and losing dollars? And even if Henry didn't authorize the trip, Jackson had a legal and ethical obligation to Dr. Randolph to complete the discovery process by going to Idaho and finding out what had happened there.

So there it was: My hero Jackson had screwed up.

The second thing my subconscious spit out was the wholly convoluted notion that maybe some of this—the attempted murders on Dr. Randolph, the rifling in the files, my mugging—might have been the nefarious doings of the good-parents, Mr. and Mrs. Goodacre, in an artless attempt to end the litigation before they were found out. Or to hide something, steal something, see if I'd found anything out. There were definitely possible motives floating out there. The parents just felt like suspects now that I knew they were frauds.

But what would that have to do with poor Dr. Trusdale, dead and decomposing in his last earthly location?

Sam handed me some wine and made me explain everything again, and again.

"Hmm," he said, as I spilled my guts about Jackson's having screwed up.

Hmm? Sometimes Sam carries this strong, silent type thing way too far.

"What do you mean, 'hmm'?" Did he think Jackson would try to

kill Dr. Randolph to cover up his own negligence? That didn't make
any sense at all.

"Nothing," Sam answered.

None of this made any sense.

"Let's go to bed and sleep on it," I said, finishing the wine. I meant,
of course, together, but Sam was still sleeping on the futon in his second
bedroom. But I saw the way he looked at me when he thought I wasn't
paying attention. Give it two more nights, I thought, and that futon
thing will end.

Chapter 28

Jennifer the dingbat Stairmaster wizard came prancing into my office with a well-dressed man who looked as if he was used to having his way, and she said, "Lilly, this is my special friend Marcus."

As in Welby? I thought. "Special friend," like Ashton?

"Marcus, this is my friend Lilly."

I was at the office on a Saturday afternoon, making some headway in the pile of work that triplicated every night while I tried to sleep. Because it was Saturday and I was living at Sam's out of a hastily packed suitcase, my clothes had fold marks, I wore no makeup, and I was already tired. In short, I didn't want to meet a well-dressed man named Marcus.

"Marcus is a doctor," Jennifer said. "Lilly is a lawyer."

Neither Marcus nor I spoke.

Ashton tripped into my office, completing the overcrowded effect, and he smiled and said, "Hey, there, troops. Ready?"

"Ready for what?" I finally spoke.

"Jenn and I thought you'd like to join us, and Mark here, for dinner in Tampa tonight. Ybor City, the Colombia sound good?" Ashton squinted down a bit at me, as if he were trying to bring me into focus without putting on his glasses. "You might want to go home and freshen up a bit first," he said.

Marcus smiled, showing a row of teeth so white they had to have been chemically altered. Come to think of it, his nose looked a little too perfect too. While I studied him, he studied me.

"She looks fine to me," he said.

"Marcus is, like, just one of my best friends," Jennifer trilled. "He even got me my job with the doctors' business services."

Marcus offered his hand to me. "Pleased to meet you."

Yeah, okay, originality wasn't his strong suit, I'd guess.

I took his hand. "I defend a lot of doctors."

"Yes, Jennifer told me. I'm a radiologist. We never get sued."

"Actually, I had a radiologist for a client once. He couldn't tell left from right."

Marcus smiled, touched my left shoulder, and said, "Left." He touched my right and said, "Right."

Cute, I thought. Real cute.

"You and Marcus can drive to Tampa in his Jag, and Ashton and me will follow," Jennifer said. "Marcus lives in Tampa. So, like, you know, you can, ah, ride back with us, unless, you know, you, er, want to, you know."

Like, all Jennifer's "you knows" aside, I wasn't going to spend the night with this guy. A radiologist with a Jag and abnormal, chemically altered teeth, as well as a probable nose job, who lived in Tampa and who could tell left from right. Is this who they were trying to fix me up with?

I wondered what they had told him about me. That my own associate, a woman technically my inferior and certainly within my control, had snaked away my lover? Yeah, I wanted to live that down with a perfect stranger.

"No, thank you," I said.

Then Bearess, Jennifer's sleepy-eyed Rottweiler, bounced into my office and licked Jennifer on the hand. She came up to me in a leap, gruffed a doggy hello, and licked my hand too. I petted her big head and she bounced back over to Jennifer's side.

"First we have to take Bearess over to Olivia's for babysitting," Jennifer said and scratched the dog's big head as the animal closed her eyes in an expression of doggy bliss.

"Leave her with me," I said, "and I'll take her to Olivia's when I'm done here."

Okay, so I used to be good at saying no. But Jennifer had that way about her, the pretty blonde trick of just pretending everybody was doing exactly what she wanted until finally everyone *was* doing exactly what she wanted.

Which is to say, Jennifer dropped me at my house, which Sam said the police department had declared poison-free and with no evidence of a break-in, to freshen up, leaving Ashton to protect me while she and Marcus drove Bearess over to Olivia's and swung back in half an hour. Which was all I needed to shower, fluff my hair with Brock's wonder gel, and put on a touch of Maybelline and a kick-ass pair of hip-rider white jeans with a red silk halter that showed off my long neck and firm arms, and possibly a bit too much else for a woman my age, but I worked hard at the Y and might as well show some tummy now and then. I took a funky silk jacket because it would be twenty degrees in the Colombia restaurant. So, okay: Marcus was a radiologist, and therefore dull by definition, but now that I'd had time to check him out, I had to admit he was a nice-looking man, enhanced by medical science or not. So I decked out to make an even match, not that I had any intentions of starting anything with him.

I did think to call Sam and leave a message on his machine that I was going to run up to Tampa with my law partner, Ashton, and a client and would be late.

I mean, it wasn't as if Sam and I were going steady. In fact, I didn't even have a clue as to why I was staying at his house. That is, a clue from his point of view. Speaking strictly for myself, I was staying there because I didn't figure any assassin in his right mind would aim for me in the house of a homicide detective. Besides, as Bonita had pointed out early on, Sam was a major hunk.

When Jennifer and Marcus showed up at my house, she overdid the cooing on the Jag and before I'd had a chance to mentally run through potentially enticing introductory conversation ideas for the ride up with Marcus, he offered to let Jennifer drive his Jag. Then Ashton wanted to talk stocks, tax shelters, and stuff with Marcus and assumed I would be bored by this, so why didn't they ride up together, he said. The upshot was that I found myself in the passenger seat of a Jag belonging to a strange man who might or might not be my date, but with Jennifer behind the wheel wearing a big grin. Yeah, whatever, I thought, naively believing Jennifer would probably be more fun on the ride up than a radiologist with bleached teeth.

Driving I-75 from Sarasota to Tampa is fundamentally boring, so I turned to Jennifer and suggested, "Hey, why don't we detour off onto 275 and take the Sunshine Skyway?"

"Isn't that, like, out of the way?"

"We have an appointment somewhere? It's a beautiful trip over the Skyway Bridge and then across the bay into Tampa. This time of day, crossing the Skyway'd be cool."

"Yeah, Ashton said that you had, I don't know, like, a thing about that bridge. Like, you're really hooked on it and go out there to, I guess, what, meditate or something."

Sure, I did have a thing about that bridge, but I didn't know my fascination was common knowledge. "Come on, let's go. It's a great bridge."

"You think it's haunted? You know, from all those people that drove off the end when it broke when that boat hit it?"

"I don't think you can have a haunted bridge."

"Why not?"

"Jennifer, you ever hear of a haunted bridge before?"

"I think the world is full of things we've never heard of before."

Well, that stopped me for a moment, suggestive as it was that Jennifer could think at a depth beyond her D-cups.

"Okay, maybe it is haunted. Let's go see," I said. But Jennifer drove right past the 275 interchange, and I sunk back into my leather seat.

With Jennifer driving the Jag at an impressive clip, we soon passed the Moccasin Wallow exit on the interstate, heading into Tampa, and a man in the middle lane crossed over in front of Jennifer, who was gaining in the fast lane. Apparently this was the guy's stupid way of passing the slower car in front of him in the middle lane—I mean, really, it makes things on an interstate so dull to actually wait until there is, you know, like, a clear spot in the next lane before you swerve into it.

Shouting out an impressively loud and crude insult, Jennifer braked and served and cursed, spinning a moment onto the shoulder and then gassing the Jag, which responded so quickly my head jerked back. Cursing with words that included some that Bonita's son had not taught me the Spanish equivalent of, Jennifer passed the jerk who had cut her off, careening around him on the shoulder and then zagging right back in front of him so close that he had to brake to avoid hitting her. The jerk spun a half circle back into the middle lane, where the slower car he had tried to pass in the first place narrowly missed colliding with him by spinning into the slow lane, where another driver showed good reflexes and spun off onto the shoulder.

"Showed him, fucking asshole," Jennifer said, and then rolled down her window and gave him the bird in a long, emphatic hand-waving gesture as we peeled off, racing ahead of him.

"Well," I said, feeling my heart racing, "wasn't that fun? You think maybe you overreacted?"

"No. Why?"

I glanced over and looked at the speedometer. Ninety-five. The Jag was smooth—I'd give it that. "Maybe you ought to slow down now that the excitement's over?"

"Marcus said this car would cruise at one-hundred-twenty-five, no problems. Let's see."

Looking at the lines of cars in the three lanes of I-75 as it approached the many Tampa exits, I thought, Oh, no, let's not. "Maybe another time," I said. Like when I wasn't in the car with her.

Jennifer eased up a bit, and I leaned back in the seat.

Then she hit the gas so hard my head jerked again and she spun around the car in front of us, and I heard the distinct sound of a siren. Oh, *mierda,* I thought.

Approaching a hundred, Jennifer turned her head and looked back. "A state trooper," she said, rather matter of fact in tone, given what later developed.

"Would you watch the road!" I shouted, and she turned back. But she continued to press the gas pedal.

"Slow down," I shouted. "You've got to stop."

"In my purse," Jennifer said, "there's a Baggie. Get it out."

I did. A Baggie with little white pills.

Mierda!

"Eat half, I'll eat the other half," Jennifer said, that matter-of-fact tone still oddly in use.

I looked in the bag. There must have been twenty of the little white pills in it. I studied them closer to see if they might be anything I'd want to hide a couple of for later, but they didn't seem to be any standard prescription drug.

"Eat 'em, damn it," Jennifer yelled, no longer matter of fact. I felt the car surge forward as she hit the gas, rapidly closing the gap on the car in front of us.

"Slow down, damn it!" I yelled.

"Eat 'em—just half, please. I'll eat the other half. I can't go to jail."

"What the hell are these?"

"Acid. LSD."

Acid, I thought, looking at the pills. Thirty years behind the times. People still ate this?

"Hurry up," Jennifer said.

Instead of eating my way into a serious hallucinogenic overdose, I poured the pills from the Baggie into my right hand. Then I rolled down the window and put my hand out, low and flat against the door, dangling it as inconspicuously as I could, and began to dribble little white pills of LSD down the corridor of I-75 heading into Tampa. I doubted this was the first time this had happened as I watched the pills rain down on the pavement and explode. Given the commanding lead that Jennifer had on the state trooper, I doubted he would notice a trail of little white pills coming out the passenger side of the car. If he did notice, I counted on his survival instincts preventing him from trying to actually gather up what would surely be just LSD dust in the wind in the dense, high-speed traffic.

Eat 'em, my ass.

"Stop the damn car," I yelled once the pills were gone, and I stuffed the bag into my bra, hoping there was no traceable residue on it but afraid the sight of a Baggie floating out of the car window might be visible and suspicious to the state trooper, who, I noted, seemed to be gaining on us. Also, littering is so tacky. I mean, those pills were biodegradable, but that Baggie would live forever.

"I can't go to jail," Jennifer wailed.

"What else is in the car?" I asked.

"Nothing. Swear."

Though I sensed a lie, I would rather take my chances with the state trooper, even the criminal justice system, than die in a high-speed multi car crash on I-75, which seemed to be Jennifer's current plan as she swerved around a car going an ordinary ninety miles per hour or so. She narrowly dodged a collision with the car already in the lane she'd just crossed into, and then she sped around it on the shoulder of the road. The siren blasted through the careening Jag, and I fingered the Saint of Somebody that Bonita had given me, which I wore around my neck.

"Stop the car. Pull over. Please. I don't want to die here," I pleaded.

"I don't have a driver's license."

"Jenn, they don't put you in jail for that. Honest. I'm a lawyer. I'd know. Now, stop."

She began to slow down. I saw hope.

"Trade places with me," she said.

"What?"

"Here." She reached for my hand. "Take the steering wheel. Climb over me. You've got a driver's license. Come on. Trade places."

And all these months we had merely thought this woman was a nitwit. Worse than that, she was crazy. Trade places while driving a car down an interstate at ninety-five miles per hour? In what universe would you live through that?

"I'll trade with you after you stop the car." I was lying, but it seemed a good thing to offer under the deteriorating circumstances.

"You will? Won't the cop see us?"

I didn't care if the state trooper did see us, especially since I wasn't planning on actually trading places with her. "No," I said with as much assurance as I could muster. "You're too far ahead. He won't be able to see us if we're quick."

She swerved over to the shoulder and skidded to a stop. Next thing I knew, Jennifer was sitting on top of me and slapping frantically at my hips with both of her hands.

"Scoot over," she said, shoving at me. "Move," she bellowed.

I scooted.

What the hell. In for a dime, in for a dollar.

While I tried to regulate my heart and breath and imagine what in the world I would say to the state trooper, I looked at Jennifer. Her face was red, her eyes big, and she was panting. Her huge, Barbie-doll breasts were heaving.

"Unbutton the third button," I said, thinking cleavage was our only weapon now. But she didn't budge, a catatonic look crossing her face.

I grabbed my wallet, pulled out my driver's license, and got out of the car. If I acted contrite and passably normal, maybe the state trooper wouldn't shoot me.

The trooper, who was young and red-faced, looked angry as he crawled out of his vehicle, outwardly cautious, his right hand free and near the holster on his belt. I'm sure I looked as crazy as Jennifer had. I didn't say a word. Delvon had told me once that there are only three things you ever, ever said to a police officer if you are stopped or questioned: "Yes, sir," "No, sir," and "I'm sorry, sir." I was silently practicing the "I'm sorry, sir" when I heard the other car door open and Jennifer popped out, the third button on her blouse opened and the bulges over her demibra radiant.

"Oh, officer," she said, sounding remotely normal. "This is all my fault, I'm afraid. I am so sorry."

You got that right, babe.

I glanced at the trooper and noticed that he had snapped open his holster and was looking down at us as if we were the Dixie Mafia personified.

At least one of us might be, I thought.

"There was a wasp in the car." She took a step closer to him, walking with a lilting spring that made her hair and hips sway alluringly, full blonde armor ready. "I'm deathly allergic. I've got these little syringes of stuff I'm supposed to carry with me in case I get bit, but I forgot. And I panicked, and I scared my friend here. She was trying to drive and swat the wasp, and I was opening the windows so it would fly out, and I told her to go faster so the air would blow the wasp out, and, oh, it finally did, and I am so sorry."

Nobody in their right mind would believe that, I thought. No bosom in the world could get us out of this.

The state trooper glanced back at me. "License and registration," he said.

I handed him my license, and then I thought, Registration, *mierda*. It isn't even my car.

"I'll get it," Jennifer said, grinning as if she were a cheerleader at the homecoming game and the trooper was the coach giving a last-minute pep talk.

"Easy, ma'am," he said, easing over toward her, his right hand hovering toward his holster.

"Just in the glove compartment? Won't be but a sec," she said.

I contemplated running like hell, but then another car whooshed in behind the trooper's car, and I turned toward the sound and saw Ashton and the doctor man get out and approach the trooper.

"Y'all stay back," the trooper said to Ashton and Marcus, his hand now on his holster.

"Hey, girls, what's up?" Ashton was grinning like a man in control of his destiny, or one deluded by substance abuse of long duration.

The trooper eyed us all. "You." He pointed at Jennifer, and she beamed as if he had announced her the winner of the Miss Blonde Something pageant. "Get over there with them."

We all watched Jennifer make a show of walking around the Jag in the shimmering heat of the late afternoon and stand beside Ashton and Marcus. "Hi, honey," she said to Ashton, and she reached out and took his hand in her own dainty little pink-tipped fingers.

"You," the trooper said, pointing at me, "get the registration, now, and go slow."

I held up my hands toward the trooper to show him I had no weapons. "Yes, sir."

The trooper followed me around to the driver's side and kept a close eye as I opened the door to reach the glove compartment. Ashton,

Jennifer, and Marcus stayed lined up on the other side of the car while I dug in the glove compartment. The state trooper watched me, right hand resting on his holster, eyes flicking back and forth between me and the trio by the side of the road. I handed the trooper a registration and proof of insurance.

"It's his car," I said, pointing at Marcus. "I was just test-driving it. We're just awfully sorry, sir, but the wasp really had us both freaked out."

And that bag of acid had us a little freaked out too.

And whatever else was hidden in the car.

"Get over there with them," the trooper said, and I did.

He walked back to his car and radioed in the registration to see if the car had been listed as stolen. Then he collected identification from each of us, accepting from Jennifer an assortment of credit cards and her library card in lieu of the driver's license she didn't have. He called all of us in on the radio to see if we had any outstanding warrants. I was pretty sure Ashton and I were all right, but I sweated out Jennifer and Marcus. But we were cleared.

Then he asked me if he could look through the Jag.

"Help yourself," I said, "but it's his car. You might ask him. I'm just test-driving it. Never met the man before late this afternoon."

Really, why didn't I say I was just a hitchhiker and whatever he found in the Jag had nothing to do with me? Surely the state trooper had never heard that one before.

"Oh, please," Marcus said. "Help yourself."

I watched Jennifer's face but saw only the vapid expression of a woman with nothing more to worry about than sweat stains on her silk blouse.

The trooper made all four of us sit in his car while he rattled through the obvious hidey-holes in the Jag. He seemed to take a long time. The Baggie in my bra scratched, but I didn't dare take it out.

None of us in the trooper's car spoke, probably for fear we were being taped or monitored.

Apparently Jennifer had told the truth and the only illegal contraband was now LSD dust in the wind.

In the end, the state trooper wrote me a ticket for speeding and left it at that. I don't know whether it was the heaving bosom, our fundamentally clean-cut, middle-class, middle-aged appearance (well, at least with Ashton and Marcus, that is), the story of the wasp, or just the state trooper's own desire to be done with all of us once he failed to find contraband or outstanding warrants. But a speeding ticket was all that happened.

That, and I made Ashton let me drive his car while Jennifer and Marcus cruised into Tampa in the Jag well ahead of us. For once I went the speed limit. Well, okay, I went ten miles over, but nobody stops you for that.

"She's totally crazy," I said to Ashton.

"No, babe, she's just high strung."

I thought, Yeah, well, I'd ask for a second opinion.

"I'll pay the ticket," he said.

"Damn right."

We drove the rest of the way in a strained silence.·

Once in Tampa, despite my attempts to get Jennifer alone and ask what in the hell that LSD thing was about, I was never able to get her outside the range of strangers who could listen in. I prefer not to discuss illegal drug contraband in the hearing of people I don't know, so I figured I would catch her later, back in Sarasota.

Oddly enough, we had a perfectly fine dinner at the Colombia, drank several bottles of fine Spanish wine, finished up with the famous Cuban coffee, and flirted our way around Ybor City, a historical area that years ago had deteriorated into a slum but, in the Florida pave-it-for-cash spirit, had been recreated into an upscale mall of bars and touristy places. After closing down the bars, we left Marcus and his Jag to whatever in Tampa. Neither Jennifer nor I had said a peep about the LSD in front of Marcus or Ashton.

Damn, Jennifer and I had a secret, and we'd had an adventure together. In girlfriend terms, I think that meant we were now officially best friends.

Best girlfriend or not, I wasn't ever riding with her behind the wheel again. "I'll drive," I said, taking the key from Ashton.

On the long ride back, Ashton and Jennifer teased and giggled and had a bit of indiscreet oral sex in the backseat while I tried not to listen.

I never did think to ask her why she didn't have a driver's license.

Chapter 29

The best-girlfriend thing went a step further the next morning.

Jennifer and Ashton had invited me to spend the night at Ashton's house, and I did out of fatigue and fear of staying alone in my own house in case the lurking would-be assassin still had me in mind, and because I figured it was too late to show up at Sam's in a sweat-stained red halter. During the night, Bearess snuggled into the bed with me and I slept soundly, notwithstanding the Cuban coffee.

I woke up when Jennifer crawled into bed with me the next morning, balancing a tray with two cups of coffee laced generously with Bailey's Irish Cream.

The caffeine and alcohol hit my empty stomach with a surge and a bang, and Bearess, to my amazement, lapped some out of Jennifer's cup without Jennifer so much as slapping the dog's nose.

"Oh, she always shares my coffee," she said when I protested.

"What about germs?"

"Oh, I don't have anything contagious. The doctors ran all kinds of tests. I'm clean."

Not what I meant, of course, but this was a new piece of information that made me wonder what doctors, noting her use of the plural, and why they had run "all kinds of tests."

"What I want to do is explain," Jennifer said, and patted my now exposed thigh. I was drinking spiked coffee, propped on a pillow in the bed, half-naked in one of Ashton's T-shirts, with a big dog nuzzling my arm and a weird Barbie-doll woman patting my leg. "Okay," I said. "Give it a whirl."

"Marcus and I are old friends, see, and Ashton and I felt bad about . . . you know, Angela stealing your boyfriend."

"Angela didn't steal my boyfriend."

"Oh, well, sure," Jennifer said, and patted my leg again as Bearess lapped another snort of her spiked coffee.

"Anyway, we just thought you and he might hit it off."

"What about the LSD?"

"Oh, I was really, really, really so glad you didn't say a word about that. I was just doing a favor for a friend, and Marcus and Ashton wouldn't understand one bit."

A favor for a friend? A wasp in the car? This girl must have gotten her excuses straight off of television. I could see she needed a course in the inventive lie. Or, as Jackson called it, the theory of the Big Lie, in which the weirder, more imaginative, and bigger the lie, the more likely it is that people will actually believe you. This was often the dominant theory of many a lesser plaintiff's case in the personal injury lottery world.

But before I could swallow the coffee and begin the tutorial on the theory of the Big Lie, Jennifer said, "The thing is, I applied for a job with Marcus, at his office. He's in with a bunch of other radiologists. But I didn't get the job. But I sorta tracked him for a few weeks, and once he met me, he, you know, kinda asked me out. We went out, and he was a really nice man, and then I decided to move to Sarasota, and so he helped me get my job. Then I met Ashton and, like, the rest is history."

Okay, I thought, you stalked the man for a date and a job, but what does that have to do with that LSD?

"So, see, the thing is, and what I was getting at, is that Marcus is really a good guy. He's not nearly as boring as you'd think. You are so *cooool*. I just thought you'd like him. That's all."

So *cooool?* Nobody except Jennifer had said that about me since before I'd gone to law school, where apparently being forced to study the penumbras of the Constitution had totally stripped me of any coolness.

Jennifer squeezed my thigh with her free hand, while the dog drank from her coffee cup in the other hand. Her fingers curled around my flesh as she held on to that rather sensitive part of my leg. As little twirls of heat spun off from her fingers on my thigh, I wondered who exactly this woman was and what she was up to.

"I'm so glad you can keep a secret," she said, and let go of my leg. "I mean, you know, the acid. Keeping a secret is really important between girlfriends, isn't it?"

"Yes," I agreed.

"So, anyway, what would you like for breakfast? I just eat fruit."

"Fruit is good," I said, and lifted my cup of coffee out of reach of Bearess as she aimed her long tongue at my cup, having apparently finished most of Jennifer's.

It turned out that Sam had been worried, which made him mad, and he actually raised his voice at me for not telling him where I had spent the night.

This took place while I was sorting papers at my desk around noon on Sunday, having earlier had a predictably weird breakfast with Ashton and Jennifer and Bearess, who actually had a place mat just for her on Ashton's breakfast table, where Jennifer fed the dog scrambled eggs. After that, I'd showered at Ashton's, admired his collection of lotions and potions, wondered how much of those Caswell-Massey products the law firm had paid for, and borrowed a long linen sundress from Jennifer in furtherance of our new status as best girlfriends. Without a stitch of underwear on (best girlfriends or not, I wasn't wearing somebody else's panties unless I'd washed them myself), I headed to the office. I hadn't been at my desk more than an hour before Sam was banging on my window, and I let him in.

"Okay, so what exactly is going on here?" I demanded after he yelled at me.

"What do you mean?"

"Am I a suspect, or what? Why am I supposed to stay glued to your side?"

There was a long pause. An awkward pause. He didn't say anything for a minute or two, and then came out with the entirely unoriginal and repetitive, "Where were you last night?"

Oh, I got it. He was jealous.

"Like I tried to tell you, I went to Tampa with Ashton and his girlfriend and a client. It was business, then it was late, so I spent the night with them. Want their number? Check up on me?"

This felt like a high school romance, and the man hadn't even kissed me.

"Dr. Randolph has hired a bodyguard. We don't know what is going on. You need to be careful," Sam said, and stood up, apparently ready to leave.

"I am careful."

He walked out without another word.

I finished the work that absolutely, totally, and without a doubt *had* to be done, left a series of notes for Bonita and also for Angela, who should have been in the office but wasn't, and I went to my house, checked all the door locks and windows twice, and took a very long shower. I put on matching bra and panties in red under a red-flowered rayon sheath with cap sleeves and a hemline too high for the office, a pair of casual sandals so I wouldn't look too dressed up, brushed and flossed twice, and drove to Sam's house. He answered the door on the first knock.

Time for Sam to fish or cut bait, I thought, and sauntered into his house without saying a word. I had a package of condoms in my purse in case he wasn't a Boy Scout about such things, and I waited patiently for him to get the picture and act on it.

He got the picture.

For a man who wasn't eighteen anymore, Sam was pretty impressive, and I felt such sweet tenderness when I looked at his face afterward that I knew this wasn't just about sex.

But the thing was, I explained, after basking in the postcoital closeness for about one and a half minutes, I had to go back to the office. "There are at least two things I really ought to finish tonight if I'm going to survive Monday," I said.

"I'll go with you. Take a look at that Trusdale file."

Okay, so much for his version of whispered lovey, dopey, great-first-sex sweet nothings.

Sam had already gotten copies of the pleadings, which are public records, from both the Dr. Trusdale and Dr. Randolph files at the courthouse, and he was still pursuing a subpoena to get the rest of the materials in the files that were not public record. I'd turned responding to the subpoena over to Jackson as the firm's managing partner. But now, all toasty and warm and completely satisfied in the arms of the man who might still harbor vague suspicions about me, I agreed that he could look at the Trusdale file. After all, the doctor was dead, so what kind of attorney-client privilege could there be? More important, who was left to enforce it?

Back at the law firm of Smith, O'Leary, and Stanley, I warmed up the copy machine and my computer and started churning out a rough draft of a preliminary response to Stephen's petition for mandamus, which sought in legally hysterical words to force Judge Goddard to set a trial date in the Jason Goodacre case. Angela had done a bang-up job of research and composing a rough draft opposing Stephen's petition, from which I was freely pirating. Our response wasn't due until Friday, but I knew I'd do five or six versions and, as with Tommy Glavine's historical bad pitching in the first inning, I just needed to get this part over with as quickly as possible.

Sam sat on the couch with the Trusdale file.

There was something rather nice and homey about this, like we were a real couple. I kept this to myself, made myself forget Sam, and typed like a madwoman.

But by the time I had the first draft of the legal argument done, the room was too full of Sam for me to move on to the next part of the response. I could see him. I could smell him. I could catch the currents of wind he threw off as he moved. I wanted to taste him. I remembered the feel of him too well. Also, my back was stiff and I needed to move around.

I stood up, stretched, peeked out the window. Though it was Sunday night, three cars besides my own 1987 Honda were in the parking lot, so I suspected that at least a few lawyers still lurked in the building.

As I was stretching, Sam got up from the couch, where he'd been reading through Dr. Trusdale's files, and locked my office door.

I guess this startled me, because he grinned and said, "Don't look so worried."

I grinned back and let him come toward me.

We didn't bother to undress completely. That's a nice thing about men's pants and the way a woman's dress can be lifted out of the way.

"My God, you are beautiful," Sam said, while pushing my dress up around my hips and staring right at my face, my eyes.

I don't believe this, that I'm beautiful, but I never deny it when anyone says it to me. "You are too," I said, and meant it, but Sam was thinking with his body now and didn't appear to hear me.

A half hour later, though we had smoothed out our clothes and I had giggled a few dozen times, my legs were still quivering when somebody knocked on my door.

"Lilly?"

It was Angela, and I could tell from the tone of her voice that something was wrong. I crossed in front of Sam in a hurry and unlocked and opened the door. Angela was holding Crosby in her arms and crying. For a moment I couldn't tell if the dog was alive or not, and I was suddenly afraid that Jackson and I had kept Angela here too long doing our work. Then Crosby opened his eyes for a moment, looked at me with some kind of doggy recognition passing through them, and then closed them.

"Oh, Angie," I said, and I opened my arms and took her in them, hugging her carefully, conscious of the weak, tiny dog in her arms.

"He's not going to make it much longer," she said.

"I know, Angie. Oh, I am so sorry." And I was. The obvious platitudes danced into and out of my brain, but there was nothing to say. Her pain was real, and it hit me harder than it should have, for reasons I didn't understand. I let her out of my hug but kept my hands on her forearms as she held on to Crosby.

"We're leaving now for Mississippi," a voice behind her said, and I looked up and saw Newly.

"He's been sedated. We've got some meds for him," Angela said, a catch in her voice. "My mother is expecting us. Crosby was her dog as a puppy. They need to say good-bye."

I understood this perfectly, again for reasons I couldn't have articulated.

"I've got to go. I put Jackson's antitrust brief under his door last night. Will you tell everybody tomorrow?"

"Of course. Don't worry. You've got your week, you know that, the compassionate leave the executive committee agreed on. Don't hurry back too soon."

"Thank you." Angela pulled out of my hands, and I saw Newly look at me, then over my shoulder at Sam.

"Drive carefully," I said.

Angela had already started walking off, but Newly stood there, continuing to stare at me, and I felt a flush creep up my face, as if I'd been caught in some infidelity.

Then Newly too opened his arms to me, and I went into them, and we hugged. He whispered, "I'll always love you," and then he dropped his arms and went out after Angela, to drive her and her dying dog back home to Mississippi, through a long, dark night, taking his new sweetheart to the arms of her mother, alerted and waiting to comfort her strange, orange-haired child.

Newly would be a good father, I thought, and turned back to Sam.

Ten minutes later, my office phone rang, and Newly's voice came through, loud and clear as if he were shouting over traffic.

"Hey, hon," he said. "I forgot to tell you something. I don't know, but this might have something to do with all that mess you're in. But Friday, this guy, the bum-knee guy who was suing Dr. Trusdale, he comes into my office. Saw my ad in the Sunday paper. Wants to hire me to sue Trusdale's estate, or his own HMO. Not sure which. Seems like his health insurance is all messed up. Looked like Dr. Trusdale was trying to defraud this guy's HMO by filing a bunch of claims for physical therapy this guy swears he never got. Not for the bum leg, but for a hip. Swears he wouldn't go back to Trusdale in a hundred years, even to use his physical therapist. Came to me to see if I could get his insurance straightened out. It's all a big mess, and his company is claiming he's way over some limit for physical therapy or something. Might just be a mistake—I don't know. But I thought you ought to know. Call my secretary for the file, and I'll let her know you'll call."

So much for attorney-client privilege, I thought, but Newly always was a bit loose on the rules. Questions bubbled in my brain, but then I heard Angela say something in the background, and then there was a long pause, and then Newly came back on the phone and said, "Gotta go, hon." His voice was sad.

I felt like crying. I looked up at Sam to see if he looked sad, and he did.

He'd had a dog once, so I guessed he remembered this part.

"Let's go home," I said.

But whose home? I wondered, for a moment facing up to the fact that despite those flashes where he seemed like a soul mate, the truth was I really didn't know a thing about this man. Except he was older than me, he was an expert lover with obvious experience, and he didn't seem to have much of a sense of humor. Also, he didn't seem to be much of a detective, judging from the Trusdale and Randolph investigations, but then, maybe I was being too harsh.

My phone rang again.

"Oh, gosh, hon," Newly said. "I forgot to tell you. I dropped off Johnny Winter at your house. You never changed your lock or anything. I put him in the bedroom. Olivia can't keep him with all those dogs at her house, and I can't take him with me to Mississippi. Angela's just too upset to deal with Johnny. I knew you'd take care of him. Let him out of the cage now and then, okay?"

I didn't say anything. But I remembered now why I'd wanted Newly to move out.

"You don't mind, do you, hon?" he asked, the sound of traffic coming through the phone.

Of course I minded. What if the ferret wizzed on my new couch and matching chair? Even used, they weren't cheap. But then, the ferret was already inside my house, and Newly and Angela and Crosby surely were in the next county by now. What could I say? At a loss, I didn't say anything at all.

"Thanks, hon. I knew we'd always be friends," Newly said to my silence.

The line went dead.

"Damn that Newly. He didn't forget to ask or tell me. He knew perfectly well that once the damn ferret was in my house and he was in the next county I wasn't going to make him come back and get it. Another Newly trick—why he—" I stopped, inhaled, looked at Sam, who had surely heard what Newly had said.

Okay, memo to file: Don't complain about the old boyfriend to the new boyfriend.

"What'd he say about the Trusdale bills?" Sam asked.

What had Newly said? "Something about Trusdale billing the guy's insurance for procedures he didn't do. On his hip."

"I didn't see anything in your file about hip procedures or charges. Are your medical records complete?"

"Yeah, they should be." I went over to the couch, where Sam had been studying the file, and I looked at the records myself, as if somehow he would have forgotten something he'd looked at no more than an hour before. "Could just be an insurance company screwup."

I had the records that Dr. Trusdale had provided me, and nothing about a hip showed up in them. Of course, if the dead doctor had been defrauding his patient's insurance company, he'd hardly have supplied me with documented evidence of it, so it was no big deal that his records didn't show anything.

I flipped over to the computer printouts of the bum-knee guy's health insurance claims for the last few years. One of my first steps in any malpractice case is to get copies of the plaintiff's health insurance claims for at least the last ten years. A good defense attorney can usually find something in such records to use either as a defense at trial or to coerce a better settlement before trial. Sometimes it is a bitch to get this information and takes a hearing and a court order, but I remembered that in this case it had been surprisingly easy. Standard interrogatories on my part and the bum-knee guy's attorney supplied the records from the insurance company. I took my time looking at them again. The first time, I'd looked at them just for something really embarrassing to the bum-knee guy, something he naturally wouldn't want revealed to a jury of his peers, or for something that suggested a predisposition toward infections. Of course, I'd concentrated on the surgery and presurgery records.

In other words, I hadn't paid much attention to anything after the fateful knee surgery once I saw that there was nothing outrageous in the guy's health records that I could use to my advantage.

But now I looked.

Nothing about any hip.

But something was amiss. The next to last sheet of the insurance claims summaries ended on March of one year. The next sheet started in January of the next year. True, it was possible to go that long without filing a single insurance claim. But not when you've been hit with the kind of catastrophic infection that this man had suffered. Quickly, I double-checked the claims printouts with Dr. Trusdale's records and saw a couple of things in the records after that March date that were not on the claims printouts.

At least one sheet of the insurance company's claims records was gone from my file.

I would have noticed this gap in the dates if these insurance claims forms had come to me that way. That's the curse and the blessing of the obsessive compulsive.

"Somebody took something out of this file," I said. And I remembered the Sunday I'd realized somebody had rifled through this file at my house and I'd gone to accuse Newly, but then we ended up fooling around, and I settled for bringing the files back to the office, where I'd kept them locked up.

"Who had access?" Sam asked.

"Newly, Bonita, me."

"Newly?"

"Look, Newly wouldn't steal something out of my file and then tip me off about it in a phone call, okay?"

I noticed I hadn't said that Newly wouldn't steal something out of my file, period. I wondered if Sam had caught the distinction.

"This is my copy of the file. A duplicate. I keep duplicates at home and in off-site storage. CYA," I said, hoping to talk past the implied taint on Newly's character. "The original file is probably still upstairs in the master storage closet. We tend to keep closed files there for a couple of months, in case something comes up, then they're moved to our warehouse."

"Your firm has its own warehouse?"

Nobody except other lawyers understand how much paper a lawsuit produces. You can't throw it out until at the very least all the remotely possible statutes of limitations have run out, but I didn't bother to explain that to Sam, who, after all, should have appreciated this given that cops keep evidence for about forever. "Come on."

We went upstairs, where it took me longer than it should have to find the cabinet with the fairly modest Dr. Trusdale file in it. The cabinet was locked. I didn't have a clue who had the key, and it took me less time than it should have to break into the filing cabinet with an impressively strong letter opener and my own bad attitude. Sam showed insight in not getting in my way.

In the original file, the complete set of insurance claims summaries showed a couple of office visits, an ultrasound, an X-ray, and a series of in-office physical therapy sessions related to the bum-knee guy's hip. All these claims, missing from my set of records, were charged by Dr. Trusdale to his then very former knee surgery patient, all allegedly filed by Dr. Trusdale's office against the man's insurance.

Just like Newly had said.

"I need coffee," I said. Smashing the file into Sam's hands, I went into the upstairs kitchen. Of course there was a pot on one of the many eyes of our industrial-size coffeemaker. Grimacing at the thought of how long it might have been sitting there turning to sludge, I poured two cups, added a big teaspoon of sugar and white fake dairy chemicals to mine, and handed the other to Sam.

We drank.

Halfway through my cup, which was outstandingly evil in taste and texture but potent, the rest of my brain started working.

"Mierda," I said. Fraudulent billing to the HMO? Was that what had escaped both my attention and Sam's? Of course, Sam had been at a disadvantage: He hadn't had the Randolph files lying around on his floor for weeks, and he wasn't in the room when Newly reviewed the HMO claims and raised questions about the bills.

What had Newly asked about the records in Mrs. Goodacre's MIB file? Records that showed claims for additional visits to Randolph after Jason was born. Why would she go back to a doctor she plainly distrusted, probably hated, for ultrasounds after she had delivered her child?

Throwing the rest of the coffee in the sink, I grabbed Sam's hand and pulled him back down the stairs into my ground-floor office, where I pulled out the purloined MIB printouts Ronny had kindly provided and the medical records from Dr. Randolph's office.

Of course, there was no corresponding account of any such ultrasounds in Dr. Randolph's own records, just as there had been no corresponding account of any hip visits in Dr. Trusdale's own records.

"So somebody is ripping off the HMO?" Sam asked when I pointed this out.

"Yes, but how in the world do you do that? I mean, the claims come from the doctor's office, and the check goes to the doctor, and the company usually sends an EOB to the patient."

"EOB?"

"Explanation of benefits."

Sam nodded and furrowed his brow in the perfect cliché of a man thinking hard as I added up the numbers in my head and rounded off. Between the two sets of what now appeared to be fraudulent bills, the HMO had paid out roughly an extra grand in each file. Of course, the company would send its hounds from hell after whoever had done this for less than a grand, but the point was, as I asked Sam, "Would somebody kill to cover up a fraud of only two grand?"

"You're thinking in too small a box," Sam said.

"You mean, like the jail time is the same whether you embezzle two thousand or two million, so go for the two million?"

"That, and what if whoever was doing this defrauded a couple hundred dollars on a couple hundred patients over a period of months? That'd add up."

"Yeah. Like that case a few years back where the hotel chain—I forget which one—added a made-up surcharge of one dollar on everybody's bill. For a buck, nobody complained, and a buck on every room in every hotel in the chain turned out to be big money. While it lasted."

"Missed that one," Sam said.

"Ah, a plaintiff's lawyer figured it out. Brought a big class action. Made a ton in legal fees. Guess that wasn't played so big outside of the legal newspapers."

And then I thought, It's the same game a lot of insurance defense attorneys play. Feeling a tad like I was ratting out my fellow lawyers, I explained to Sam, in possibly more detail than he needed, the theory of the little fifteen-minute cheat, the simple trick of adding fifteen minutes to most of the entries on your daily time sheet. Myself, I had (really) never done this, because I was as busy as hell and billed accordingly without the need to cheat. But I knew it was done. An attorney attends a hearing, and it takes one hour. Instead of billing that one hour, he (or she—billing fraud not being solely a male practice) instead bills one hour and fifteen minutes. The theory is that nobody is going to notice, or check, or bitch about fifteen minutes. But then you repeat it, over and over, and the ten-hour day an attorney legitimately puts in working on a variety of cases for a variety of clients suddenly becomes at least a twelve-hour day. Multiplied by an average work year, that's roughly, rounded off, an unearned bonus closing in on an additional hundred grand. All raised in little increments of fifteen minutes.

"So, lawyers cheat, huh?" Sam said.

"Oh, yeah, and there aren't any crooked cops," I snapped.

"But, yeah, couple hundred here, a couple hundred there from the HMO, and it adds up. Small enough claims on a variety of patients and the company doesn't see anything amiss. No heart transplants or anything like that, just a few ultrasounds and some physical therapy. But how would it work? I mean, if all these bills were being done by the same doctor, I could see how it might work, with the checks coming into his office. But two different doctors?"

"I don't know. I don't get it."

But under the influence of adrenaline and stale caffeine, something was ticking inside my head. My own little neurotransmitters were connecting the dots even as I said I didn't get it.

Explaining the theory of the little fifteen-minute cheat made me think of Ashton. Ashton espoused that theory, had explained it to me when I was still a pup wet behind the ears. He had acted offended when I politely declined the chance to join the club.

No doubt Ashton had explained it to Jennifer.

Jennifer, who worked at a "service" that did medical transcriptions and billings and filed insurance claims, and did who knew what else for doctors too cheap to hire their own employees. How closely would the doctors monitor that service?

Grabbing my cell phone from my purse, I punched in Ashton's number. Then I hung up.

"What are you doing?" Sam sounded like a cop.

"I don't know," I said, telling the truth and not liking his tone one bit.

If Ashton was involved in some way, I didn't want to get him in trouble. Beyond that personal loyalty thing, a code I'm pretty big on, a code Delvon and I had lived by in the rough years, there was the immediate problem that if a partner in Smith, O'Leary, and Stanley went down the tubes as a major crook, then the firm was done. The publicity would kill us. I still had a huge mortgage on my apple orchard. I needed at least five more years of the Smith, O'Leary, and Stanley gravy train.

But then another little dot got connected. The Trusdale file had been in my den the Saturday Jennifer and Ashton had come home with me. Jennifer had disappeared into the powder room and could have detoured into the den and taken the now missing evidence of insurance fraud. Or she could have unlocked the back door and then let herself in later that night while Newly and I were playing in the pool at Ashton's.

Anger bubbled up in me until I thought of Jennifer curling beside me in bed that Sunday morning after the I-75 car trip from hell, squeezing my leg and saying how glad she was that we were best girlfriends, especially now that she knew I could keep a secret. Somehow, she'd wiggled into being my friend, and friends kept each other's secrets.

Okay, get a grip, Lil, I thought. Not ratting out somebody for transporting a bag of LSD was one thing. But not ratting out somebody who had killed someone, had tried to kill someone else, and had possibly tried to kill me was too much.

No, I couldn't keep this secret.

I wondered where Jennifer was on this Sunday night. With Monday morning's workday looming, she probably wouldn't be at Ashton's now, as least I hoped not. I saw no way out of making the phone call, so I picked up the phone on my desk and punched in Ashton's number. At least I'd keep it off the cell phone airwaves.

Sam walked out to Bonita's desk and picked up her phone to listen.

Ashton answered on the fifth ring. "Yo."

"Ashton, you alone?"

"Hey, babe, want to come over?"

"What exactly does Jennifer do?"

"Anything I want her to do."

"I mean, at the medical services place where she works."

"Why do you want to know that?"

"It's a long story, Ashton. Now, what's she do?"

"She does all that paperwork for the insurance claims. Files the claims for the patients, processes the checks when they come in, you know, stuff like that. She's a great bookkeeper. I told you she wasn't as dumb as you make her out to be."

Apparently not, I thought.

"Ashton, ah, you need to protect yourself, I, er . . ." I saw Sam wave his hand for me to stop, but this was Ashton. For better or worse, he was my law partner. For better or worse, he was my friend. I spit it out quickly. "Jennifer has been filing fake bills with an HMO. It shows up in Dr. Trusdale's and Dr. Randolph's files. You've got to—" Sam crossed back into my office and slammed down my phone.

We glared at each other but didn't have the time to explore our sudden mutual anger.

"I've got some work to do now," he said. "Stay here or get a ride to my house. Stay off the phone and don't go to your house."

Assuming, apparently, that I would explicitly obey, Sam then turned and slammed himself out the back door.

Immediately I called Ashton back, and he answered equally immediately and without preliminary greetings.

"Lilly? You didn't call the cops, did you?"

Okay, technically I hadn't *called* the cops, and I didn't want my law partner thinking I was ratting him and his girlfriend out to the police, so I wordsmithed my answer with careful legal precision. "Ashton, I haven't called nine-one-one, but you need to protect yourself. Are you—"

"Gotta go, babe." Slam.

Visualizing Ashton rushing toward his personal shredder, I wasn't particularly offended he hadn't stayed on the line long enough to chat about whether he was involved in Jennifer's scheme or not. Still bristling at Sam's order, I decided to go home and call Ashton later to pursue his potential culpability.

Sam's car wasn't long out of the parking lot before I found the first associate I could, a first-year still toiling away in the Smith, O'Leary, and Stanley library, and I demanded he take me home, which, in true toadlike associate fashion, he did posthaste.

As it turned out, this was not a particularly bright move on my part.

Chapter 30

I have no idea exactly why I went to my own house, except that Sam had told me not to and I don't take orders from my lovers. Taking orders from Jackson is about all I can stand. So I went to show my independence. Oh, and to make sure Johnny Winter was really in his cage and not dousing my new secondhand couch and matching chair with Eau de Tomcat Piss.

Sure enough, Johnny Winter, the errant and nearly homeless rodent, was in his cage, and he shared his feelings about that by kicking some cedar chips on the floor and then lifting his leg and peeing on me when I moved too close.

By the time I got the ferret wiz off of me and changed clothes—I mean, after making love in it, solving a murder in it, and getting pissed on by a small animal, that red dress was totally done—the doorbell was ringing. Thinking it was Sam, and eager to see him even if he was going to fuss at me for warning Ashton and then coming home, I blithely went out to answer it, *blithely* being a very nice word for "plain stupidly."

I opened the door, and Jennifer glared at me, Bearess by her side.

"You bitch," she yelled, pushing the door open as I tried frantically to close it in her irate face.

As they shoved into my house, side by side, Bearess wagged her tail and woofed at me, licking in my general direction in a kind of doggy air kiss, and Jennifer repeated, "You bitch."

"Me! You're the one who shot up my car."

Okay, so I missed the more obvious point, but I was under a lot of pressure.

"Yeah, but I wasn't trying to kill *you*."

"What were you trying to do?"

"Kill Randolph."

Oh, well. Ask a silly question.

"See, it worked out so good with that other doctor. Once he was dead, you closed the file and I knew you wouldn't make the connection about the fake insurance claims."

Well, sure, Jennifer the Underestimated did have a point there.

What she also had was a gun. Pointed at me.

I smiled and put on my best-girlfriend tone of voice, and said, "But why kill the first doctor?"

"Ashton was always bragging about you, how smart you were, how you always looked at everything. Anal-retentive, a real detail queen, he said. He told me you even got computer printouts of, like, the entire medical and *insurance* records of guys who sued your doctors. When he told me you had a case with Dr. Trusdale and that you'd already gotten the guy's insurance records, I got worried. So, like, I was going to go through the file and tear up the fake claims that day you were in trial. But the lock code was changed and I couldn't get in. So I waited for you behind the stairs, and after you punched in the code I tried to choke you, just till you passed out, so I could get in and steal the file. But Ashton came up."

I remembered the mugging, the reenactment, Sam's assessment that the mugger was a rank amateur. So, okay, maybe Sam was a better detective than I'd given him credit for. He just didn't know what to do with that information.

And I remembered the odd, perfumy smell on the mugger, how it smelled like the flea spray Olivia used, how that had made me suspect her.

"You use that all-natural flea spray on Bearess, the one Olivia uses?"

"Yes," Jennifer said, looking puzzled. "What's that got to do with anything?"

"Nothing," I said. "Why'd you kill Trusdale?" As if we were gossiping over tea.

"That's what I was trying to tell you. Then, I asked Ashton, you know, about the case, Trusdale's, I mean, and, like, what would happen next. He said you'd probably settle it if you could, so I decided to push that along. If Trusdale got sick or died from smoking pot, I figured, you know, that you'd have to settle it. Quick. Before you saw the fake bills."

How had Jennifer gotten such a good grip on the litigation process? "How would you know about settlements and stuff?" I asked.

"Oh, Ashton talks that shit all the time, like he's some college professor and I'm the girl in the front row. You wouldn't believe what I know."

Apparently not.

"Then, after Trusdale died, I knew you wouldn't be looking at the insurance records once you'd settled his case, and I thought the whole mess was over. But then Ashton told me Jackson had dumped the Randolph case on you too. I didn't figure Jackson would notice the fake claims, not after what Ashton told me about him. But you would notice them, being—what is it? Obsessive-compulsive?"

Well, Ashton certainly is the little motormouth, I thought, and edged toward the kitchen door, thinking about potential weapons and how fast I could run.

"So I had to kill Randolph too, once it was your case, 'cause you'd look at the insurance records and stuff. So I had to end the case before you compared the insurance claims with the actual medical file."

Trying to kill Randolph was so half-brained, so digging the hole deeper, so weird, and so pathetic, I thought, and so pathological. "Jenn, you ever think you might need some help?"

Jennifer shook the gun at me, which, while scary, wasn't nearly as scary as shooting it at me would have been.

"You're the one needs help," she said, stating, I thought, the obvious. "Stop moving to the kitchen."

"Aw, Jenn, come on. You're not going to shoot *me*."

"No. I'm not. I'm going to shove you off the Sunshine Skyway. Like, you know, a suicide. Now come on, let's go."

"Jenn, don't be crazy. What the hell good will that do?"

"Don't you be calling me crazy," Jennifer screamed, a wholly new and horrible expression distorting her features. "I spent a year showing 'em I wasn't crazy. In Miami. After my husband was killed. Poor, sweet Elliot," she said, her voice softening, her eyes dreamy. "You didn't even know I was married, did you?"

Inside my brain, I could practically hear little pinging noises as the last dots were connected.

"Jennifer, you're not . . . you weren't . . . Are you Mrs. Jobloski, by chance?"

She inhaled and started sobbing. I took that as a yes.

"So, you were faking bills . . ." Filing fake claims by Dr. Trusdale and Dr. Randolph for revenge? Jennifer seemed to recover, and she shook the gun at me again.

"Those men killed my husband, same as if they'd poisoned him. And nobody would do anything. So I was filing fake bills under their names and diverting the money to a separate account. Setting them up for fraud and stealing money from the HMO that killed Elliot."

"But, then, why worry about me figuring it out? I mean, why kill Trusdale if you wanted him fingered for defrauding the HMO?"

"Oh, that's just how I got started. When I learned Trusdale and Randolph probably wouldn't even go to jail for the fake bills, I started thinking about a better plan. Then I realized that it was the HMO that killed Elliot, and that the only way to get even was to steal as much money from that damn HMO as I could. So I, you know, I branched out some. Added some doctors. You wouldn't believe how it added up, all the money I got outta that HMO."

In a sick sort of way, this was brilliant, I realized. Compliments seemed inappropriate at the moment, though, so I asked, "But why kill me?"

"I heard you and Ashton on the phone, and knew you figured it out. But you said you hadn't called the police."

Damn, she had been at Ashton's. Another miscalculation on my part.

"But Ashton knows too. So killing me doesn't help you." But I wondered, and not for the first time, if Ashton was part of this plan.

"Ashton knows how to keep a secret," she said, and flashed a cheerleader smile that scared me down to my toes. I figured that meant Ashton was already dead. I envisioned his mangled body bleeding beside his really big pool.

"Why the Skyway?" I asked, then wondered if she planned to dump Ashton off the bridge with me, like some lovers' leap thing.

"I told you, to look like suicide. Everybody knows you've got, like, this nut thing about that bridge." Jennifer's blond cheerleader simper was gone now.

Dizzying as it was, I tried to think as Jennifer was thinking. Ashton was either dead or would be, or he really wouldn't tell, and I'd be a suicide, and Jennifer was what? She thought she was off scot-free because I hadn't called the police? What about Sam? If I told Jennifer that Sam also knew, would she kill him too? Wasn't he a big boy, with a big gun, who could take care of himself and who presumably wouldn't blithely answer his door to a murderess?

But if I told her the police did know, she had two choices—leave me alone and sprint for the hills, or figure she might as well just shoot me for ratting her out and then sprint. I didn't have a clue which way she'd go, and fifty-fifty odds on getting shot or not didn't appeal to me. Besides, letting her play out faking my suicide gave me more time, and more time seemed suddenly enticing.

With my palms sweating, I figured my best hope was to stall here long enough for Sam to find me. I mean, Sam would know to come to my house, but he wouldn't know to go to the Sunshine Skyway. If I told her Sam knew, Jennifer would be less likely to let me dillydally around, stalling, and more likely to just plug me. So that was my plan: Don't tell Jennifer the police already knew, and stall her until dutifully rescued by my new lover.

"Why bother making it look like a suicide?" Okay, I think I got this already, but stall, stall, stall was my new mantra.

"Like, 'cause, then nobody will suspect me. Ashton keeps quiet, 'cause, you know, we're in love and all, and you're dead, and I'll get your files and throw them off the Skyway too, and then I'm okay. See? Nobody connects me to you and Trusdale, then I don't have to leave Ashton. Not just yet, anyway."

Okay, that made it sound as if Ashton wasn't dead by the pool or stuffed in the trunk waiting for a plunge off the Skyway. So she was going to fake my suicide so she could stay with Ashton and not just flee right now? So this thing with Ashton was real?

"I won't tell. Jenn, we're friends. Come on, I didn't tell about the LSD. And, you know, Ashton's my partner. I didn't call the police, did I? I called Ashton."

"Ashton won't tell because he loves me. But you I can't be sure about."

"You trust Ashton that much? Is that because he's in on it with you?"

"Ashton? No way. Yeah, I mean, I kind of got the idea from him.

You know, that little fifteen-minute cheat theory he has. After he explained that to me, I figured, you know, I'd do a version of that on the insurance claims."

"But how'd that work? Damn, they hardly pay the real claims, and you got them paying fake claims?"

"Yeah, about half of them. The bills they denied, I let go. I mean, I wasn't going to hassle them over the fake claims."

Well, no duh, I thought, but I wondered about the mechanics of her hair-brained yet brilliant scam. "How'd you get the money? Don't the checks go to the doctors?"

"Not right off, not for the ones with our services. We collect the checks, do the bookkeeping, eventually deposit the checks in their accounts, send them copies of everything."

"But, Jenn, insurance companies send copies of the paperwork to the patients. Didn't you think somebody might call and say, 'Hey, what's with this hip X-ray I never got?'"

"Come on. Cost-containment shit—this HMO doesn't send an EOB unless the patient asks for it. You think a patient's gonna ask for it when he doesn't know a claim is filed?"

"Health insurers don't send out explanations of benefits anymore?"

"Not this HMO. And I only fake-billed it. I just took from the HMO that wouldn't let Elliot have a heart transplant after Trusdale infected him. It doesn't send out EOBs, and some of the other HMOs don't anymore either. It's a different world with all this managed-care shit. There are things they routinely deny—ER claims, like, almost always get rejected, most surgeries—but ultrasounds, physical therapy, and office visits are usually still paid because of the tight limits on the number of these claims the patient is allowed. So I maxed those out, you know, and moved on to the next patient. You'd be surprised how often I got paid."

What surprised me was how efficient Jennifer had been at filing fake claims. What she was talking about required a great deal of surreptitious paperwork and memory, detail work—the sort of thing I excelled at but for which Jennifer had shown no inclination at all. Guess I had read her wrong.

"But, okay, so you filed the fake claims and collected the checks," I summed up, thinking, again, Stall, stall, stall. "But those checks were made out to the different doctors. How'd you cash them?"

"I told you once that I worked for a bank in Miami. My boss was a jerk, but he handled the coke dealers."

Oh, yeah, the crickets and petty-revenge stuff, because her banker boss didn't respect her.

"Before Elliot married me and took me away from all that, I helped my boss clean the dealers' money. You don't think I learned a thing or two, like how to set up an offshore account?"

"So," I said, still hoping Sam would come barging in and rescue me, "exactly how did that work?"

"Come on, do you think I don't know you're stalling?"

I looked at the gun, remembered she wasn't a very good shot, and calculated my odds of running, screaming, or jumping on her. In the end, stalling continued to seem like the best thing to do.

"Hey, you've got to tell me how you did it. I mean, how'd you get Trusdale to smoke the joint?"

"He was easy to seduce. Told him the pot would make him more potent—no problem at all. Like, he didn't even notice I wasn't smoking any."

"So, okay, but tell me this, were you a biology major or what? How'd you know how to poison both doctors?"

"No. I got the oleander idea from that book. You know, the one they made into a movie? Woman kills her lover with oleanders when he dumps her. It was an Oprah book. For the LSD, I tracked down one of the Miami dealers."

LSD? Marcus? That's what all that was about? "So, Jenn, you

mean, Marcus was on your hit list?" Though my panicked brain was still shouting at me to stall, this actually did interest me.

"Marcus was on the review board with Dr. Randolph and voted against Elliot's heart transplant. He didn't use our service, so I couldn't fake bills from him. I needed to get him some other way. So I was going to spike his wine with the LSD."

"You set me up on a date with Marcus on the same night you were going to kill him or drive him nuts?" I practically screeched.

Jennifer gave me a round-eyed, blank look. "Yeah, whatever," she said, and then she refocused. "For the Datura, I got a book at the library."

"A book on poisoning people?"

"A book on toxic native plants in Florida. You'd be amazed."

No, at this point I was pretty much past the point of amazement. As the seconds sped by without Sam smashing my door down, I was pretty much into the realm of contemplating death, wondering if God would really let me into heaven on the basis of a last-minute plea.

"Come on," Jennifer said, "we're going to the bridge. Now."

Chapter 31

Okay, so there was this good chance I was going to die within the next half hour or so, the timing depending on traffic on the Tamiami Trail and the Skyway this time of night.

And, damned if I didn't respond to the great looming void by thinking like an attorney.

Staring down Jennifer's gun, I happened to remember I had never quite gotten around to making a will. As I had neither spouse nor child, my estate would pass by state law to my parents.

That was the rub. I didn't want my parents to have my 180 acres of apple trees and good pine forest in north Georgia because they would evict Farmer Dave, who was still hiding out from the Georgia Bureau of Investigation, and then they'd sell the pine trees to the first logger that came along. No, I wanted Delvon, my mad-hatter brother and best friend, to have the apple orchard. I wanted Dan, my sweet, shallow-thinking delivery-man brother, to have my Florida house and half of my other assets. I quickly calculated that with half of my more liquid assets Delvon could pay off the mortgage on the orchard, especially because he makes far more than he likes to discuss, plus his profit is tax free. My insurance would pay off the mortgage on my house for Dan, and he and the wife and kids could have a winter place in Sarasota, or a prime rental property. Dead, I was in good shape financially. This was an oddly comforting thought.

While Jennifer stood four feet in front of me, contemplating casting me off the Sunshine Skyway as a possible suicide, I realized I needed to write a quick will.

Very quickly, from the look on Jennifer's face.

"Ah, Jenn," I started, pausing to frame just the right words, "could I, uh, make a last will and testament? You see, I have this apple orchard in north Georgia, and I want my brother to have it, and if I don't make a will my mean, crazy mother will get it." Forsaking entirely my vague father, who had no use of an apple orchard, as he had his fishing dock, but knowing he wouldn't stand up to her when she booted Farmer Dave off and sold the place.

"A will?"

"Yeah—it won't take me long. Just a couple of minutes to write it. Please?"

The inscrutable face on the evil Jennifer flustered me a bit.

"I mean we . . . are friends. Just this last request. Please?" *Were* friends, the past tense being more technically accurate, as it's hard to feel warm, fuzzy feelings toward someone planning to force you over the side of a monstrously high bridge. But claiming to still be her friend might warm her hard heart more than the harsh-sounding past tense.

"Don't try anything," she said.

"Ah, yeah, like I'd shoot my felt-tip pen at you?"

Mierda, I thought, easing over to the desk as a wary Jennifer and a tail-wagging Bearess followed. What I was talking about was a holographic will—a will in the dead person's handwriting and signed but not witnessed. I had no idea if Georgia would probate a holographic will; Florida will not. I needed a witness—two, probably, but at least one.

"Okay, don't get antsy. I'm just getting out a notepad and a felt-tip, all right?"

Quicker than a high school typing exam, I wrote out: "I, Lillian Rose Cleary, being of sound body and mind, do hereby leave my 180 acres of apple orchard and woods in north Georgia, in the county of Habersham, to my beloved brother Delvon Williams Cleary. To my other beloved brother, Daniel Taylor Cleary, I leave my house in Sarasota, Florida. The remainder of my estate should be divided equally between Delvon and Daniel."

This probably wouldn't win me an A in any estate-planning class, and I wasn't even sure it would work in the probate courts of Georgia and Florida, but I had to try, as the thought of my mother evicting Farmer Dave and selling off my timber rankled me.

Now the tricky part.

"Ah, Jenn, I need a witness. Could you sign below my signature and date it?"

"You got to be kidding."

"Uh, no. It doesn't count without a witness."

Jennifer stood over my shoulder, glanced at what I had written, and said, snidely, I might add, "Why don't I just sign a confession?"

"No—oh, no, everybody knows we are friends. This will make it look like, you know, we are friends, not like you're the one who, ah, killed me. I mean, really, who witnesses somebody's will and then kills them?" I paused, stunned by the pictures my mind was throwing at me. "If you make me jump off the bridge, then this looks like a suicide note. Sort of."

Actually, I was pretty certain I needed two witnesses, now that I thought about it. As Jennifer hesitated, I pushed the needle.

"Jenn, ah, maybe we could, ah, stop at a gas station on the way to the Sunshine Skyway or something and get two signatures from the clerks or something. I mean, if you aren't cool with this."

"Hell, no. Are you totally nuts?"

Probably. A little, anyway. Might be genetic. Delvon and my parents definitely were around the bend. But a full contemplation of the madness that might run in my gene pool was not something I had the luxury of pursuing at that precise moment in time. I needed to get a credible will signed.

"All right, if you'd just sign it. Be my witness."

"Like I'm really Jennifer," she said. But she reached over and signed and dated my hasty will.

"You any good at forgery?"

"Stop stalling," she snapped.

"Just one more signature. I don't care, some woman's name. Anybody's."

Jennifer leaned over me again while I sniffed her perfume—White Shoulders, I thought—and again contemplated grabbing the gun from her. She scribbled some nearly undecipherable signature that maybe was Della Street. Wasn't that Perry Mason's secretary? Did Jennifer have a sense of humor, or had I just misread the forged signature? Did it matter in the overall scheme of things?

"Great. Thank you." As if we were in an office and this was a normal will.

"Sure." As if it were nothing. As if she weren't planning to kill me.

"One more thing . . . ah, two, actually."

Jennifer waved the gun at me and said, "No more stalling. Get up."

"The ferret. You know, Newly's ferret, Johnny Winter. Let me put down some more food and water in his cage. I mean, no telling how long it will be before somebody thinks to look in the guest room and feed him." Stall, stall, stall, my desperate brain commanded, and I obeyed. "You don't want that poor animal to starve, do you?"

Jennifer squinted her eyes, but she apparently had a soft spot for animals, as she finally nodded.

"Bearess, stay," she ordered, and the dog sat.

Then with her as a shadow I moved into the second bedroom,

where I checked on Johnny's still full water tube. I poured the whole box of food in there with him. Johnny Winter blinked his little pink weasel eyes at me and chittered, almost friendly-sounding. I briefly wondered if Angela would accept Johnny Winter lovingly into her and Newly's apartment now that Crosby, peacefully doped on doggy Valium and in the loving arms of his mistress, was on his last road trip to his final resting spot under the pecan trees.

I left the door unlatched on Johnny Winter's cage and left the guest room door open. What possible difference could it make now if he had a misadventure on the furniture?

That done, there was only the very last thing: Pray.

"Do you mind if I take a moment to kneel and pray?"

"Make it quick."

Jennifer was being entirely too indulgent. Apparently, killing someone with whom she had shared Stairmaster tips and drunk spiked coffee was harder than poisoning doctors she blamed for the death of her husband.

I had hope yet. Sam would be driving into the driveway at any moment. In the meantime, I planned to kneel and pray—really pray—and then if Sam had not jumped in to rescue me by them, I would leap up headfirst into Jennifer's torso and butt the gun out of her hand.

First, I knelt and prayed. "Dear God, please get me out of this mess. I promise to try to be a good person if you save me."

So spank me—in my near-death moment of religious fervor, I wasn't original.

Chapter 32

Delvon later explained to me that it was the unseen but no less divine hand of the Great Savior that led him to knock on my door and enter with a key I had long forgotten he had at the precise hour that Jennifer the Stairmaster wizard came to shove me into kingdom come.

That God would send the Georgia Bureau of Investigation into Delvon's tiny corner of bug-infested backwater Georgia with a search warrant and a herd of trained pot dogs, sending him on the lam straight toward me, might, I thought, technically be a bit outside the established dogma of most churches, but then Delvon wasn't a member of most churches. He was a deacon at the First Pentecostal Church of the Holy Ghost and the Savior Who Will Return. At any rate, I was glad for the help, and I have thanked God.

Though, technically Delvon's claim to have been led by God to save my ass would have made better propaganda if Delvon had in fact actually saved my ass.

Instead, all irony aside, it was Johnny Winter, the wiz-spraying ferret, that saved me. What happened was this:

As I knelt, praying, the doorbell rang, and I thought it was Sam, said my "thank you" to God, and hopped up to answer the door. Of course, Jennifer knocked me down with a pretty strong backhand for a skinny girl, though the gun gave her some added weight.

I landed on the terrazzo floor with a painful thunk, and Bearess came over and licked my face.

"Don't even think about screaming," Jennifer said, "or I'll shoot you."

Well, I was going to be dead either way, so I was thinking I'd roll into Bearess and scream on the theory that Jennifer, being a bad shot, wouldn't shoot at me if I were near her dog.

But before I had a chance to try that, the lock on the front door made that little clicking noise and the door opened, and there stood Delvon, looking every bit the mad-hatter dope grower on the run. Apparently these last years John the Baptist had been his fashion guru, as my brother actually had sticks and weeds stuck in his long tangled hair.

"Praise the Lord, thank you, Jesus," he said, and raised his hands in thanksgiving.

I stood up. "Jennifer," I said, my best manners forward, "this is Delvon, my brother. Delvon, this is my friend Jennifer."

Delvon stepped forward and offered his hand. "Pleased to meet you," he said.

"And this is her dog, Bearess," I added.

Jennifer didn't accept his offered hand, but Bearess accepted the head pat.

"Jennifer is planning on killing me by making me jump off the Skyway Bridge," I added conversationally. "What brings you to visit?"

"Got GBI and narcs over my place like roaches on the leftovers," he said, and I watched his eyes flit to the gun, the dog, Jennifer's face, and back to the gun. Taking it all in. Delvon is cool that way—he studies up on things.

"Delvon grows marijuana and poppies for a living," I added, smiling at Jennifer.

"We had a bit of a tussle before I got away," he said. "Hitchhiked to here down the interstate. Rough ride."

Well, no duh. Who would pick up a wild man with sticks in his hair and torn clothing?

"Come on, both of you," Jennifer said, pointing the gun. "Now you're both going to have to jump off the bridge."

I waited for Delvon to do something. Apparently Delvon was waiting for the Second Coming or a rapture. We all kind of stood around doing nothing.

"I mean it," Jennifer said, sounding testy. "You don't march out to my car right now, I'll shoot you both in the stomach and leave you here. Know what that feels like?"

No, I didn't, but I could imagine. Still I stood, stuck to my spot on the floor as if I were suddenly a well-rooted oak tree.

Then there was this little scamper noise and a little chitter, chitter, chitter, and in wandered Johnny Winter, the inquisitive ferret.

Nature took its course in rapid succession. Bearess saw what to her dog brain must have looked like a rat, or something she was supposed to kill, and she pounced at the ferret, which jumped away, chittering up the side of the new secondhand chair until it had a vantage point on the dog, and it squealed its banshee squeal. Bearess lunged into the chair, closing the vantage point. But Johnny wasn't down and out yet, not by a long shot. He turned his back, raised his tail, and sprayed.

None of us, especially Bearess, had any notion at all that a ferret has the same built-in defense as your basic, garden-variety skunk. Well, technically, not nearly as strong as a skunk's, but definitely pungent. Pungent enough that Bearess howled and spun back against Jennifer, knocking her off balance. As Jennifer struggled to stand, Johnny aimed at her, lifted his tail, and repeated the performance. So much for her White Shoulders.

We were all gagging and gulping and backing up, and Bearess, in a hysterical dog pounce, vaulted at Jennifer, as if hoping Jennifer would scoop her up in her arms and make that terrible, terrible smell go away. Instead, Jennifer fell down under the panicked dog's full-body hurl and dropped the gun.

Delvon, living deep in the woods and more tolerant of wild smells, recovered quickly from the next-best-thing-to-a-skunk drenching. He snatched the gun up before Jennifer could grab it. I was mostly trying not to throw up.

And, yeah, it did cross my mind that this was the second set of furniture that Johnny had killed off in my house, but in light of the overall circumstances I overlooked this.

Jennifer and Bearess sprang to their nimble feet and ran like greyhounds for the door. Delvon and I ran outside, not so much to follow but to breathe fresh air.

Jennifer and Bearess jumped into her car, and she drove away.

After gulping air, Delvon, still holding the gun, said, "Whoa. Praise Jesus, what *was* that all about?"

"Dev, I've got to call the police."

"No, Lilly Belle—I'm in enough trouble."

Delvon is the only one allowed to call me Lilly Belle without getting knocked upside the head for it. And he had a point about the police coming anywhere near him. So I said, "Let's follow her." Since this was from the same brain that had blithely opened the door to a killer, I wondered a bit about all those youthful indiscretions in the world of mind-altering substances. Maybe there was a tad bit of brain damage there.

But, lacking sense or not, chase her we did. Jennifer had a commanding head start, but my ancient little Honda rallied to the challenge, and, besides, I was pretty certain I knew where Jennifer was going. I remembered her hysterical "I can't go to jail," and I wondered if she'd already been there or whether her two stays in mental institutions were close enough to jail to persuade her to seek other alternatives, no matter how rash.

Given the late hour, traffic was light, and we dodged a few cars and stayed steady on the tail of the car we thought was Jennifer's, racing toward the Sunshine Skyway in the night.

We reached the top span of the bridge in less than half an hour, but Jennifer had enough of a lead on us that she was already out of her car and had climbed over the railing. She had taken off her jeans and stood there, perched on the edge of eternity, in a blouse and a pair of midnight blue bikini panties.

"Jennifer, don't," I cried out. I meant it. "I'll help you. We'll all help you. We're a whole law firm of lawyers. We can get you off. They killed your husband. A jury will understand." Not likely, of course, but a modest lie at such a junction seemed forgivable.

"Jesus will help you if you open your heart," Delvon tossed in there.

Bearess stood beside Jennifer and whimpered so loudly I could hear her, even at the distance I stood from Jennifer.

"They'll think I'm crazy. I can't go back," Jennifer said.

As Delvon and I shouted for her not to jump, Jennifer peeled off her blouse and arched her back, pointed her toes, and sprang up and out, off the bridge, 192 feet into the dark, hard waters below. Whether she pulled off her clothes because of the indelible smell of Johnny the skunklike ferret or in some final show of glory or rebellion, we'd never know.

But one thing I did know. Jennifer didn't just jump. She executed what looked to me to be a perfect dive. In the lights off the Skyway, I saw her hands come together, her feet push off, and her thin little body pull itself into the traditional jackknife position for a high dive, before she dropped below the line of lights and my vision into the night below us.

"I've got to call nine-one-one," I said, holding back a sob as Bearess howled into the void.

"Oh, man. Listen, I'm gonna, you know, drift down to the other side and pray for that girl's soul. You want to look for me, pick me up later?"

"Hang on," I said, digging in my purse for my cell phone. "I'll call, then give you a ride to the bottom, and we'll make plans to get you out of here, safe. Get you some money, good clothes. You can hang at the apple orchard with Farmer Dave. 'Sides, it'll take 'em a few minutes to get here anyway."

"We'd better get that dog," Delvon said, as Bearess howled in utter desolation and moved toward the railing.

I saw what was about to happen and dropped the cell phone and threw myself at Bearess, grabbing her tail as she jumped up over the railing. Delvon, right at my back the whole time, grabbed me and held on, even as the raw muscular strength of a full-grown Rottweiler in grief nearly pulled me over the railing with her.

The dog's howling continued for a long, eerie moment, then ended.

So it was, some twenty-odd years after the first time he'd grabbed me on the remaining span of the original Skyway, that Delvon reached out and saved me in the nick of time, just before I careened off the Skyway in a thwarted attempt to save Bearess, the loyal Rottweiler, as she leaped off the high girders of the great bridge into the waters below after her beloved mistress, Jennifer the mystery woman.

When we were standing straight up again, Delvon took my hand and I cried, hard, heaving sobs. Delvon, my best ever friend, pulled me into his arms and said, "Oh, Lilly Belle. We'd better pray, then you call the cops."

Epilogue

I have a nearly endless capacity for driving those around me crazy.

That's why Ashton and Angela were both sitting at the counsel's table, twirling their respective poufs of hair and chewing their lips and telling me how to pick a jury. Only the oddly pleasant Dr. Randolph, acting as if his unintentional Jimsonweed hallucinogenic trip to the ER had been a lobotomy of sorts, sat sedately while I let Stephen LaBlanc alienate the jury pool with his kind of Miami big-shot penetrating and insulting questions. Of the thirty people now sitting in front of Stephen as he talked down, through his nose, to them, prying into their personal beliefs about just about everything but oral sex, some six of them would eventually become the jury in *Goodacre versus Randolph*.

Me, I was cool. So cool that Angela had been poking at me with her finger and whispering in my ear, and jotting me little notes about things I should ask the prospective jury members. So cool that Ashton was Mr. Antsy-Pants and kept leaning over Angela to hiss little suggestions at me.

Me, I was so cool that even the migraine crashing against my skull didn't rattle me. I just pulled out my bottle of Dr. Trusdale's last prescription for Percocet and took one.

Angela sucked in her breath. A bit self-righteous, if you ask me, for somebody living in sin with a man still technically married, and somebody who had induced her brother to commit a computer crime and steal valuable secrets from his own employer.

"For heaven's sake, Angela," I said, ever the Zen master of mentors, "it's just voir dire."

Angela tsked-tsked another minute. But Ashton stuck out his hand. "Got one for me?"

I popped out a pill for him.

Then Dr. Randolph eyed me suggestively.

"You want one too?" What I started to say was "Write your own prescription," but, then, sharing is the minimum standard for civilized behavior, so I rolled out a pill for the now transformed and weirdly affable doctor.

Angela tsked again.

Me, I was totally cool with voir dire, which is a fancy lawyer phrase for a session to ask the pool of perspective jurors (known in fancy lawyer talk as voirdiremen) questions designed to help a lawyer see into their souls and pick the ones who would naturally resolve any conflicts in that attorney's favor.

See, my thought was simple: I didn't care who was on my jury, because I was going to win.

After all, I had Mrs. Goodacre's irate sister cooling her heels in the Holiday Inn on Lido, just chomping to get before the jury and impeach her sister by spilling the whole thing about Baby Sister stealing her insurance card, going to Boise, and finding out through amniocentesis and ultrasounds that the baby she was carrying had CMV birth defects.

This same sister, when Angela and I had appeared at her door in Idaho, had been more than willing to spill it all once she found out that her own baby sister had turned down a $2 million settlement offer and had not even mentioned to her, the big sister, that she even had this lawsuit going. Big Sister's view was obviously that a fair split should have been envisioned by Little Sister, whose fraudulent ways apparently included keeping her own sister's hand out of the cookie jar. Then, of course, there was the small matter of the big sister's potential role in defrauding her insurance company, which, of course, Angela and I were more than willing to straighten out for her once we were assured of her testimony—testimony that would not only doom the formerly saintlike Mrs. Goodacre but subject her and her dapper little attorney to some interesting sanctions for defrauding the court.

Big Sister, née Nell Bazinskyson, was most indignant at being presumptively cut out of the Jason Goodacre litigation lottery pie. Calling Baby Sister a bitch and a cheat, among other things, Big Sister agreed to be our surprise witness, used to impeach Mrs. Goodacre's testimony, who we could sneak in without listing her on the pretrial witness list because Angela had found an exception to the rules against "trial by ambush" that allowed us to do just that. Dr. Jamieson, my expert witness, had seen the light indeed once he was confronted with the amnio and ultrasound reports, which Big Sister had been kind enough to get for us from the Boise clinic, because, after all, at least in the eyes of the Boise clinic, these were *her* patient records and there were no patient-client privilege issues that required involving Mrs. Goodacre or her able though jackassy attorney, Mr. LaBlanc. Dr. Jamieson, confronted with the irrevocable evidence that the fetus already showed damage in the ultrasound and that the amnio established a primary CMV infection during Mrs. Goodacre's pregnancy, had backed off his concurrent-cause theory in a hurry.

In short, migraine or not, I had an ambush witness, the plaintiff's own big sister, who would establish that the good-mother was a lying, cheating fraud who knew by her fifth month that the child she carried had birth defects, defects caused not as she now claimed by any act of Dr. Randolph but because of an altogether common virus.

I had an expert witness who looked like Robert Redford, had impeccable credentials, and could not be impeached with prior, inconsistent
testimony or a history of testifying for filthy lucre. He had been added to
the witness list and had been deposed by Stephen, who didn't ask any
questions about the amnio or the ultrasounds, no doubt because he was
clueless about them, or he assumed I was clueless.

Angela had been awarded the second chair position at trial
because she had the good luck of having a computer guru brother,
who had hacked into the MIB records in the first place. In sulky contrast, Ashton was being punished by being assigned the second, second chair and working for free as his act of contrition because his
crazy girlfriend had tried not once but twice to kill Dr. Randolph, our
client. Despite my antsy cocounsel, I was so cool during voir dire
because it simply didn't matter who in the jury pool actually ended up
on my jury.

I could win this case with Mrs. Goodacre's own family tree on the
jury.

So I didn't have any questions to ask of the prospective jurors, in
contrast to Stephen, who was now prying into their beliefs on when the
soul entered a fetus.

While Stephen prattled on with his meddlesome quest, I checked
my watch. Nearly noon. I eyed Angela and pointed at my watch.

One of us had to sprint to my house at the lunch break and take
Bearess for her noontime frolic about the neighborhood.

See, in the way of the miracles, Delvon's showing up and Johnny
Winter's turning into a skunk in the nick of time were not the only
claims to genuine miraculous events.

Bearess, who had jumped into the dark waters of Tampa Bay after
Jennifer, survived. A fisherman out at dawn had spotted a dog paddling
in a circle and had pulled her into his boat. Bless his heart, he had taken
the dog, which had suffered a broken leg, some broken ribs, and assorted
other injuries, straight to his own vet, who had tended her and then

traced her rabies tag back to Jennifer. When the vet realized what she had—by then the story of Jennifer and her dog's diving off the Sunshine Skyway had been blasted off every Bay-area radio station and cable news channel and got a page-one mention in the *Sarasota Herald-Tribune*—she contacted me, as I was prominently mentioned in the story as an eyewitness who had tried to save the dog and had "ties" to Jennifer. Naturally, I claimed the dog. Though the story leaked out, and various and sundry good-hearted people came forth to offer to adopt Bearess, whose noble nature and physical strength could never be questioned, I paid the bills, tipped the fisherman and the vet both, and brought Bearess home.

She was a distraught and emotionally wounded beast.

Angela came home, a distraught and emotionally wounded woman, having buried Crosby under the pecan trees with the "others," who as it turns out included a grandparent and a cousin and a host of other dogs and one billy goat named Earl Gray.

I took both of the wounded, heart-weary females into my home, and Newly too for a couple of nights, though he tiptoed into my bedroom not once, but twice, and acted hurt when I verbally chastised him and sent him back to Angela. I nursed Angela and Bearess the best I could, which is to say I listened a lot, made them do wind sprints with me until they were too tired to cry, and fed them both copious amounts of Häagen-Dazs ice cream, which, I might add, had the unpleasant side effect of making Bearess throw up in equally copious amounts. But Johnny Winter, the now hero ferret, ate a whole carton with no ill effects at all. Needless to say, he has the run of the house now. I mean— what the heck?—Brock and I can pick out new secondhand couches and chairs every few months, and with the windows open during the days, it's not so bad.

During all this, Delvon, who was still technically on the lam, stayed at Angela's and out of the watchful and still suspicious eyes of Sam, the detective, who had indeed yelled at me for going home and almost getting killed, but he more than made up for it in the usual way. While

Sam was a bit cop-like about Delvon, the John the Baptist look-alike, at least Sam didn't ask too many questions, and eventually Delvon, who can't physically stand to be outside the state of Georgia for too long a period of time, headed up to my apple orchard in north Georgia to chill for a while.

Not long after Delvon settled into the apple orchard, Bearess and Angela fell in love with each other, just as Bearess and I had fallen in love with each other, and the only fair thing was a joint-custody arrangement. We take turns caring for the dog, though, having a yard, I get dibs on keeping her most of the time.

Newly is whipping up a king-size class-action suit against nine different HMOs for violation of the prompt-pay provisions, and if the HMOs don't have him killed, he'll probably end up famous and the subject of a movie. Did I mention he stole the pink tap pants when he moved out of my house? I assume he will marry Angela if he doesn't woo me back from Sam.

Sam remains the steadfast, noncommunicative but ardent lover he was the first week. Frankly, I still don't know if he is a good detective or not, but he takes his turn walking Bearess when Angela and I are too tied up to do so. Eventually, Sam, I figure, will have to break down and talk to me, really talk to me, or I will just go back to Newly after he and Angela get divorced.

The mystery of who Sam really is remains, but it is not the only remaining mystery. Jennifer's body was never found. The HMO she had been defrauding in hundred-dollar bites sent its hounds from hell and tracked some of the waylaid checks to a bank in the Caymans. But by the time the HMO had all its little legal ducks in a row to claim the proceeds in the account, someone beat them to it. The money was gone—poof. Withdrawn well after the date of Jennifer's skinny-dip dive off the Skyway.

The accepted theory espoused in the newspapers and by the official spokespersons for the various law enforcement agencies involved was that Jennifer had an accomplice. In fact, Ashton was a key suspect, but after a sustained period of police harassment he skated clear.

My theory is different. Me, I remembered Jennifer's dive from the bridge. The way Jennifer's toes bounced and pointed, her hands in a serene triangle in front of her face, the lovely arch of her body in the jackknife formation of a high dive as she went out and over and down out of my sight. See, I think she lived, and some fisherman somewhere picked her up, dressed only in her midnight blue panties, and she and the fisherman are living somewhere in the Carribean, no doubt happy enough until the stolen HMO money runs out.

Or else Ashton really did snake the money out of the Cayman bank.

I'll have to figure this out later, just as Angela and I will eventually have to decide who gets custody of Bearess and Newly.

Who knows?

What I know right now is this: I'm going to stomp all over Stephen LaBlanc in *Goodacre versus Randolph*.

Let the show begin.

Acknowledgments

Indulge me, please, in first acknowledging and thanking these most fabulous members of my family: my husband, William Matturro, for believing and loving and listening and being my living dictionary and never once complaining when I quit my day job to write mysteries; my parents, John and Della Hamner, who have bestowed on me many gifts, including their lifelong examples of honesty, compassion, and hard work, and for banning television from my childhood home until I was addicted to books; my brother, William Hamner, for not letting go and for being, unfailingly, friend and fan; and Mike Lehner, who with no blood or marriage ties to make him part of my family simply became so through the force of enduring friendship.

In addition to the help and support of my family, in writing this book I was blessed to have the help of friends, fellow lawyers, the HarperCollins family, and even perfect strangers. I cannot thank each of you enough but will try once more.

Steven Babitsky, esquire and president of SEAK, Inc., and a man that as of this writing I still have not met face to face, provided a most gracious gift in enthusiastically awarding an excerpt of this book first prize in the SEAK National Legal Fiction Writing for Lawyers Contest. Not only was he one of the judges in that contest, but he became chief cheerleader for me during a low point when, by phone and e-mail, he strongly encouraged me to finish the book and offered his help to me in getting it published.

The SEAK prize proved to be my toe in the door with Carolyn Marino, my editor and a vice president at HarperCollins. Not only did Carolyn let me sneak in without an agent, she has edited, encouraged, brainstormed, and answered a hundred questions or more, all with gentle good graces and patience. Her time and talents made this book sharper, funnier, and immeasurably better. I offer sincerest thanks to both Carolyn and her able assistant, Jennifer Civiletto, who not only has her own way with words and an instinct about plots but also could and did answer every question within minutes.

It would be wholly remiss of me not to acknowledge and thank Gary Larsen, one of my former law partners and the funniest lawyer I've ever met, perhaps even the funniest person I've ever met, for the loan of his "Anything wrong with your mouth?" story. Thank you, Gary.

Martin Levin, lawyer and retired publisher and author of *Be Your Own Literary Agent,* shared his vast knowledge with me, both through his book and his words. I had the great pleasure of assisting him in revising his book and researching another, and the lessons learned during those months have proved invaluable. His book *Be Your Own Literary Agent,* his advice, and his friendship helped me navigate wholly new waters.

On a legal note, let me acknowledge that the type of brain-damaged baby case that Lilly defends in this novel would more than likely be outside of the tort system under Florida's current law. In an attempt to curb the costs of liability insurance and create a no-fault system for catastrophic birth-related neurological injuries, that state adopted the Florida Birth-Related Neurological Injury Compensation Plan, Chapter 766, Florida Statutes, in which an administrative law judge determines such claims rather than a jury.

Acknowledgments

Perhaps the hardest job of the friends and spouse of any writer is that of telling the writer that something in a manuscript doesn't work. And that job fell repeatedly to Bill, my husband, and Mike Lehner, my friend. Both men had to convince me that about ten thousand words of the first draft of *Skinny-dipping* were utter garbage and had to go. For that unsparing honesty, I thank you both.

And on that note, let me end where I began: with my family. My husband, Bill, and my father, John, proved repetitively to be talented sounding boards and editors. Their logical minds, their command of grammar, and their awesome vocabularies kept me from many a stumble. My mother, Della Johnson Hamner, proved to have the ablest ear for dialect and language, and thus, taught me early in my writing to reach for exactly the right word. My brother, Lieutenant William Hamner of the Selma, Alabama, police department, served earnestly as my technical adviser and helped me rewrite my police officer's dialogue to realistically reflect the speech patterns of that honorable profession. There was no detail too small, no question too obscure, and no forensics query too weird for my brother to answer for me.